DESIGNED *with* LOVE

Books by Tracie Peterson

For a complete list of Tracie's books, visit TraciePeterson.com.

*with Kimberley Woodhouse

TRACIE PETERSON

BETHANYHOUSE

a division of Baker Publishing Group
Minneapolis, Minnesota

© 2025 by Peterson Ink, Inc.

Published by Bethany House Publishers
Minneapolis, Minnesota
BethanyHouse.com

Bethany House Publishers is a division of
Baker Publishing Group, Grand Rapids, Michigan

Printed in the United States of America

Library of Congress Cataloging-in-Publication Data
Names: Peterson, Tracie, author.
Title: Designed with love / Tracie Peterson.
Description: Minneapolis, Minnesota : Bethany House Publishers, a division of
    Baker Publishing Group, 2025. | Series: The Hope of Cheyenne ; 2
Identifiers: LCCN 2024041937 | ISBN 9780764241116 (paper) | ISBN
    9780764245107 (cloth) | ISBN 9780764245114 (large print) | ISBN
    9781493450879 (ebook)
Subjects: LCGFT: Christian fiction. | Romance fiction. | Novels.
Classification: LCC PS3566.E7717 D46 2025 | DDC 813/.54--dc23/eng/20240906
LC record available at https://lccn.loc.gov/2024041937

Scripture quotations are from the King James Version of the Bible.

This is a work of historical reconstruction; the appearances of certain historical figures
are therefore inevitable. All other characters, however, are products of the author's
imagination, and any resemblance to actual persons, living or dead, is coincidental.

Cover design by Peter Gloege, LOOK Design Studio

Baker Publishing Group publications use paper produced from sustainable forestry
practices and postconsumer waste whenever possible.

25 26 27 28 29 30 31   7 6 5 4 3 2 1

For Rainy,
the most amazing of granddaughters.
You've faced many hard knocks and difficulties,
and defied doctors and medical prognoses
to prove God has something else in mind for you.
We are so blessed to have you in our lives.

Prologue

Cheyenne, Wyoming Territory—July 4, 1874

Emma Johnson, you must surely grieve your ma and pa." The man who gripped Emma by the ear had started his rant at the park and continued as he practically dragged her several blocks. Once they stood in front of the jail, he seemed to have reached the end of his tirade.

"You're hurting me, Mr. Gibbons!" Emma let out a howl of protest just as a uniformed police officer stepped from the building.

He eyed them with grave concern. "What's going on?"

"She stole liquor from me," Mr. Gibbons offered up, pushing Emma toward the man. "I want her dealt with."

"Hank, she's just a kid."

"Edward Vogel, are you going to do your job or not?"

Emma watched as Mr. Vogel seemed to think about the question. She let out another wail and tried to break away from the older man. He had a firm grip on her ear, however, and she had no choice but to settle down. It already felt like he was about to rip her ear right off her head and take a handful of hair with it.

Mr. Vogel reached out and took hold of Emma's arm. "I've got her now, Hank. Just let her go."

"You'd better have a firm grip. She's a wildcat."

"I've got her." He tightened his hold on Emma's upper arm. "Now, Emma, tell me what's going on. Did you steal from Mr. Gibbons?"

Emma knew better than to lie. "I didn't want to. It wasn't for me."

"That doesn't answer my question, Emma. Did you steal liquor from Mr. Gibbons?"

"It was whiskey," Mr. Gibbons said. "Two of my best bottles."

Mr. Vogel looked at her with the hint of a smile. He seemed to understand that she didn't really want to be bad, but her friends—well, really her brother's friends—had dared her to do it, and Emma was always up for a challenge.

"Did you steal them, Emma?"

She lowered her head and glanced up. She'd found this look quite effective. Giving what she hoped was her saddest, most regretful expression, she nodded.

"I'm really sorry. I didn't want them for myself."

Mr. Gibbons made a huffing sound. She wasn't sure what he meant by it. Could be his way of disapproving, or he may have just swallowed a fly. There sure were a lot of flies this Fourth of July.

"Well, let's go inside. Hank, you'll have to sign a formal complaint. Emma, I'm going to have to lock you up."

"In a cell?" All at once she was profoundly sorry for what she'd done. "I won't do it again. I swear!"

"I don't want her arrested, Deputy. I just want her folks to control her. If she'd gotten away with it, I'd be out ten dollars."

Mr. Vogel continued to hold her fast but tipped back his

hat with his free hand. "That's some mighty expensive whiskey, Hank."

"It was, at that. Fine Scottish whiskey. Old too. The longer it ages, the more expensive it is. Maybe just hold her and send for her parents. They need to know what she's capable of." The man turned to go. "I don't mean to stir up a hornet's nest, but young'uns like that need to be taken in hand."

"Old coot," Emma muttered under her breath.

"What was that?" the deputy asked.

She gave a sigh and gazed upward at the man once more. "Nothing. I'm just upset."

"I'll bet you are." He chuckled, only serving to further Emma's frustration.

To make matters worse, Connor Caffrey, her brother's best friend, happened to walk by just then. Emma silently wished the earth would swallow her whole.

"Emma Johnson, as I live and breathe," the young man declared, sounding more than a little bit sarcastic.

"Connor, I need you to do me a favor." Edward Vogel's grip remained firm.

"Anything at all, Officer. I'm always happy to help the law."

"Yeah, I can imagine you are. Emma, where are your folks?"

"At the picnic. They were visiting with the Aldrich and Taylor families by the bandstand."

"Connor, go tell the Johnsons that I need to speak with them right away."

"Sure thing!"

He sounded more than a little eager to get Emma in trouble, and she threw him a glare that she hoped gave him a pang of conscience. After all, he would have been first to sample the wares had she gotten away with her thievery.

"Oh, and don't make it a public ordeal. Understand? Just tell them in private and ask them to come see me at the jail."

"I understand."

Connor's tone was rather deflated, but Emma had no doubt he'd enjoy his duties. Connor and her brother, James, were seventeen and loved nothing more than seeing her in trouble. And if not her, then someone else. Just as long as it wasn't one of them.

"Get to it, then, Connor." Mr. Vogel turned, pulling Emma along with him into the jailhouse.

Emma couldn't help but gawk around the place. She'd never been in the jail before, although she had heard terrible tales from her brother and his friends about it. James had never been taken to jail. In fact, as far as Emma knew, no one in her family had ever been in trouble with the law.

Leave it to me to be the first.

She regretted the honor, if it could be called that. Consequences were usually far less pleasurable than the hoped-for rewards when nefarious deeds were done.

"I want you to sit in that chair and not move. Do you understand me?" Mr. Vogel said, pointing to a round-backed, wooden chair. "I don't want to have to put you in a cell."

Emma swallowed the dry lump in her throat and nodded. Now that her folks had been sent for, there was no getting out of whatever punishment was headed her way.

She plopped into the chair in a most unladylike fashion and stared at Mr. Vogel as he took a seat behind a small wooden desk opposite her.

"Why'd you want to go and ruin such a great day by doing something like stealing liquor?"

Emma shrugged. "I get talked into a lot of things, and it didn't seem like it would be all that hard. Mr. Gibbons was busy with his customers, and I'm not so big as to be noticed."

"Big enough, apparently."

Emma gave a sad nod. "It would seem so. I really don't set out to be bad."

"Oh, Emma, you aren't bad. You just make bad choices sometimes."

She heard sympathy and kindness in his tone and knew she could use it to her advantage. She continued to nod. "I do. It's true. I try to be good. I really do."

He chuckled. "I was a boy once. I remember very well how hard it was to behave. I was probably twice as rowdy as you. I will say, however, I've never had to take a young lady into custody. I expect this kind of behavior from the boys, but honestly, it comes as a surprise to hear that a girl like you was stealing whiskey."

Emma lowered her head in a dejected manner. Putting her hand up to cover her face, she poked a finger into her eye to create tears. It had been most effective a few months earlier when the cook caught her stealing cookies. She felt her eyes water sufficiently and glanced up with a sniff. "I'm just as sorry as I can be."

Mr. Vogel smiled. "Well, don't get too riled up. Your folks seem like decent people, and once they realize that you were encouraged to do it, I'm sure they'll understand."

Emma dabbed at her eyes with the back of her sleeve. "They are good people. It's not their fault that I do bad things."

That was probably the first time she'd really spoken the truth that day. Her folks didn't deserve the blame for her actions. Emma had always been a wild card. She was born the day after the War between the States started. Her father had once joked that she started her own kind of war as well.

But how could the fault be assigned to her? If she had been out of control since coming into the world, wasn't that more or less the fault of someone else? She couldn't help it if she was easily bored and fixed on the idea of having a good time. She liked to take a dare and thrilled at the excitement that followed. It was just how she was created. How was that her fault?

She sniffed again for good effect and waited a few more minutes in silence. Down the street, she could hear the band playing a march. How she wished she were at the picnic instead of sitting in the jail. In fact, she wished she could be just about any place else but here, waiting for her parents to come and show their disappointment in her once again.

It wasn't that she didn't want to be good. She had tried, but it grieved her. There was no fun to be had in being good, and she wanted to have fun. A lot of fun. Mama said it was unnatural the way she was constantly looking for a good time.

"Life is full of responsibilities and tasks that must be done," her mother often said. *"Good times are the reward for the hard times of work."*

Emma recalled just a few weeks back when her mother had declared that once again, and Emma's response had perfectly summed up her thoughts. *"I don't want to have responsibilities and tasks that must be done. I can hire someone to see to that. I just want to enjoy my life and the good times."*

Mother had just shaken her head. *"That would be nice, I suppose, but not at all in the plan for us. Since Adam and Eve sinned in the garden, we have been tasked with hard work. Even before that, Adam was given the job of seeing to the animals and garden. And now we have responsibilities to see to our various roles of work. Believe me when I say it makes the rewards all the more enjoyable."*

But Emma didn't see it that way at all.

She heard footsteps on the boardwalk outside, and the door opened to admit her parents. She glanced up and saw her mother's reproving glance while her father looked to Mr. Vogel.

"Edward, good to see you again. Sorry for the circumstances."

They shook hands, and only then did Papa turn and look at Emma. "What'd she get caught doing?"

"Stealing whiskey."

"What!" Mama's tone was one of complete shock. Emma felt bad for having upset her. Genuinely bad. She didn't want to hurt either one of them.

"Emma, why don't you explain yourself? Why were you trying to steal anything, much less whiskey?"

"Papa, I couldn't very well buy it," she began. "And James and the others . . . well, they kind of encouraged me to sneak over and take it."

Papa rolled his gaze toward the ceiling. "James. Somehow that figures. I'll thrash that boy when I get ahold of him. He knows better than to put his little sister up to such a task."

Emma gave her most contrite expression and nodded. From the side, however, she could see that her mother was unconvinced. Mama always knew whether Emma was innocent or guilty. She had a special gift that way. She called it discernment, but Emma called it very inconvenient. It seemed impossible to fool her mother.

"Emma has a mind of her own, Rich. She's fully capable of saying no when it pleases her to do so." Mama gave her a look that dared Emma to deny it. She knew better, however, and remained silent.

"What do we need to do to make this right, Edward?"

"Hank Gibbons doesn't want to press charges. He just wanted to make sure you knew what she'd done. He was more upset that she'd gotten a hand on his good stuff." Mr. Vogel smiled, and her father actually laughed.

"Emma's always had expensive taste."

"Yeah, well, she's all yours to deal with. We've got no hold on her."

"Then let's just go home," Mama declared. "I'm in no mood to continue with a celebration."

Emma started to protest. She wanted to see the fireworks that had been promised. She wanted to have freshly churned ice cream and maybe get a chance to dance at her first grown-up party. But she knew the consequences of her actions had not yet been dealt, and to argue with her mother would only add to the punishment. So, in silence, she followed her parents outside and down the boardwalk.

The sun was hot, as it was most July days, and for once there didn't seem to be much of a breeze. It was like the world was holding its breath . . . watching, waiting, for Emma's punishment.

Mama didn't say another word to her until nearly five hours later. Emma was washed and dressed for bed before her mother came to speak with her. What was most startling was that Emma could see from her reddened eyes that Mama had spent a good part of the time crying. And those tears were Emma's fault. It made her feel a little sick, like the time she'd been walking on the top rail of the fence and lost her footing. She'd hit her stomach hard on the rail, knocking the wind out of her and leaving her wanting to retch.

"Emma, I don't know why you have to do the things you do. I can understand wanting to have fun, even wanting to run a little wild. But for sure, stealing is beyond the pale." Her mother's Irish roots were showing, as they often did when she became emotional. "It oversteps the bounds of wanting to have fun and takes you into breaking not only man's law but God's."

Emma knew that this was more egregious to her mother than anything else she'd ever done.

"You know how your father and I feel about obeying God's laws. I know you can recite the Ten Commandments by heart. I've heard you do it."

"Yes, ma'am. I can recite them again, if you like."

"What I'd like is if you'd live by them. You call yourself a Christian, Emma, but you don't live as one."

Emma had given this some long and serious consideration. "I don't think I want to be a Christian anymore. Not if it means never having any fun, and Christians don't have fun." Emma's words spilled out, not considering her mother's feelings. "Seems to me that Christians just worry about all the 'don'ts' in life. Don't do this, and don't do that. They hardly ever smile. I don't want to be like that."

"Oh, Emma." Mama's eyes filled with tears. "Being a Christian has so much more to do with love than rules. As people, we're given easily to sin. Doing the wrong thing comes far more naturally. But sin only leads to sorrow, and it forever separates us from God."

"But if heaven is like church, then I don't wanna go." She was surprised by her own declaration. But now that it was said, she could hardly take it back. It was the truth of how she felt. What good was an eternity of sitting around singing mournful hymns that spoke of how terrible she was for her sins?

Mama shook her head, and a single tear slipped down her cheek. "Emma, I wish you could understand the goodness of God. The love He has for each of us. He loves us so much that He sent Jesus to die in our place. Our sins are worthy of death, but Jesus took the debt and paid it with His life. He's giving you a free gift—a chance to be forgiven—and all you have to do is accept Him as Lord."

"And stop having fun, right?" Emma shrugged. "Doesn't sound like much of a gift to me."

Emma regretted her words. She saw the pain she'd caused her mother and almost took them back. Almost.

She really had tried her best to understand and believe the things her folks believed, but it was just too hard. God wanted too much from her.

1

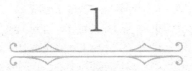

DALLAS, TEXAS—JANUARY 31, 1889

I t was a surprisingly warm day for the end of January
in Texas. Emma stood dressed in her expensive white
Worth wedding gown and waited for the minister to
declare that she and Tommy Benton were husband and wife.

Tommy grinned at her, then made a face of boredom, and
Emma nearly laughed out loud. At twenty-seven, she supposed that they should take their wedding day with a degree
more seriousness. But that wasn't her nature. Life should be
one good time followed by another. At least, that was how
she'd always seen it—and lived it.

Nine years ago, when the chance to leave Cheyenne for her
married sister's ranch in Texas came up, Emma had jumped
at it. Some folks in Cheyenne weren't overly fond of her.
There were quite a few who'd had their toes stepped on by
Emma, and some who bore worse than that. Leaving the
area was the perfect solution after breaking her engagement
to a local boy in order to take up with another man—a man
who soon afterward deserted her. It gave her an easy way to
avoid all the folks who thought her worthless and difficult.

Besides, her sister, Clara, wasn't overly demanding. She

needed help with her children, and the children enjoyed having fun. Emma was just the right person for rowdy games and horse races. As the children grew up and attended school, Emma had more free time. This allowed her to escape the boredom of the ranch and do what she wanted to do. Clara was usually far too busy with her responsibilities to worry about monitoring her little sister's actions.

Emma did just enough to satisfy Clara and give her the relief she needed, and in turn Clara kept her mouth shut when Emma took off on one of her escapades. It was a good arrangement, one that had allowed her to meet Thomas Benton, the youngest of four wealthy Benton brothers, the previous January.

Tommy was sweet—more boy than man. He loved having fun just as much as Emma. He agreed with her philosophy of there being plenty of time to focus on religion when old age was upon them. Youth was supposed to be spent exploring options and opportunities. It was no wonder most adults were sullen and serious all the time. And many were still all bound up by religious rules from the minute they struck out on their own. Emma considered herself lucky to have figured out that such things were a waste of time.

She glanced sideways and saw her father and stepmother. They didn't look all that happy. Goodness, she'd maintained her purity and given them a church wedding, they should be delighted, especially after years of worrying about her moral standings. Her father and mother had never accounted for Emma having her own standards—standards that she had refused to yield on no matter how persuasive Tommy had been. That was the reason for the wedding. Emma might love a life free of rules and regulations, but when it came to the physical aspects of love, she was quite guarded. She'd heard far too many horror stories about women who allowed themselves to be compromised. Then, too, she had to look no further than her sister to see what a life of marriage and motherhood did to a woman's spirit. Clara said she was happy, but, goodness, she never got to do much of anything but see to household duties and child care. Frankly, Emma hoped she never had children.

Tommy didn't care about having them either. He said maybe later, in another ten years or so. Maybe by then Emma would be ready for them as well. Still, being married would put them at risk of that coming sooner rather than later. It was the only real reason Emma had hesitated when Tommy begged her to marry him.

Tommy was saying something, so Emma turned her attention back to the wedding. With the heat, she just wished they'd conclude with the ceremony. Worth gowns were beautiful creations, and this one was no exception, but it was hot, and a simple cotton dress would have suited her better.

Tommy took hold of her hand. "With this ring, I thee wed. With my body, I thee worship. With all my worldly goods, I thee endow. In the name of the Father and of the Son and of the Holy Ghost. Amen." Tommy slipped the ring on her finger.

Emma was impressed with the ring they'd chosen. Tommy had insisted on sparing no expense, and given that he'd inherited a hefty sum of money the previous year, he could afford the best. Diamonds and sapphires set against gold. She'd never owned anything like it, and Tommy had given her plenty of jewelry. One thing about Tommy, he was more than generous with his money. Emma glanced up and met his gaze. This marriage was going to be a happy one. They were good at finding things to do, and marriage would open up even more doors to good times.

The minister, an ancient old man who headed up a church Emma and Tommy didn't attend but had given a large tithe to, pronounced them husband and wife. Tommy pulled her into his arms and kissed her soundly.

"Well, I'm glad to know that you can keep your word to someone," a feminine voice called out.

Tommy pulled away, and Emma turned to see who was speaking. A woman gowned in black with a heavy veil moved down the aisle toward them. Emma looked at Tommy, who had gone as white as a ghost.

The woman lifted her veil and smiled. "I don't suppose you expected to see me today, did you now, Tommy?"

"Stella." He barely whispered her name.

"That's right. Stella." The petite blond woman looked at him for a long moment, then turned to Emma. "Did he tell you he'd love you forever? Sweet talk you into doing things you swore you'd never do? Did you lose your innocence to him and then find yourself in a bad way?"

"Young woman, this is the House of God," the minister protested.

"Well, that's why I'm here." She turned back to Tommy. "You took my innocence, all while promising to marry me. Now I'm carrying your baby, and you've married another."

Emma wanted to do something . . . anything, but found herself frozen in place. Tommy turned back to her with a sad look of regret.

"It'd be best for all concerned if we just ended this family here and now."

Confused by Stella's statement, Emma looked back to her. Somehow, the young woman had produced a revolver and now aimed it at Tommy's head.

When the gun went off and Tommy crumpled to the ground beside her, Emma still couldn't move. She watched as Stella turned the gun on herself as several men rushed her. There was a scuffle, and the gun went off a second time before someone managed to get the piece away from her.

A woman screamed, and Emma turned to see that it was Rosie Benton. Tommy's younger sister. Poor girl. Emma's own family was pointing and starting to cry.

Several people rushed forward to where Tommy had fallen at Emma's feet. For the first time she looked down and could see for herself that Stella's aim had been true. The bullet had pierced Tommy's left temple. Blood pooled around his head. His eyes were still open.

It was only as she studied her husband's lifeless body that she saw the spread of red across the waist of her white wedding gown. For a moment it seemed unreal. Where had the blood come from?

Emma touched her stomach and realized a hot pain spread across her abdomen. The second bullet had struck her. She looked up to see her father rushing forward. Tommy's brother Colton was right behind him. The men took hold of each of her arms as her knees gave out and the room went black.

It would seem Stella had claimed more than one victim.

"Emma, can you hear me? Emma, please wake up, darlin'."

It was her father's voice. Emma knew it well, and for just a moment she was back home on the ranch outside of Cheyenne. It was early morning, and Papa was urging her to get up.

He was always so cheerful as he called her and Clara. *"Rise and shine, my darlins."*

Mama would be downstairs fixing breakfast and would send Papa up to wake Emma and her brother and sister. Of course, Papa had been up since before dawn, getting a start on the ranch chores. In the early years, he didn't keep a staff, and Mama didn't have any help with the house or meals. It was just the family, and they all pitched in to help.

"Emma, please wake up."

Fighting against the blackness, Emma struggled to open her eyes. Instead of finding her childhood bedroom, she found herself stretched out on a desk in a small office. Papa held her hand. His expression was grave. Another man seemed quite intent on cutting away her wedding gown.

"Oh, sweetheart." Papa smiled down at her. "I feared I'd lost you."

"What . . . happened?"

She saw her sister crying into a handkerchief while their stepmother embraced her.

"You were shot, Em. The doctor isn't sure how bad it is, but you're losing blood."

Her father's words made no sense. Shot? Then the memory of the wedding flooded back in such a rush that Emma tried to sit up.

"Tommy!"

"Stay still, Mrs. Benton." This from the man who had destroyed her wedding gown. Well, she supposed the bullet had actually done that deed.

"I want to see Emma!" a woman all but screamed from somewhere outside the small room. "Emma!"

"Rosie." Emma had grown quite close to the younger woman. "Let her come to me."

Her father shook his head. "The doctor needs to stop you from bleeding to death. It would just upset her all the more to see you like this. I'll go speak to her."

Emma nodded at her father. "Please tell her I'm all right. Tell her I'll see her very soon."

"I will, Em. I will. You just stay still and let the doctor do what he needs to do."

"I'd like to get her over to the hospital and into surgery. Better lighting and equipment."

Lucille, Emma's stepmother, spoke up. "You think this will require surgery?"

The doctor straightened. "I can't tell just yet. I've got the wound covered, and I've slowed the bleeding."

"The pastor sent for an ambulance." This came from Clara, who moved to Emma's side. "Oh, Emma, I'm so sorry this happened."

Emma closed her eyes as the pain became more evident. She supposed the shock of everything had kept her from feeling it too much, and she couldn't help but moan.

"As soon as we get to the hospital, I'll give you something for the pain." The doctor pressed the bandages tight to her body.

It was all too much. Emma could hear the pandemonium and shouts of someone in the other room. Once again, her vision began to blur, and rather than fight it, she gave in. She could hear the doctor telling someone that she was losing consciousness from the loss of blood. After that, nothing more.

When Emma woke up the second time, she was tucked away in a hospital bed. She felt her waistline. A thick layer of bandages was beneath the overly large white cotton nightgown she wore. Her vision was somewhat hazy from whatever medicine they'd given her.

"Emma?"

Was that her sister? "Clara?"

"It's me, Em." Her sister took hold of her hand. "The doctor said you're going to be just fine. The bullet sliced across your abdomen. A little deep where it entered. He had to put in quite a few stitches but said if you'd been standing straight on instead of sideways, you would be dead."

"Tommy?"

Clara's brow scrunched together. "Don't you remember?"

Emma had a vague recollection, but she hoped she was wrong. "She shot him in the head."

"Yes." Her sister's tone was so matter-of-fact. "I'm so sorry, Emma. He's dead."

The finality of the words hit Emma harder than she'd expected. Tommy was dead. His life was over. Just like that. In the blink of an eye. Blink of an eye . . . Why did that phrase ring in her ears? Oh, it was like a twinkling of an eye. She had once asked her father about the phrase after he'd read a passage in Corinthians, and he had told her a twinkling was like a blink. Just that fast. Why had that stayed in her memories?

"I know he's dead. I saw him." She heard herself say the words, but still they made no sense. "Did someone take care of him?"

"Yes. Colton and his brothers arranged to have him taken to the funeral home."

"Who was that woman?"

Clara patted her arm. "It's not important now. Rosie wants to see you. She's beside herself."

Emma nodded. "Please let her come to me."

Her sister left, and Emma closed her eyes. How could so much have changed so quickly? In a blink . . . a twinkling. She was being kissed, and then Tommy was dead. Why didn't the thought bring tears? She cared for him deeply . . . even loved him in her own way. So why couldn't she cry over him?

The door opened, and Rose Benton rushed in. For all her twenty-three years, she was in so many ways so innocent of life. How this must have devastated her. She adored Tommy. She was even set to come live with Emma and Tommy after they returned from their wedding trip.

"Oh, Emma, I'm so glad you're alive." Rosie bent over and kissed Emma's cheek. "Colton said that Tommy probably didn't even know what hit him, so he didn't have any pain. But now he's dead." Tears came to her eyes. "She shot him dead." She began to sob.

"I know. I'm . . . so . . . sorry."

Rosie stifled her tears. "Oh, Emma, what are we going to do?" She didn't wait for an answer but hurried on. "Does your stomach hurt? I saw the blood on your dress. Your beautiful dress was ruined."

Emma forced a smile. "It's going to be all right, Rosie. It was just a dress. As for the pain, they gave me medicine. I'm sure I'll be fine."

"I was so scared that you had died too. I prayed and asked Jesus to save you, and He did. I would have prayed for Tommy, but Colton said God doesn't bring people back from the dead anymore. I was one of the last ones. But I'll keep praying for you." She sniffed and wiped her face on the back of her sleeve.

"Thank you." For once, the words pierced Emma's heart. Mama had told her so many times that she was praying for Emma to yield her life to God. Clara had sometimes mentioned in passing that she was praying for Emma to learn the truth before it was too late.

Was it too late?

A wave of guilty conscience washed over her. Tommy knew about Jesus. They had scoffed at religion and the rules that God laid out for man. Emma had agreed with Tommy that the Bible wasn't for them. Maybe they'd reconsider when they were old and close to death. Now he was dead.

"Emma?" Rosie stroked Emma's cheek with her slender fingers. "Are you scared?"

"I was. I was so scared I couldn't move." Visions of what had happened began to trickle back to mind. The young blond-haired woman all dressed in black—like someone attending a funeral instead of a wedding. A specter of death.

"I screamed. I couldn't help it."

Emma saw the fear in Rosie's eyes. "It's over now, and you're safe."

"I didn't care if I was safe. I was scared for you and Tommy. I love you so much, Emma." Rosie bent over her once again and pressed her cheek to the top off Emma's head.

"Come along, Rose," Clara said, taking hold of her. "Emma needs to sleep now."

"I'll come back with Colton. He promised we could see you when you're better. He said I could help take care of you."

Emma nodded and gave a wave. The pain was starting to feel more pronounced. Once Rosie had gone from the room, she turned to Clara. "I'm hurting."

"I'll tell the nurse. They said they would give you something when you needed it."

With Clara gone, the room seemed so very silent. Emma couldn't help but think back to Tommy lying dead on the floor. She had been pronounced a wife, and just as quickly, it was taken from her.

"Emma?" Her father peeked at her from the open door.

"Come in, Papa."

He smiled and crossed the room in two long strides. "I'm so thankful to see you awake. Clara said you were in pain, so I won't stay long. Lucille wanted me to make sure you had everything you needed. Can I bring you anything from Clara's?"

She had moved most of her things from the ranch to the Benton house. She and Tommy planned to get their own place soon, but for the time being, they were moving Emma in to share Tommy's room. Rosie had been so excited.

"I don't know what I need." She moaned and pressed her hands to her stomach.

"Doc says you're very lucky. I told him you were blessed, since we don't believe in luck."

"I know. I'd be dead if I'd taken the bullet while facing the gun." She could still see the hopelessness in the expression of the young woman who'd shot them. "What happened to her?"

Her father immediately understood. "They took her to the jail. She's there now. Won't say another word. Just sobs." He moved closer to the bed. "Did you know . . . I mean, was it a shock to learn that . . . well . . ."

"That Tommy had another woman?" Emma had avoided thinking about that revelation. "Tommy never told me."

"He betrayed you."

"I suppose that's true. I don't know what to make of it all. I can't really even think clearly." She rubbed her eyes and tried to eliminate the image of the woman who'd ruined her wedding.

"I'm so sorry, Emmy." It had been a long time since anyone had called her by her childhood name. "This was supposed to be your happiest day."

Emma nodded, but in her heart, she couldn't help but wonder if justice had been served. They'd made vows to God without either of them meaning a word. They'd even laughed after the rehearsal. Tommy had said he'd never expect her to stay with him if times were bad, and although the thought had troubled Emma for a moment, she'd assured him that she felt the same way.

Clara had known Emma and Tommy's feelings on the matter. She'd asked Emma why they bothered with a wedding, then.

"Because everyone expects it. You can't go setting up house together or travel together and such without a ring and piece of paper to say it's legal."

That had been Emma's answer. Now as the words came

back to her, she was stunned by the coldness and heartlessness of them. What was wrong with her? Why had she ever agreed to marry Tommy that way?

Nearly dying was awakening feelings and thoughts that Emma had fought for years to bury deep inside.

The nurse came in just then carrying a small bottle of medicine. "I've brought something to help you sleep and numb the pain."

Numb the pain. Hadn't that been what Emma had been doing all of her life? Perhaps *pain* was the wrong word. It was more of a void. Her life had always seemed so empty, and yet no matter how she tried, she couldn't find a way to fill that abyss. She was always sure that one day she would find something out there in the world that would make her feel whole and happy.

"Here you go." The nurse handed her a shot glass with a reddish-brown liquid.

Emma lifted her head and reached out for the glass. She instantly regretted her actions and grabbed her waist. "Oh, the pain is so bad."

"Just drink this and you'll feel better in a couple of minutes," the nurse insisted, helping Emma to put the glass to her lips.

The medicine tasted foul, but Emma swallowed it and eased her head back against the pillow. Once the nurse was gone again, Papa stepped forward and took hold of Emma's hand. The look on his face betrayed his own pain.

"I thought I'd lost you."

"I'm so sorry, Papa. This day wasn't what any of us wanted or expected."

"I am sorry about your husband. It's hard enough to lose someone to death, but to have that kind of treachery exposed . . . it's a lot to bear."

"He wasn't treacherous. Tommy just enjoyed life to the fullest. He'd tell you that he had no regrets."

"I wonder if he still feels that way." Her father shook his head. "I know neither of you had much use for God, but maybe now you can see where that gets you. Emma, you have another chance to make things right with God, but that young man of yours . . . well, he made a bad choice, Emma. I'm hoping you won't make the same one."

The medicine was starting to take effect, and Emma could feel herself drifting away. She looked at her father, unable to tell him that his words pierced her heart. Without Jesus, Tommy would go to hell. If she died now, she would go there too. She didn't want that . . . not for either of them.

It's too late for Tommy.

Too late.

2

Colton Benton walked away from the city jail in a stupor. He'd gone to check up on the arrest of the woman who'd killed his brother only to learn she'd hanged herself the night before. Had the world gone mad? Only the day before Colton had watched helplessly as Stella Mikkelson shot his brother dead and wounded the only woman Colton had ever loved.

He'd never told Tommy or Emma about his feelings, but from the moment he'd first met Emma, Colton hadn't been able to stop thinking about her. He was forty years old and had never given his heart to any woman. At first it was to devote himself to his studies and education in the law. Then it was because his father had wanted him undistracted in learning the family railroad business and handling the legal affairs for anything related to the Bentons' financial and business matters.

But a year ago, Tommy had brought Emma Johnson home, and everything changed. Tommy had announced his intention to marry the vivacious brunette with her dark brown eyes and full lips. She was possibly the most beautiful woman Colton ever met, and she was smart too. Emma's quick, witty responses and knowledge about affairs that usually bored women impressed Colton. He remembered one conversation they'd had at length regarding the cattle industry. This was Emma's background, and although she wanted nothing to do with being a rancher, she knew everything about it. Once, when Colton and his father had questions regarding cattle shipments, Emma's thoughts on the matter helped them to make their decisions. She was no wallflower, nor a simpering belle.

But she was Tommy's lady.

That alone forced Colton's hand. He had stayed away from her and did what he could to avoid ever being alone with her. Most of the family thought he disliked her, but the very opposite was true. He loved her. And now she was widowed and lay injured in the hospital, and Colton had a funeral to plan for his youngest brother.

Tommy had lived life fast and loose since his birth. He was never one for sitting still. Colton was seven years old when Tommy was born. He hadn't been overly impressed with getting yet another brother. He already had to share his mother's affection with Walter, age four, and Ernest who was two and constantly ill. Now came Thomas, and while his father delighted in yet another Benton boy, Colton was less than pleased. He'd hoped this would be the last of his siblings. And for years it seemed that it was, until his mother announced one Christmas that she was once again with child.

On May 30, 1865, a baby girl had been delivered after a most difficult time. The doctor announced her stillborn as the cord had been wrapped three times around her neck and suffocated her airway. The nurse quickly wrapped the baby in a blanket and set her aside.

Moments later, however, Mother had told Colton that she heard the tiniest mew from the baby and insisted the nurse unwrap the child. The nurse had thought her in error—

thought that sorrow had caused her to hear what she so longed to hear. But soon enough the baby's cry grew louder, and Rose Benton was truly born. The doctor informed the family that Rose would most likely never be able to learn or function on her own. Having been deprived of oxygen, her brain had no doubt suffered damage.

Colton remembered learning the news and later making a solemn promise to his mother on her deathbed two years later that he would always look out for Rose. And he had. He'd looked after all of them, Tommy included. Yet he'd been unable to keep a young woman from walking into Tommy's wedding and putting an end to his life.

Colton made his way into the funeral home and paid for the final arrangements for Tommy's funeral. They would hold it the following day at Trinity Cemetery. There would be no full church service and no open-casket viewing. Tommy, much as his brothers, had found religion to be a waste of time. He wouldn't want a church service.

The funeral would be for family only. Emma would be unable to attend, but even if they'd held off on the funeral until Monday, she couldn't have made it. The doctor said she would be in the hospital for at least a week, longer if an infection set in. No, it was best to just get Tommy buried and grieve his passing. His death would change a great deal for the family, and Colton's mind was already on how he should proceed.

The previous November, their father, Lawrence Benton, had passed away due to heart failure. He left his entire fortune to be split four ways between his sons, with the provision that they would each supply a portion to always care for their sister. Colton had been made guardian over her, considering her difficulties, but Tommy and Emma had wanted Rosie to live with them. Colton had agreed to this, knowing they would probably stay nearby, but he remained in charge.

Now Tommy was dead, and Colton had no idea what Emma would do. She might want to return to her sister and brother-in-law's ranch. Or she might even desire to head back to Cheyenne. Colton had heard her father say that he'd like very much to take her home. Colton would just as soon she stay with the family there in Dallas. Rosie would prefer that too.

How could he convince Emma to stay, however? She was now legally a Benton. In fact, Colton, as the family lawyer, had already changed Tommy's will to leave everything to Emma upon his death. Neither had anticipated that the day would come anytime soon, but here they were. This brought up another difficult situation. Tommy had inherited his equal share of railroad stock, but he had also been given their aunt's share prior to their father's death, which left him majority owner. Now that would fall to Emma.

Colton heaved a sigh and headed home. There was just so much to consider. He would have to sit down with Emma once she was feeling better and explain what was going on and what he hoped she'd find acceptable for her future. But what he really wanted to do was somehow convince her that he should be a part of her future. Yet how could he speak of love with her husband—his own brother—not yet cold in the ground?

As he approached the three-story Queen Anne that his father had built six years earlier, Colton frowned. He'd never liked the place. It was lavish and ostentatious. The kind of place you built to show others that you could. The hipped-roof building with its lower cross gables and multiple turrets was accented with a delicate spindle-work frieze that extended around the entire wrap-around porch. The house itself was over fifteen thousand square feet and boasted a third-floor ballroom that was seldom used.

Father had said that with the coming of electricity to Dallas and the success of their railroad, the Bentons' deserved to be noticed. He studied the city and chose his land carefully, then paid an enormous sum to have the city extend water and electricity to his new creation. Once the word was out that the Bentons were moving to this location, other moneyed people quickly bought up the surrounding land and began to build their own mansions. It wasn't long before an entire neighborhood of palatial estates had been fashioned.

Colton preferred their old house, where memories of his mother could be had in every corner and room. He supposed that was the reason, however, his father insisted on the move. He'd not been happy since losing her and seldom spoke of her. Upon his death bed, though, Colton had heard him murmur her name more than once. Theirs had been a great love.

Now his brothers, Walter and Ernest, were married with their own families and living elsewhere in Dallas, and Tommy had been looking to find his own place. That left just him and Rose in the big house . . . maybe Emma, too, if he could convince her. He supposed it was his decision entirely, however, as to whether they stayed in this monstrosity of a house or left for something smaller.

"I knew it was you!" Rosie said, coming to greet him in the oversized foyer. She stretched up on tiptoe and embraced Colton as she had done every day for as long as he could remember. "Can we go and see Emma?" She stepped back and fixed him with a hopeful expression. "I want to know how she's feeling."

"It's too soon. Maybe tomorrow."

Rosie frowned, and she lowered her gaze to the floor. "She's all alone now."

"She is not. She has her father and stepmother, as well as her sister's family."

"She'll think we don't love her anymore."

Colton shook his head and put his arm around Rosie's

shoulder. "We can go see her first thing in the morning. She needed today to rest. The doctor had to put in a lot of stitches, and that hurts."

"Can we bring her home tomorrow?"

He considered this question for a long moment. "I don't know where Emma wants to live, since Tommy won't be here."

"Do you think Tommy's in heaven?" Rose was always changing the topic with lightning speed.

The last thing Colton wanted to do was talk religious matters with his sister. He wanted to curse Aunt Clementine for her religious beliefs and how she'd convinced Rosie they were important, much less true.

Clementine Benton Nelson had come shortly after Mother's death to take care of her brother's youngest children. Father had been most grateful for her help but less than happy when he learned of her insistence that the children attend church with her. He relented to allow Rose to go but let the boys decide for themselves. Tommy blamed God for his mother's death and refused. Walter and Ernest went a few times, but when Colton remained home, they were soon persuaded to remain there as well. As Rose grew older and her condition caused more questions, Father insisted Aunt Clementine keep her home. But that didn't stop the older woman from "Training a child up in the way they should go," as she always said.

"Did you hear me? I wondered if you thought Tommy was in heaven?"

"I don't hold with such things, Rosie. You know that."

"But, Colton, God is real, and if you don't have Jesus as your Savior, you can't go to heaven."

He looked at her for a moment. "And you think that's fair? You think God is loving to act in such a way? Sending people to hell?"

"God doesn't want them to go to hell." She shook her head and furrowed her brow. "He sent Jesus so they didn't have to go." There was a decidedly childlike innocence to her reasoning on the matter. "People go to hell because they choose that instead of God."

"Oh, bother. I don't want to discuss this now. Look, if you're good, then we'll go see Emma in the morning. But for now, let me get some work done."

She smiled. "Do you want some coffee and pie? The cook made your favorite pecan pie."

The thought did intrigue him, but it was getting too close to suppertime. "No, I'll wait and have some with dinner."

Rose hugged him again. "I'll go out to the garden. Miguel is getting the dirt ready to plant new flowers. He said I could help."

"All right. You go ahead."

Colton watched her all but skip away. Recently Emma had been working with her to walk in a more ladylike manner. For years they'd done very little to train Rose in any particular etiquette, certain that she would be unable to learn anything difficult. Father had even forbidden his sister to impose rules upon the child. It was to their benefit Rose had such a sweet and simple nature. A more unruly child might have brought the entire house down.

Still, she surprised them all by picking up little things. She especially learned from Emma, who thought it nonsense to keep Rose hidden away without any training. Perhaps she was right. Maybe they'd been wrong to shelter Rosie and keep her from outsiders. Father had feared her being embarrassed or, perhaps even more so, feared her being an embarrassment to him. But Emma didn't see things that way. Emma had taught her about numbers and the alphabet, certain Rosie could learn to read. She went proudly for walks with Rose, and from time to time Tommy accompanied them. Last year they'd even taken Rose to the fair, where after brief instruction, she had won a game of ring toss.

The memory brought a smile. "I believe we've underestimated you, Rosie girl."

But that thought gave him hope for the future. Rose needed them more than ever, and that was how he would convince Emma to stay. He'd explain how she was the only one who could help Rose live up to her full potential.

Emma fought nausea along with the pain. The doctor said she was running a slight fever, which wasn't unusual, and encouraged her to drink plenty of liquids. But no sooner did she drink than it all came back up. Lucille and Papa had visited earlier and brought some peppermint lozenges. Emma had to admit they did help. She just wished things could go back to normal. She wanted to get up. To go for a long ride. Anything but lie in bed . . . thinking.

As the sun set and she faced another long night in the hospital, Emma couldn't help but relive the shooting all over again. She longed to wipe away the image of Tommy dead on the floor, but it haunted her. Worse still, she could recall every sermon she'd ever heard about salvation. It played over and over in her mind.

She had memorized Acts four verse twelve as a child. It was that verse that echoed in her thoughts. *"Neither is there salvation in any other: for there is none other name under heaven given among men, whereby we must be saved."*

That name was Jesus. Neither she nor Tommy had given it much consideration. Tommy had gone to church as a child, and so had she. Both had been told of the need for Jesus, and both had prayed as directed, asking for salvation. But neither had any real purpose for God or religion as they grew older.

They had talked more than once about their encounters with the Gospel message.

Tommy related accepting Jesus as Savior at his mother's knee. She had been a woman of great faith and held the Gospel dear. However, when she passed away, Tommy had been quite angry at God. It was unfair, he told Emma. Unfair that a God supposedly full of love should take a mother away from her children. He wanted little else to do with God, and neither did his brothers.

From how Tommy had described her, it sounded like Aunt Clementine had worked to undo his anger. She had loved Tommy quite dearly, seeing in him the son she might have had. As a childless widow, Aunt Clementine had lavished love on all of the Benton tribe, but Tommy and Rose received the lion's portion.

She had babied Rose, hiding her away from the world as instructed by their father. Tommy had told Emma how Aunt Clementine often explained that Rose was a special kind of being. Not quite an angel, but more than human. Rose recognized spiritual things easier because her mind wasn't bogged down with earthly woes.

Emma wondered at times if that was true. Rose did seem closer to God. She was always speaking of things in the Bible she'd been taught by Aunt Clementine or had heard from the pulpit. Emma found the young woman's ability to recall such things nothing short of a miracle. Rose could neither read nor write, and yet she memorized Scripture like no one Emma had ever seen.

She was also quite adamant with Emma about seeking God. Emma had once confessed to having accepted Jesus quite young, but then told Rose about the time she had decided she didn't want to be a Christian. That Christians had no happiness in their hearts.

"Oh, Emma, you are silly. Of course we have happiness. God is love, and love makes me happy all the time."

Emma fought back tears. How she wished Rosie might be with her right now. Rosie always had a way of comforting her, even if it was with her religious views.

Never had Emma's heart been so heavy. Not even when she'd hurt Mama by declaring her desire to forgo God and Christianity. Then, Emma had ignored the sense of guilt, but at the moment she couldn't begin to avoid it. Guilt consumed her. Overwhelmed her.

How she wished she could pace the floor, but the medicine they'd given her clouded her mind and made her body feel incapable of obeying directions. She was swimming in a haze of regret and despair.

Had Tommy gone to hell?

She was so uncertain of how it all worked, despite having a dozen memorized Scriptures come to mind. Why hadn't she paid more attention? She knew she'd heard plenty of sermons about souls who were condemned without Jesus, but what about those who had accepted Jesus and then hid from Him after that?

"Who are you fooling, Emma John—Benton? You didn't just hide from Him; you denied Him. Denied Him like Peter did in the Bible. You didn't want to follow His rules. You wanted to have fun." Her whispered voice seemed to echo in the silent room.

Tears flowed at this thought. She had done so many foolish things. She'd ignored doing anything of value with her life, and she most assuredly had ignored God. Could she be forgiven? Would God be willing to take her back again? How she wished there was someone she could ask. It might be too late for Tommy; she didn't know. Maybe in the moment he faced that gun, the truth had come back to him. Maybe he sought forgiveness. She couldn't know.

To her surprise, the door to her room opened just a bit, and her stepmother, Lucille, peered inside.

"I hope I didn't wake you," she said, smiling.

"No, no." Emma sniffed back tears and dabbed her face with the edge of the sheet. "Please come in. I was just wishing I could talk to someone."

Lucille slipped into the room. "I know it's past visiting hours, but I felt the need to come here. I told your father that something compelled me to see you."

"It's God." Emma's tone was hushed and filled with awe. Did He still care for her after all she'd done?

"God?" Lucille came to Emma's bedside and took hold of her hand.

"Yes." Emma nodded and met Lucille's kind gaze. "I've been so wrong to put God from me. You can't imagine the guilt I feel. It's pressing down on me like nothing I've ever known before. I fear the worst for Tommy and can't bear to go on without making things right with God."

"Oh, my dear girl, that blesses my heart to hear. I know how hard your mother prayed for this day. We both did."

"You prayed for me?"

"Of course. Your mother and I were good friends; you know that. She used to grieve over your desire to put God out of your life. She asked me to pray with her. On her death bed, she made me promise I would never stop praying for you to find your way back to God. She just knew that you would."

"She did?" Emma felt the first tiny bit of hope. "How could she be so sure?"

"She knew the truth, and that God would one day make it clear to you. You were her prodigal son—or daughter, in this case." Lucille brushed back Emma's hair from her face. "A mother never gives up hope that her child will find their way home."

"Oh, Lucille . . . I want so much . . . I want to make things right. I don't know how. Please tell me what to do." Emma reached for her stepmother and sobbed against her, ignoring the pain from her wound.

"Seek the Lord's forgiveness and recommit yourself to Him, Emma. He stands willing to receive you. He loves you and has never stopped."

Emma closed her eyes, and her mother's face came to mind. She could hear her mother's words from the time she had led Emma to Jesus. *"Pray and ask Him to forgive your sins and come into your heart, Emma. Believe in Him as your Savior, and you will be saved."*

Mama then shared a verse from Romans ten. *"'That if thou shalt confess with thy mouth the Lord Jesus, and shalt believe in thine heart that God hath raised him from the dead, thou shalt be saved.'"*

Emma's voice was barely a whisper. "Please, Lord, let it be so. Forgive me for the way I've acted. Please forgive me for my disbelief. Cleanse me, Lord, and take me back. I want You for my Lord and Savior."

A peace unlike any she had ever known settled upon her. Emma looked up at Lucille, who was also crying. They shared a smile, and Emma knew without any doubt that God had taken her back.

"Do you think my mama knows?"

Lucille nodded. "I'm sure she does. I'm sure all of heaven is rejoicing, and she's the loudest of them all."

Emma settled back in the bed. "Thank you, Lucille. Thank you for listening to God and coming here tonight. I wouldn't have known the way if you hadn't come."

Her stepmother gave her cheek a gentle touch. "God is faithful to draw us to Him. If not me, then He would have sent another. He always hears His children when they long to come home."

3

Saturday morning, Emma was surprised to see Colton accompanying Rosie. He brought Emma a large bouquet of flowers and seemed almost embarrassed when Emma fussed over them.

"They're so beautiful." She drew the flowers to her face and breathed in. "Oh, and they smell so sweet."

The collection of roses and other blossoms reminded Emma of times when Tommy had brought her flowers. The memory was bittersweet.

"Are you better now?" Rosie asked, coming to kiss Emma's cheek.

"Much better. I made them stop giving me so much medicine for the pain. I don't like feeling so strange, and that medicine left me confused. I told them I didn't want to take it unless things got really bad. The doctor told me I should begin feeling better and better."

Rosie nodded and smiled. "You will, because I've prayed for you."

"I'm glad you did, Rose. I think when I get out of here, I need to do a bunch of that myself."

Colton cleared his throat and glanced toward the door.

The conversation appeared to be making him uncomfortable. Emma took pity on him.

"What did you learn about the woman . . . at the wedding?" She found it difficult to speak of what Stella Mikkelson had done.

"She's dead," Colton replied matter-of-factly.

Emma put her hand to her heart. "What? Dead? How?"

"She hanged herself. That same night."

Emma could hardly believe it. "How could that happen?" The woman had tried to turn the gun on herself in the church. It shouldn't be such a surprise that she'd find a way to end her life, but still, it was shocking. After all, she was carrying a life within her. Tommy's child. A baby innocent of all wrongdoing.

"The jailer said he'd checked on her at bedtime, and she had asked for a Bible. When he came to wake her for breakfast, she was gone."

"How terrible." Emma hated what Stella had done, but somehow she couldn't bring herself to hate the woman. Instead, she felt great pity and sadness.

Colton stepped to the edge of Emma's bed. "I know this might seem awfully soon to discuss, but have you decided where you'll go after the doctor releases you?"

"Emma's going to live with us." Rosie spoke as though the matter were settled.

"I haven't really thought about anything except Tommy and what happened."

"We're burying him this afternoon at Trinity Cemetery. I felt we might as well proceed. Forgive me for not asking you first. You were in so much pain, and the doctor said you most likely wouldn't be out until next week. Even then he felt you'd be too weak to attend a funeral."

"There's nothing to forgive. Thank you for managing everything. I know Tommy would have wanted it that way."

She looked toward the window and thought again of the Mikkelson woman. Had her family come to claim her and her unborn child? What would they do? Suicide was not at all an acceptable means of death. Was there a special cemetery for such people?

"We'll bury him by our parents and Aunt Clementine. There's a large plot of land for any of the family who needs it." Colton looked down at her. "I'm so glad we won't be needing another space for you."

Emma drew in a long breath. "It could have been very different. Of course, that woman didn't aim her gun at me. I don't know why."

"You did nothing wrong. You were as much a victim as she was," Colton declared. "Tommy was the one at fault."

Emma tried to move, but she was too weak. "Colton, could you help me to sit up? I'd hate to call the nurse."

"Of course."

Emma handed Rosie the flowers, and Colton moved in to put his hands under each of her arms. "I hope I'm doing this right."

He lifted her and helped her settle back once again. Emma ignored the pain and gave him a nod of approval once he stepped back. "Thank you. That's better."

Rosie started to hand her back the flowers, but Emma waved her off. "I think you should probably take them home with you. I can come and see them there later. The nurse wouldn't approve of them being here in the room."

"I wasn't thinking. Sorry." Colton glanced around the room. "Seems pretty sterile and stark."

"I'm sure it's all about keeping things clean and tidy." Emma folded her hands against her bandaged midsection.

"You are going to live with us, aren't you?" Rosie asked without prompting.

"I hadn't really thought about it." What little she had considered of the future had been focused more on her decision from the previous night.

"We want you to come and stay with us. You are a Benton, and it was Tommy's desire that you both live at the house until you found another place." Colton was most encouraging.

"My father and stepmother want me to move back to Cheyenne and live at their ranch. Clara suggested I come back to live with them."

"But you said no, right?" Rosie asked. "You said I could live with you."

Emma knew the arrangement they'd agreed upon, but with Tommy dead, she seriously doubted Colton, as head of the family, would allow his sister to go off with Emma. Besides, she and Tommy had never planned to leave Dallas permanently. They intended to travel plenty and part of the time take Rosie with them, but moving away wasn't proposed.

Colton cleared his throat. "You can hardly travel to Cheyenne until you're healed. And even the ranch is too far. I suggest you come and stay in Tommy's room as you had planned. Your family is welcome to come there and visit you as much as they like."

"And I can take care of you." Rosie gave Emma a big smile. "You'll be my patient."

Emma chuckled. "I suppose that does sound like the best solution. I just wasn't sure you'd still want me."

"We do want her. Don't we, Colton?"

Emma met Colton's dark eyes. For a moment he just stared at her. Sometimes she didn't think he cared much for her. She always feared that he thought she was only marrying Tommy for his money.

"Yes, we want her." His voice was so low that Emma barely heard him.

"So when can you leave the hospital?" Rosie asked.

"I don't know. The doctor said it would be a few days, Rosie. We must just wait and see. He wants to make sure my wound doesn't get infected."

"It won't. I prayed that you would get well fast, and you will."

Emma loved Rosie's childlike faith in God. "I'm sure if you've prayed, then everything will go well."

Colton frowned, but Emma ignored it. Rosie, however, leaned in to kiss Emma on the cheek once again. "I'm so glad God kept you from dying like Tommy. I miss Tommy. He liked to make me laugh."

"He did. He liked to make me laugh too. I guess there won't be quite as much laughter now."

"Do you think Tommy went to hell?" Rosie asked.

Emma felt a catch in her throat. "I've been thinking about that. I had a long talk last night with my stepmother."

"Last night?" Colton asked.

"Yes, she snuck in after visiting hours. She said she felt compelled to come to me, and it turned out she was right. It gave me a great deal of comfort. She prayed with me."

"But you don't believe in that stuff."

It was hard not to look away, but Emma continued to keep her gaze fixed on Colton. "I walked away from God for a great many years, but after nearly dying, I was forced to revisit my convictions—or lack thereof."

"So now you're religious?"

"Not exactly. I did ask God to forgive me. I'm not sure what it will mean for my life. I just felt so alone last night, as well as guilty."

"Guilty for what? You did nothing wrong." Colton's tone was firm and insistent. "This is what I hate about religion."

"I did plenty wrong, but—"

The room door opened, and Clara gave a light knock just

as she spied Colton and Rosie. "Oh, I see you already have visitors."

"We were just leaving," Colton announced. "We're burying Tommy this afternoon at three. Trinity Cemetery, if you're so inclined to join us. It's just family."

Clara nodded. "Thank you. I'm sure my folks will want to be there. David took the children back to the ranch with the exception of the baby, so I won't be able to attend."

"It won't be a long service, nor all that formal. You can bring the child if you want to be there."

Clara looked to Emma and gave a slight nod. "Thank you."

Colton moved from the bedside and took hold of Rosie. "We'll see you tomorrow, Emma."

"I love you, Emma," Rosie said, giving her yet another kiss.

"I love you, Rosie. Don't forget to put the flowers in water."

"I won't."

Emma watched them leave. She wished so much that she might leave this place too. A sigh escaped her lips.

"You sound tired."

"Weary of this place." Emma looked to her sister. "Hopefully, I'll be able to leave soon."

"Will you come back to the ranch or go to Cheyenne with Father and Lucille? I know they want you to be with them."

"Neither. I won't be up to travel for a while, so I'll go stay at the Benton house as I had figured to do after marrying Tommy. Rosie is adamant that I come and let her nurse me."

"Is that really appropriate?"

"Why wouldn't it be? I did marry Tommy. We might have had no chance to live as man and wife, but I'm still legally a Benton."

"Yes, but it'll be just you and Rosie and . . . Colton."

Emma chuckled and felt the pull across her stomach. She pressed her hand against the pain. "And a staff of ten who live on the premises. So if you're worried about any improprieties,

I assure you there is never a private moment in that house. Besides, Colton has no interest in me."

"I wouldn't be so sure. I've seen the way he looks at you."

Emma shook her head. "He studies everyone in great detail. Colton is an observer of everything and everyone." Yet even as she said it, Emma couldn't help but remember the way he'd looked at her just moments earlier. She'd had the strangest feeling that he wanted to say so much more than he had.

Colton stared down at the open grave and felt a sense of emptiness. Was that all there was left to a soul after death? A hole in the ground? A wooden box? A handful of mourners to say prayers and sing hymns?

His mother would have said that there was all of eternity and that if Colton wanted to spend it in happiness and love, then he needed to make peace with God. As a child, Colton had accepted her words as truth. He had prayed many prayers at her prompting. But his father held no respect for such things, and because of that Colton had put them aside as childish. Even though his mother continued in her beliefs, Colton felt no such need.

There was something about death, however, that caused a man to reflect upon such things. He had never expected to bury any of his brothers, much less Tommy. Colton had been too busy working at his father's side to get very close to Ernest and Walter. In fact, their father had insisted on putting Colton in a position of authority over them, making it clear that they were subordinate to him. It was hard to have a brotherly relationship with someone you were encouraged to see more as an employee than a sibling. But Tommy was different. When Colton was firmly established and trained,

Tommy was still young enough that they could interact as brothers. Tommy often sought Colton out for advice when he'd been young. Young and impetuous. And now he was young and dead. It tore at Colton's heart like nothing else could.

"'O death, where is thy sting? O grave, where is thy victory?'" the pastor read from First Corinthians.

Colton wanted to walk away. This man didn't know Tommy. If he had, he would never have been able to speak those words. The sting of death was a searing pain. The grave would swallow his brother, and Tommy would be no more. The pastor spoke on of Christ having victory over death. For those who could accept that as truth, Colton supposed there might be comfort, but there was no comfort for him. That gentle, fun-loving young man was taken from them. No amount of religiosity could bring him back. The loss tightened a band around Colton's heart and brought tears to his eyes. Even Rosie questioned Tommy's eternity.

Rosie, gowned in black, stood beside him crying softly. The loss she felt was as deep as his own. Colton put his arm around her. What were they to do without Tommy to lighten their days? Colton held Rosie tight. He couldn't help but wonder what would become of her. He did what he could to be there for her, but he was always caught up in business. Just as their father had been.

Father had had little to do with Rosie. First, because he didn't know how to deal with the fact that she wasn't perfect. Second, because she was a female, only furthering her imperfection in the eyes of Lawrence Benton. The only woman Father had ever gotten along with had been Mother.

Then there was the fact that Father was loud and boisterous, especially when he was angry, which was often. But even in his contentment, Father could be deafening. He frightened Rosie. But knowing this, Tommy always made a game of it.

Father was the dragon and Rosie the princess. Her brothers were knights pledged to keep her safe. Colton thought it all ridiculous, but it comforted Rosie as a child and kept them from enduring her tears.

"'For dust thou art, and unto dust shalt thou return,'" the minister recited, then nodded to the casket handlers. The two men immediately lowered the simple box into the ground. Although there was plenty of money for an elaborate coffin and lavish funeral, Colton had seen no sense in spending the money. Tommy was beyond caring.

Rosie startled at the scene and grabbed Colton's arm. After attending their aunt and father's funerals, Rosie knew what to expect, but still it upset her.

"It's all right, Rosie. This is how it must be."

She looked up at him and nodded before burying her face against his coat. Nothing about an unexpected death was easy. He held Rosie close and let her cry, but holding her only served to remind him of Emma. If she could have attended the service, it might be her Colton held. He pushed the thought aside in disgust. How could he stand at his brother's grave and covet his widow? Yet here he was. He couldn't help himself. The pain of Tommy's death only served to make him want Emma all the more. He had loved her in silence for an entire year, and he would go on loving her.

At least they'd convinced her to come live at the house. She could heal there and be close to Tommy's memory. Hopefully Colton could convince her to stick around long after that by reminding her of how much she benefited Rosie. No one could deny the changes Emma had brought about in their sister.

In a matter of minutes, the funeral was concluded, and they were heading back to their buggies. Emma's father and stepmother caught up with Colton and Rosie and once again offered their condolences.

"I'm truly sorry for your loss," Rich Johnson said, extending his hand.

Colton shook hands. "Thank you. I'm glad you could be here to represent Emma. I felt bad that we couldn't delay the funeral."

"It's understandable."

"Emma's going to live with us," Rosie declared, pushing back the veil that continued to blow across her face.

Rich nodded and fixed Colton with a look. He wasn't quite disapproving, but he looked none too happy. "I know she can't travel yet, but I hope if she wants to return to Cheyenne that you'll do everything in your power to help her."

"I will, of course." If it comforted the older man to think that Emma would return to the Wyoming Territory, then what of it? Though in time, Colton hoped to convince her that Dallas was the best place for her now that she owned a majority in the family railroad. With her living under his roof, Colton intended to guide her in their plans for the future. Perhaps even convince her that she should love again.

"I'm so glad to be out of the hospital," Emma told her sister and stepmother as they helped her settle in at the Benton house. "It's a huge house, as you can see, but so amply furnished. Tommy even purchased a brand-new bed for us. The mattress came all the way from the East Coast and has springs inside. I am looking forward to giving it a try. Tommy said it was amazing."

Rose strained to listen to their conversation from the open bedroom door. She had thought about joining them but didn't know if that was polite. There were so many rules for interacting in the company of others.

"I hope you'll consider coming back to the ranch to live."

This came from Emma's stepmother. "You know you will always be welcome there."

"Thank you, Lucille. I appreciate that." Rose braved a peek and watched as Emma embraced her stepmother. "Thank you for everything."

"I hope we can be close," Lucille replied. "I have missed your mother so much. It would be like having a bit of her in my life to have you back in Cheyenne." She pulled back and looked at Clara. "Both of you were so precious to her. She prayed for you constantly. Your brother too. You were her entire world. You and your father. Just as Frank and my children were to me. But we had such a special arrangement in our little part of the territory. Your family and mine and the Hamiltons. How blessed we were to share those friendships."

"I have considered coming back to Cheyenne," Emma said, surprising Rosie. "I thought maybe I could open a dress shop or something. I've learned a lot about women's clothing designs since Tommy bought the very best for me and wanted me to keep up with what was considered the height of popular fashion. I know a great deal about Worth and the various houses in New York and Paris." She paused. "I suppose, however, I'll be wearing black mourning for a time."

"If you come to Cheyenne and want to live in town, your father and I would be happy to help you find a house."

"If you start a dress shop, I want to come too," Rose said, forgetting herself. She hurried into the room. "I'm sorry for spying."

"It's quite all right, Rosie. I would never go anywhere without thinking about you first." Emma reached out and hugged her close. "Although, I doubt your brothers would want you moving that far away."

"Colton will say yes if I ask. He told me he just wants me to be happy."

Emma smiled. "He loves you very much, but I'm not sure he would approve. It's a very long way to Cheyenne."

"Yes, but my brothers say I'm a burden. I heard them, and when I asked you what a burden was, you told me it was a heavy load to carry." This brought a frown to Emma's face. Rosie worried she'd said something wrong.

"You are never a burden, Rosie. They were wrong to say that, so just forget about it. I'll do what I can to make sure that where I go, you go."

Her words made Rosie smile. She loved Emma like the sister she'd never had.

4

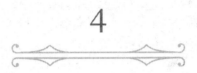

Emma felt much better now that the stitches were gone. The last two weeks had been a challenge in many ways, but most vital to her was deciding about the future. Strangely enough, the more she considered it, the more Emma wanted to return to Cheyenne, partly because she wanted to forget about Texas and all that had happened, but also because it felt like she'd left things undone there.

She had only been home once in the nine years since she left the territory, and that was for her father's marriage to Lucille last fall. She hadn't even been able to return home after their mother died because Clara and the children had been so sick that they'd needed her in Texas. There was a good portion of guilt associated with that originally, but Emma was never one to dwell on such things for long. In keeping with her good-time nature, she spared little time for regret. That had changed with the shooting.

Now it seemed regret haunted her day and night. She hated that the last time she'd seen her mother had been tense. Her mother's words had been full of warnings and stern reminders that her reputation might be forever ruined if Emma failed to curb her zest for living.

The black gown she wore was evidence that her zest for living had come to an end. Emma didn't mind it at all, as it rather matched her mood. She grieved for her husband as any woman might, but even more than her personal loss, she grieved for his soul. They had forfeited so many important things, all in order to enjoy the moment. Emma seriously wondered if she would ever enjoy life again.

Staying at the Benton house had helped in some ways. She felt Tommy's presence here, but in a shared sense. With Colton and Rosie ever present, it was as if they bore the grief together. With a houseful of servants, there was also no reason to worry about cleaning or mending or cooking. At Clara's, Emma had helped with a little bit of everything.

Clara had wanted Emma to return to the ranch, where she could care for her now that Papa and Lucille had returned to Cheyenne. But coming to the Benton house had been an easy decision. It allowed Emma to say good-bye to Tommy in degrees, and that was so much easier than saying good-bye all at once.

Colton was congenial in every way. He checked with Emma daily to ascertain her needs and had driven her out to the cemetery to see Tommy's grave. Perhaps most impressive of all, he arranged for them to sit down to meals together each day. And what meals. The Benton cook was Chef Antoine, who hailed from Lyon in France. He was quite the master chef, creating some of the most mouthwatering meals Emma had ever sampled. Tommy had once told her that the family hadn't eaten together in years, so Colton's gesture to see them sharing three meals a day surprised Emma. Nevertheless, she found it quite pleasant, as did Rosie, who was now her constant companion.

Rosie helped Emma not to feel so lonely and sad. Without Tommy, Emma's entire perspective on life had changed. Add to that her prayer for forgiveness and desire to live a life more acceptable to God, and Emma was almost confused as to what to do next.

For now, it was tending to business. Tommy's last wishes had been dictated to Colton, the family lawyer, and witnessed. Tommy had already told her he intended to provide for her, so Emma was curious as to what he exactly meant by that. It might very well help her decide her future.

"It's time for the reading of the will, Mrs. Benton," Lydia said, bringing Emma a black shawl. "Turned kind of cold, and I thought you might like this. There's a fire in the library, but it might not be enough."

Rosie came in just then. She was also dressed in black and came to Emma for approval. "I am wearing the brooch Tommy gave me. Do you think that's all right?" she asked, pointing to the ruby, rose-shaped pin. "Lydia said no one wears jewelry in mourning."

"That is the custom." The maid glanced from Rosie to Emma. "But it doesn't seem a bad thing since it came from Mr. Benton."

"I think it's just fine." Emma got to her feet and took the wrap from Lydia. "I suppose we'd best make our way downstairs, or your brothers will be vexed with us."

Rosie nodded and helped Emma with the shawl. "Why do we have to be there? I hate business meetings."

"This isn't just a business meeting. This is the reading of Tommy's will. People write wills so that everybody knows what they want done after they die."

"What do you think Tommy wants us to do? Will he want us to stay here with Colton? What if he doesn't want us to be together?" Rosie sounded quite worried.

"It's not exactly like that, Rosie," Emma explained as they made their way downstairs. "A will is Tommy's instructions for what to do with his possessions and money. See, Tommy sat down with Colton and told him exactly what he wanted him to do with his things after he died."

"So Tommy knew he was going to die?"

"No. A will is just something wealthy people put together before they die so that their things can be dealt with whenever they die."

"Oh, I see. Do I have a will? I don't remember ever making Colton write down anything about my things."

"Perhaps you can ask him about it later."

They came to the library, where the three remaining Benton brothers were speaking with two other men. She had met one of them at a family party once but didn't know the other.

"Ah, here are the ladies," Colton said, coming to Emma's side. "Emma Benton, this is Roger Aniston and Simon Glickman. They were both witnesses to Tommy's will. Of course, you know Walter and Ernest."

Emma nodded toward Tommy's brothers. They were cold and indifferent, quickly looking away as if bored with the entire affair.

Colton continued. "And this, gentlemen, is my brother Tommy's widow, Emma Benton, and my sister, Rose."

The men gave slight bows and offered their condolences. Still Walter and Ernest said nothing. Colton led Emma to a chair, and Rosie followed, claiming the one beside her. With that, the men also took their seats, and Colton took his place behind the large oak desk.

Emma glanced around the room without trying to look obvious. She'd never been in the library. For all the times she had been invited to the Benton house, the library had never been one of the rooms frequented by Tommy. She found it quite appealing with the floor-to-ceiling bookshelves and large windows to let in the light or air.

Lydia had been right. There was a fire burning in the hearth, but it was too far away to feel any real sense of warmth. This, added to the cold stares she was receiving from Walter and Ernest, caused Emma to pull her shawl close and hope this ordeal would soon be over.

"We have come here today for the reading of my brother Thomas Benton's will. Tommy wasn't about a lot of procedures and ceremony, so we will make this quick and to the point." Colton looked up from the paper he held. "Tommy asked me to change his will just before he and Emma married. It was his desire to leave the entirety of his wealth and possessions to his wife, Emma Johnson Benton. Mr. Aniston and Mr. Glickman were witness to this testament." He paused and looked at the men. "Gentlemen, would you confirm your signatures?"

Each man rose and came to the desk.

"That is my signature," Mr. Glickman assured.

"And are these the contents of the will as you remember them?" Colton asked.

"They are."

"Thank you. And now Mr. Aniston?"

The routine was repeated, and then the men took their seats once again. Colton looked at Emma. "This means you are now the owner of all that Tommy possessed. He left no exceptions. His money, as well as furniture, clothes, carriage, horses, investments, and anything else, is now yours."

Emma hadn't thought Tommy would leave her everything he owned. That would make her a very wealthy woman in her own right. Wealthy enough that she'd never need to open a shop to support herself. She could easily move anywhere and do just about anything she wanted.

Colton dismissed Mr. Glickman and Mr. Aniston with thanks for their having come. The housekeeper, Mrs. Lansdale, showed them out before Colton spoke again. "Well, that's that. Do you have any questions, Emma?"

"If she doesn't, I do," Walter interjected. "Why did Tommy

leave her the railroad stocks? It's our family's heritage, not hers."

"I agree." Ernest brushed lint from his trouser leg. "She may have married Thomas, but she wasn't a wife to him. At least not while legally wed."

"I beg your pardon?" The words were out of Emma's mouth before she could think them through. "How dare you?"

Ernest gave her a look of boredom. "We all know what Tommy was like, so don't pretend to be so offended."

"I don't have to pretend. I am offended." Emma got to her feet. "Your brother has only been gone a short time, and this is the focus of your heart?" She looked at Colton. "I've given it a lot of thought, and I plan to move back to Cheyenne."

"And I want to go with her," Rosie declared, shooting up to stand beside Emma. "You said I could live with her and Tommy."

"Yes, but Tommy is gone now, and you are our responsibility, not Emma's," Colton replied.

Rosie gave her foot a stomp. "Emma is our sister now. Even if Tommy is dead. She loves me and wants me to live with her."

Emma felt all eyes turn to her. "It's true. I do love Rose. I would be happy for her to live with me in Cheyenne, and since Tommy has left me so amply endowed, there is no reason I can't use that money to take care of your sister."

"We can discuss this at a later time." Colton glanced at his brothers before continuing. "I'm sure you're tired and should rest."

Emma wasn't sure what his plan was, but there was something in the way he spoke that encouraged her to comply.

"Then please excuse me." She headed for the open library door with Rosie at her side.

"Please don't let them keep me here in Texas without

you," Rosie whispered. "I'm all grown up now. Twenty-three is old enough to tell them what I want even if . . . even if I'm not as smart as they are."

Emma smiled and looped her arm with Rosie's as they started up the stairs. "You are plenty smart, Rosie. I won't leave you alone. I promise. If they won't let you come with me, then I will remain here with you."

"Thank you, Emma. I love you so much." Rosie gave her a sideways hug. "Oh, why don't I go tell the cook to send someone up with tea? He might have cakes too."

Rosie did love cake, and Emma couldn't help but chuckle. "I think that would help my mood considerably."

Colton shook his head at Ernest. "Don't you think that was a little uncalled for?"

"I'm concerned about our railroad. She now owns the majority control."

"Emma's not foolish. She'll listen to counsel. She knows how we feel about the railroad."

Walter got to his feet and poured himself a drink. "Why did you let Tommy make such a change to his will?"

"How was I to stop him? He was determined to leave everything to Emma. If I didn't draw up the will, he would have had someone else do it."

"Well, you could have done it without witnesses. That way you could have changed it," Walter declared. "She doesn't deserve to have his fortune."

"She loved him and married him. They planned a future together. I believe she deserves it as much as you do." Colton sat back down and refolded the will.

"Do you suppose she's with child?" Ernest asked.

"Why don't you just run upstairs and ask her?" Colton's

sarcasm was more than evident in his tone. "I'd like for Emma to give you what you have coming for being so rude to her."

"It's not rude," Walter said, coming back to where he'd sat for the reading. "It's just pragmatic to know whether or not there's a baby. After all, they did get married rather quickly, and that other woman claimed to be pregnant. At least she had the decency to end her life."

"Walter, I pity your wife and children. You are utterly without feeling. Tommy put Miss Mikkelson in a very bad situation. Her options were not many. As for Emma and Tommy, they had been talking about a wedding since last summer. I hardly see it as a rush to the altar." Colton knew his brothers were worried about Emma's control over the family railroad. Especially now when they were in negotiations with the Southern Pacific to sell it. Her signature would be required in any dealings they had regarding the family's rail line. He had his own concerns, but what was to be done now?

"But she could cause us trouble, especially since she isn't of a mind to remain here where we can control her."

Colton might have laughed at his brother had it not been such a serious matter. Walter did well to give a pretense of controlling his own family. The idea of him controlling Emma was too ludicrous to imagine.

"She's a sensible woman. If you would have spent any time at all with her, then you'd know she's also quite insightful. I'll speak to her about our plans when the time is right."

"But she's leaving for Cheyenne. It will break all connections."

"Not exactly," Colton replied. "She wants to take Rosie with her."

"Let her." Walter tossed back his drink. "She's nothing but a burden to all of us. I was delighted when Tommy said he wanted Rosie to live with them."

"Yes, let her take Rose to Cheyenne. That way we'll remain tied together. You would have to make frequent trips to see to it that Rose was being well cared for." Ernest sounded quite enthused.

Walter put his empty glass on Colton's desk. "Yes, yes. That would be perfect, and even better, what if you were to show interest in Emma as time went on? Woo her and then marry her? You could then ensure that the family things Tommy inherited as well as the stocks would remain in our control."

"I'm not marrying Emma for control of her railroad stock." Colton did his best to remain calm, but he had to admit that the idea of courting Emma was ever in his thoughts. His brothers had no idea of him being in love with her, however. He'd gone out of his way to keep Emma at arm's length for fear Tommy might see how he felt about her.

"But Walter makes a good point. You could marry her and solve everything. Good grief, we're not asking you to fall in love with her, but as the leader of this family, and an unmarried one at that, you could solve all of our problems. The railroad and our plans for it could be placed on hold while you convince Emma that you have fallen in love with her. It shouldn't be that hard. After all, she needs to be comforted." Ernest studied his fingernails for a moment. "Women are easily manipulated if you know what you're doing. I didn't have any great love for my wife when we courted. It was more financial benefit than romantic, and yet I convinced her of my undying passion for her. If I can manage such a thing, I'm sure you can."

Colton could hardly believe what his brothers were saying. He supposed had it been anyone other than Emma, he might have been less offended. But knowing that marriage to her would fulfill his deepest desires made Colton feel awkward about the entire matter. It sickened him to imagine using Emma in such a fashion.

"The matter is closed to further discussion. But I agree that it's a good idea to allow Rosie to go with Emma to Cheyenne. They are very close, and given both are mourning Tommy, they will be good for each other. I know Emma will take good care of our sister—probably better than we do."

"And you could go with them to Cheyenne and see them settled in," Walter added, rubbing his beard. "Maybe stay on a little while just to make sure the transfer of funds and such goes without a hitch."

Ernest got up and walked to the fireplace. "And you could incorporate business. I've read that cattle ranching in the territory is picking back up after that bad winter. Perhaps you should consider it as an investment. Wasn't Emma's family involved in such things? You could speak to her father about it."

Colton felt guilty for even considering all that they were saying, but at the same time, it intrigued him. It was the perfect excuse to stay close to Emma. Perhaps in time he could convince her of his feelings for her.

"It's not the worst idea," he admitted. "I could look into those things with Emma's help."

Walter jumped up from his chair. "It's settled, then. We'll let Rosie go with Emma to Wyoming. Now I need to go. I have another meeting. Let me know when you have it all arranged, Colton."

Later that night, Emma couldn't sleep. Restless and hungry, she made her way downstairs. Chef Antoine always left things available for snacking, so she figured she could at least put an end to her hunger.

She found sliced roast beef in the icebox, as well as the cook's horseradish sauce, and decided to make herself a sandwich. She had just brought the bread to the kitchen table when she heard footsteps in the hall.

Emma quickly checked to make sure her robe was properly closed and glanced up just as Colton entered the room.

"I heard a noise and figured to check it out."

He was fully dressed, as though he'd not yet gone to bed. Emma wondered if he was missing Tommy as she was.

"I couldn't sleep and wanted something to eat. Are you hungry? I was just about to make myself a sandwich."

"I could definitely go for one, thanks." Colton went to the stove. "I'll work up the fire and put some water on for tea."

"Could you also grab a couple of plates, please?" Emma returned her attention to slicing the bread. "Tommy told me about coming down here for midnight snacks and how Chef Antoine got so annoyed at his messing things up for the next day that he started leaving food in a specific place for Tommy to eat."

Colton brought her two dinner plates, then went to the stove. "He did. As you probably found, there's usually sliced meat and cheese in the icebox and bread in the bread box. There are also cookies in several jars and a cake under glass on the far counter. And one of the servants keeps a small fire going in the stove throughout the night. That way it's always hot for morning meals. Antoine is quite insistent on no delays."

"That's very accommodating. It's a wonder Tommy wasn't as plump as a partridge."

Colton finished tending the fire, then went to the sink and filled the teapot. "He was always too busy to get fat. Our mother said he had more energy than all of the rest of us combined."

"Well, I think we all know that Tommy was energetic and

ambitious." She thought of Stella and frowned. "Then again, sometimes I don't think I knew Tommy at all."

"I know he loved you."

Emma was surprised at the gentleness of Colton's tone. For so long he had been stern to the point of dismissiveness with her. "That's kind of you to say. I believe he did love me in his own way."

"Did you know about Stella? I mean, before the wedding?"

"No. Not in particular. I knew he was popular with the girls. The first time I met him he was surrounded by women all vying for his attention." She smiled at the memory. "I had gone to a party given by someone my sister was friends with at church. It was a garden party, and I remember the lush and beautiful flowers. They were everywhere. Roses as big as plates. It was like nothing I'd ever seen. And there across the way was Tommy. He was laughing and telling some story. The ladies were hanging on his every word."

"I've seen him like that too." Colton brought the cups to the table and sat down.

Emma could see a weariness in his eyes and wondered what was troubling him so much. Perhaps it was simple grief, but if it was something more pressing, maybe she could help.

"You look like you have something weighing on you."

Colton leaned back in the chair. "No more so than any other time. There's a lot of business to deal with, and losing Tommy has been such a shock. I never figured to bury my little brother. It won't be the same without him. As much of an irresponsible knave as he could be, I loved him. I will miss our talks. Tommy could be quite thoughtful, as you know. His insight was sometimes astounding. The loss will be immense."

Emma finished slicing bread, then reached for the sauce. "I'm truly sorry. I know you cared for him more than anyone. Tommy knew that too. He told me that you were the only one he could trust in the family—that you were the only one who cared about him as an individual. Which seems evident by the fact that your brothers seem far more worried about my inheritance than Tommy's death."

"Walter and Ernest were always closer to each other than Tommy. They're serious-minded regarding their business dealings. I must allow, however, that both of them pay very close attention to their own families, although perhaps more out of obligation and society's watchful eye than love."

"Well, at least there's that. But again, they have each other and their families in which to find comfort. You don't have anyone, it seems."

Colton shrugged. "Since I was a boy, I've always had to be the strong one as the eldest brother. Our father trained me up that way—told me one day it would be my responsibility to see to all the others once he was gone. He wanted me isolated."

"That's a lot to put on a child."

"I suppose it was, but then again someone had to do the job."

"Still, I'm sorry. I prefer to see children have a chance to enjoy childhood. We're burdened with responsibilities soon enough. When I was young, I have to admit, I was indulged. Too much, in fact." She shrugged and continued focusing on the sandwiches. "I wanted to have fun, to live life like it was one big party. I found that same attitude in Tommy, so we fit well. Tommy said I was the only woman he'd ever met who wasn't pursuing a husband like it was a life-and-death matter."

Colton chuckled. "I can hear him saying that."

"I wasn't looking to get married or fall in love. In fact, Tommy and I both agreed that such things weren't needed in order to enjoy life together. We only married because . . . well, Tommy wanted more from me than I felt I could give without the benefit of being married." She felt her cheeks grow hot.

"But you did love each other. I know Tommy loved you."

"In his way, and the same was true for me." He looked at her oddly, and she smiled. "Does that shock you? We understood how we felt and what was important to each other. It wasn't at all conventional, and I don't know that I could ever hope you'd understand. But that's why I'm not angry about Stella." She looked up. "There were probably a great many Stellas."

"How can you not be enraged? Your husband, the man who pledged his life to you, was cheating on you with another woman."

Emma gave a long sigh. "I know, but I also know it meant nothing to Tommy. Only I meant enough to him to marry. The others did all they could to convince him to choose them, but Tommy wanted me. I have that thought to comfort me despite how much his betrayal hurt."

"But it's not enough. That's not what love and marriage are about. You deserved more than that."

Emma thought Colton sounded almost angry. "It was enough at the time. And I agree it's not what most people consider when they think of love and marriage. I guess I really never thought of myself as needing a conventional marriage or love."

She wished she could explain how things had changed with her. Colton probably thought her so unfeeling, so lacking in commitment. But what could she say? That was who she was before her brush with death.

"I know you don't understand what I'm saying. I hate who I used to be, Colton." She placed the sandwiches on the plates. "Tommy and I neither one had much sense. We only knew about having a good time, and only my prudish morals brought me to the altar. You can hate me if you want to, and I'll understand because I hate myself. At least, I hate the woman I used to be."

"I don't hate you, Emma." Colton reached over and took hold of her hand. "I could never hate you."

She felt her breath catch in her throat. The way he was looking at her caused a strange feeling to course through her, but Emma ignored it. She searched for something to say in reply, but the words wouldn't come. Thankfully, the teapot began to whistle, and Colton dropped his hold on her. Emma hurriedly cut her sandwich into fourths. She didn't understand the things she was feeling or the thoughts that were coming into her head. Everything was so different now that she allowed herself to have a conscience.

5

I'm glad you were able to stop by." Emma signaled a young man waiting by the door to bring the refreshments.

"Well, your message sounded urgent." Clara pulled off her gloves, then removed her sunbonnet. "Are you eating properly?" She nodded toward Emma's black crepe de chine gown. "That gown is awfully big on you."

"This was one of the ready-made gowns purchased for me. It's quite light and, given the humidity and heat, is more comfortable than bombazine. I'm grateful for what I could get. My regular seamstress went to all of her friends and the stores where they work and brought me samples once I was out of the hospital. For such a large city, the selection wasn't that great."

"You could have just dyed a couple of your old gowns."

"They did that as well, but of course it took a little time, and we wanted to keep the waist loose because of my incision anyway. I can hardly do that in my fitted gowns. They require a corset as well, and until a week or two ago, I was still unable to manage that without it irritating my wound. Now I'm corseted, and it makes this gown seem all the bigger."

"Do you plan to wear black for a full year? I mean . . . well,

I don't discredit the fact that you were legally wed, but it seems a bit much to—"

Emma waved off the comment. "I don't know yet what I plan. Tommy wouldn't have wanted me to wear black for even a week, but it suits my mood right now and makes my status clear to anyone who sees me."

The footman arrived with the tea cart and wheeled it near Emma. "We'll serve ourselves, thank you." She waited until he was gone, then turned back to Clara. "To answer your concerns about my eating, I'm doing just fine. I even occasionally raid the icebox in the middle of the night."

Clara got to her feet before Emma could stand. "I'll serve us. Tell me why you asked me here today." She held up a small plate and gave a nod to the tray.

"Tea with cream and one of the little sandwiches would be fine for now." Emma wasn't hungry, but given her sister's worries, she wanted to prove she was eating.

Clara put it together and handed Emma the tea first and then the sandwich plate. She chose for herself, then reclaimed her seat.

Emma sipped her tea and then set it aside. "I'm moving back to Cheyenne. I've made up my mind that I need to do this. I want to put the past behind me, but I feel like there's much in Cheyenne that I need to tend to. Pardons to be asked, forgiveness sought."

"And just how will you do that?"

Shaking her head slowly, Emma contemplated the question. "I've asked myself that over and over. I suppose to those I've wronged, I could apologize and ask if there's something I could do to show my regret."

"But some things can't be bought and paid for." Clara picked up her tea. "You can't pay to mend someone's broken heart or wounded feelings."

Memories of the various young men Emma had courted

came to mind. "Who's to say how such a thing might go? All I can do is apologize and ask forgiveness. If they don't give it—and I wouldn't blame them if they didn't—then I have to accept that."

"I suppose there's little else to be done," Clara admitted.

"I want to start with my family. I spoke to Papa before he left, and of course he said I owed him no apology and that no forgiveness was due because he held nothing against me. I can't very well seek it from Mama, except I did ask God to tell her how sorry I am. I don't know if heaven works that way, but God knows my heart. I want more than anything for her to know that I've made a change to my life.

"As for other people, honestly, I'm not sure of what to say or, in some cases, of any particular wrong to point out. I do want to seek your forgiveness, however."

"Mine?" Clara looked at Emma for a few moments. "I can't think of thing that I need to forgive. I used to worry about you something fierce, I suppose. You did upset me on several occasions, but usually that was experienced secondhand. Mama would write letters and ask me to pray for you. She'd never say exactly what trouble you were up to, but she asked me to pray."

"And did you?"

Clara laughed. "All the time. For you and James. You were both such ambitious souls. Always going your own way and doing things that were considered unacceptable. To tell you the truth, there was a part of me that envied your ability to throw caution to the wind and dare to do things that were dangerous. I remember that time when you stood on the back of your horse at a full gallop. My heart nearly stopped. I know Mama felt faint."

"I was ten, and I remember it well. There was something inside me that was willing to risk life and limb. But not anymore."

"You came too close to death."

Emma sipped her tea. She had seen death up close, and it was too intimidating. She didn't care to see it again. At least not in that horrible state of being alone. Of hearing the loud beat of your own heart and wondering if it might stop at any given moment.

"A lot of the things you did were just antics based on a desire to feel that sense of elation and excitement that you craved." Clara shook her head. "I never longed for that. I liked things safe and simple. David takes enough risks for us both. But I don't feel you owe me an apology for anything."

"There were so many times that I worried you. You're ten years older than me, and I know people said things. I overheard a good many of those conversations. People were only too happy to point out my failings, be they teachers at school, store clerks, or church folk. I wasn't polite enough. I spoke my mind too often. I didn't come home when I should have. I didn't abide by our parents' rules. Just as I ignored God's rules for most of my life."

"Worse still, you ignored His love."

Clara's matter-of-fact statement caused Emma's breath to catch. That was it. She had chosen to live like the prodigal son and in doing so had missed out on the love that her heavenly Father offered. She'd cast off His love, His security, and His protection.

"Well, things are changing now. I still don't know exactly what it all means or how I will live, but I have sought God's forgiveness."

"That's a wonderful place to start. Now you need to know Him for yourself. You knew Him through Mother and Father, since children learn that way. But you need your own relationship with Jesus—something that will get you through the truly bad times with comfort and the good times with great joy."

"I suppose that makes sense." Emma put her cup down and wiped her hands on a linen napkin. "Look, I want you to know that while you might not think I owe you an apology or anything else, I appreciate that you took me in when Mama was at her wit's end with me."

"I needed you. With all the work on the ranch and the kids so little and needy, you gave me a great deal of relief. Then there were all those times I miscarried, and you were there for me, nursing me through and comforting me. I doubt I'd still be alive had you not been with me these last nine years."

"I could have done so much more. My mind was always on doing just enough so that I could head to town and meet up with my friends and have a good time. Going around unescorted. I hate to think of the ruckus I might have raised had I been a boy instead of a girl." Emma smiled and shook her head. "I hope Rachel and Leah never give you the kind of trouble I gave everyone."

"My daughters will no doubt try my patience, but, Emma, I can assure you that no matter what they do, I will always love them. Just as Mama loved you."

Emma's brow furrowed. "I hope she did. I hope she knew that I loved her."

"She did. She even said as much in her letters. Take comfort in that. She knew."

Tears came unbidden, and Emma bowed her head. "I'm glad you think so. That eases my mind." The grandfather clock in the hall struck two, and Emma straightened. She reached into her pocket and pulled out a bank draft.

"I've been thinking a lot, as I said. I know that there are things on the ranch that you and David want to accomplish, and I want you to have this. In appreciation for all that you did for me over the years."

Clara took the check and looked at the writing. Her eyes

widened. "I can't take this. That's a lot of money, Emma. You may need this."

She shook her head. "I can honestly say that it will take very little away from my wealth. Tommy was incredibly rich. I didn't even realize how much he owned. He had stocks, land, and investments from his father and his aunt. He left the family investing to Colton, who managed everything in an amazing fashion, but he also had another man who invested for him." She lowered her voice. "I don't think anyone knew about him. He came to see me last week and told me about other investments that did very well. There's artwork that Tommy bought on whims when he was out traveling about, buildings he leased out, and an entire fleet of ships to carry freight and passengers. Those I knew about because Tommy promised me that one day we would board those ships and travel the world. For a man who gave the appearance of taking nothing seriously, Tommy was quite ingenious. I have more than I can ever hope to know how to spend.

"I know that when David inherited his uncle's ranch, it was pretty run-down. I want you to have this money to help make the ranch everything you've ever dreamed. What's the sense of my having money if I can't help those I love? And I love you and David. I admire you more than I can say. Let me do this. If you approve it, I know David will."

Clara stared at the check for a moment, then looked up to meet Emma's gaze. "This will change everything for us. Thank you."

Emma smiled and dabbed the napkin to her eyes. "You've made me so happy. I'll look forward to seeing how you two change the place."

Clara folded the check and put it into her purse. "When will you leave for Cheyenne?"

"Within the next few weeks. And I hope to take Rosie with me."

"Will the Benton brothers allow her to go?" Clara frowned and glanced toward the archway into the hall.

"I'm speaking to them about it. Colton seems positive about the idea." Emma lowered her voice again. "Frankly, I think Walter and Ernest will be glad to have her gone. They've never had much time for her. I think they're embarrassed by her, even though she's perfectly precious."

"How sad. Rose is a delightful young woman."

"She is, and I think Colton realizes she'll be better off with me. At least, I hope that he still feels that way. With Benton men, you can never tell what they're thinking. I suppose, however, we shall all know soon enough."

Emma was surprised when Mrs. Lansdale came to her and announced that Colton would like to talk to her in the library. She found him staring out the window, looking quite pensive.

"You wanted to see me?"

He turned and for a moment just stared at her. Emma found his study to be a bit unnerving. He had the most intense dark brown eyes, and they always seemed able to spy out the most intimate details.

"I did," he finally replied. "I've been thinking about your move to Cheyenne."

"So have I. I'd like to leave before the end of the month. I realize we can still get into bad weather, but I thought if we took the train, then there would be fewer worries."

Colton moved closer to where she stood. His presence seemed to fill the space around her. She'd always admired Colton and his ability to lead. When Lawrence Benton had fallen ill, Colton kept things running without so much as a pause. He knew the family business in detail and had a confidence of authority that none of his brothers had mastered.

He seemed to consider what she had said, then nodded. "The new line from Fort Worth to Denver would be perfect, and the family has free passes to ride anytime we like. Is Rosie still of a mind to go with you?"

"Yes, and I would very much love to have her. I figure it's only right I spend some of my inheritance on her care, and it would honor Tommy at the same time. He loved her so . . . not that you don't, but I know how busy you are. And Rosie and I are good for each other."

"I know you are, and that's why I believe she should go with you. Cheyenne is a long way away, though, and it's still rather wild. But truthfully, we've got our problems in Texas too. Walter and Ernest left the decision up to me, and I think the opportunity is a good one."

Emma smiled, knowing this would please Rosie. And having her sister-in-law live with her in Cheyenne would comfort Emma as well. "Thank you so much, Colton. I appreciate the trust you're putting in me."

"It's obvious you love Rosie, and she loves you. She won't get that from Walter and Ernest, and although I try to show her my love, I'm not the best at it."

"You weren't allowed to practice much with your father being so very demanding of you."

"Yes." Colton's expression was rather sad as he looked away.

Emma touched his arm, something that appeared to surprise them both. He looked at her oddly for a moment, and she released him. "I'm sorry. I just . . . well, it's never too late to change. Rosie needs your love more than ever after losing Tommy."

"Maybe it would be smart for me to come along and see you two settled in. Even stay a month or two and conduct some business with the Union Pacific."

His comment surprised Emma. Colton was seldom willing

to leave Dallas even for business meetings. He always felt it was important to remain close at hand for anything that might come up.

"I can see that this surprises you," Colton said before Emma could speak. "However, Rose is of the utmost concern to me. I made our mother a promise years ago that I would look after my sister. She knew life would be difficult for Rose and wanted only the best for her. And as you said, it's never too late to change. Plus, I can attend to some railroad business. Perhaps help you to better understand the value of what you've inherited."

"Oh, I already understand that. Maybe not what it's worth financially, but sentimentally. Tommy once told me the railroad was the very heart of the family."

"Perhaps at one time it was. Now . . . well, not as much. Walter and Ernest are concerned about costs and such. In fact, we're contemplating the future and whether or not to sell."

"Oh, but you could never sell. Your father worked so hard to leave it as your legacy."

Colton looked as though he might reply to that but then changed the subject back to Rosie. "I do hope to be a better brother to Rose. She deserves to have a good life, one of ease and comfort."

"I intend to give Rosie the best and more. Your family has never allowed her to decide things for herself or really learn anything. Rose is smart, and despite the circumstances of her birth, I believe she can be taught a great deal."

"Well, you've proven that in part. I must admit that you have a way with her. That's why the decision to let her live with you was rather an easy one. I had hoped you would remain here in Dallas, but maybe getting Rosie to an entirely different place will be all the better. What few people she's been allowed to associate with here are not likely to challenge her or treat her as they would others. They have it in their mind that Rosie is unable to understand what everyone else knows, and the folks in Cheyenne might allow her to prove herself."

"My thoughts exactly."

"I'm going to speak to Walter and Ernest later today. I'll let them know that I've decided it's for the best that Rosie accompany you to Cheyenne."

"And you'll come too?" Emma was still surprised that was even being discussed.

"Yes, if that's all right?"

"I think it would be wonderful. We can get a big house there. We can all stay together for as long as you decide to remain in town. I figured to buy a place, anyway."

"Well, it would hardly be appropriate for me to move in with just you and Rose. You are a widowed woman, and there are proprieties. I wouldn't wish to upset the community."

"I'm your sister-in-law, and your sister will be living under the same roof just as we do here."

"Yes, but there's a staff of ten who also live here. It makes things more acceptable. I know you'll hire someone to help you, but having just one or two people who come in to work rather than live there wouldn't be the same."

"Perhaps I shall hire live-in staff. It is nice to have someone available at a moment's notice. But I see your point. No sense upsetting the old ladies of the church now that I'm trying to make amends for the past."

"The past? What could you possibly have to amend for in the past?"

Emma shrugged and hugged her arms to her body. "The same wild young lady who stormed Dallas was storming Cheyenne before that." She smiled. "I didn't rob a bank, but I did occasionally take items from the store without paying." She bowed her head. "I'm not at all proud of my behavior.

Stealing was often a challenge that my friends and I thought fun. I had no regard as to how I was hurting the store owners. I was obnoxious and devious and only concerned about myself. I offended a great many people, and I'd like to make that right."

Colton surprised her by laughing. "I cannot imagine you offending anyone."

She raised her head. "You didn't know me then, Colton. With your serious nature and no-nonsense attitude, you would have quickly cast me aside."

"I doubt that. There's always been something about you that I . . . well, that I find quite appealing."

Emma could see that look on his face once again. No one ever looked at her the way Colton did. Most of time, people considered her with disdain or at least caution. Colton's gaze was one that, for the life of her, Emma didn't understand.

"Well, so long as you're warned about it. I have no idea of what I'll face once I'm there. I haven't been home in a long, long while."

"Maybe folks will forget about what you were like and give you a chance to prove who you've become."

Emma swallowed the lump building in her throat. "Wouldn't that be nice?"

"So I've agreed to let her take Rose to Wyoming, and I plan to go with them, at least for a few weeks, maybe longer."

"And you'll do your best to court Emma and get her to marry you so that we can keep the railroad stock and other investments in the family?"

Colton shook his head. "I don't intend to do that."

"But you must," Walter insisted. "She's not going to understand business. If she decides against the sale, thinking, for example, that we shouldn't sell off what our father worked so hard to create and build, then we'll be in a most difficult place."

"Besides that, there are other things Tommy inherited that belong to our family. His share of Mother's jewelry, for example," Ernest joined in.

"Those things are Emma's now. Besides, I think she's sensible and will listen to me when it comes to the railroad." Colton took a seat behind his desk. "I feel confident that she'll receive my direction and adhere to it."

"I still think you should marry her. For pity's sake, Colton, you need to marry and produce an heir."

"Why?" He gave a laugh. "If I died tomorrow, you two would inherit my entire fortune." That brought to mind that he'd not changed his will since Tommy died.

"Well, controlling Emma is the most important thing, and we need to make sure she doesn't sell those stocks to someone else," Ernest declared. "Let her have Rose, but perhaps tell her she must sign legal papers to allow you to be the proxy in all railroad votes in return."

Colton shook his head. "I'm not going to sell our sister for stocks. I'll let Emma know how Tommy felt about selling off the railroad and investing elsewhere. I'm sure she'll listen."

"And you'll not even entertain the idea of getting her to marry you?" Walter asked.

"I don't see that it's required for what we want. I think Emma will cooperate and do whatever I say."

Colton didn't intend to make any problems for Emma or Rosie, but he was certain that by stating this his brothers would feel more confident of the situation.

Walter appeared less than convinced. "She could change her mind soon enough. Especially if one of her old acquaintances happens to take an interest in courting her. Once the men in Cheyenne learn that she has money, they'll line up to wed the Widow Benton."

Colton didn't like to even imagine such a thing, but Walter's words hit him hard. Emma was beautiful and young. She must have had plenty of suitors in Cheyenne. No doubt there would be men aplenty seeking her affection and attention. Well, just another good reason for him to go along with her.

"Look, Colton, you've always been forthright with us, and we've listened to you," Walter began. "Ernest and I have talked about this and feel it's critical that you listen to us. You have to marry Emma. There's just too much at stake. It's not just that she has majority control of our railroad, but she also owns a percentage on all the holdings we inherited from our Father. We can't risk that going astray. You need to put aside your desire to remain single. This is something Ernest and I must insist on."

"You must insist, eh? Since when did you decide I was obligated to take orders from the two of you? I will marry when and whom I desire to marry. You two aren't going to bully me into anything."

"You owe us this much, Colton. We rarely ever question your desires for the family businesses."

"And I've made you plenty of money, haven't I?"

"Yes, but this time we can't risk Emma going back to her people and picking up with someone from her past. If she did that and married a man with lofty ambitions, we'd have little control over anything. We don't need a stranger coming in to wreak havoc on our affairs."

Colton had to admit they made a good point. He hadn't previously considered Emma finding an old beau and remarrying. However, she did have a new sense of purpose in going back to Cheyenne. She wanted to amend for her past wrongs, and who knew where that might lead her.

"You need to do this for us—for the family—Colton." Ernest fixed him with a stern gaze.

"And do it quickly," Walter added. "Don't give her time to consider anyone else. Marry Emma as soon as possible. We need things settled immediately."

"She hasn't been widowed that long. It wouldn't even begin to be appropriate for me to approach the topic."

"Forget what's appropriate or acceptable by social standards. Just find a way to endear yourself to her and for her to need you. It shouldn't be that hard." Walter shook his head and gave an exasperated sigh.

Colton wanted to walk away from both of them and leave well enough alone. He cared for Emma and would be delighted to court her, but now wasn't the proper time. He'd keep with his original plan and build first on friendship and their connection as family. Emma was the kind of person who had been brought up to cherish those things. And truth be told, so did Colton. He wanted very much for Emma to desire his company, just as he did hers.

6

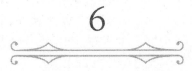

I hope you'll like the house we picked out for you," Lucille Johnson said as Emma's father drove them away from the Cheyenne train depot. She looked over her shoulder at the trio in the back of the carriage and smiled. "When you wired that you wanted something really nice, we had our doubts, but Rich and I prayed about it and learned about the Wellington house being for sale. Do you remember it, Emma?"

"No, not really." Emma adjusted her coat and pulled the lapels together to ward off the chilly breeze.

"Temperatures dropped just yesterday. We'd had some nice spring days until then," her father said with a smile. "Havin' lived in Texas these last few years, you're probably missing the heat."

"It is a lot colder than I anticipated." Emma turned to Rosie. "Are you doing all right?"

"I'm fine. I like the cold."

Emma looked to her left, where Colton was squeezed in beside them. He gave a nod. "It is different to be sure. I don't mind the temperatures, but that wind is getting stronger as we go."

"Wind blows all the time around here. When it's not blowin', we're wonderin' what's wrong."

"Papa isn't joking. Out on the ranch, you learn to steady yourself and lean into the wind." Emma smiled at memories of gusts knocking her over as a child.

"Getting back to the Wellington house," her stepmother said, "it's brick, but they painted it."

"First with a white wash, but against the brick it looked kind of pink, so they added in some sort of brown. Now it looks kind of like a pale, buttery tan," Emma's father added. "Real nice."

As they made their way past the main part of downtown Cheyenne, Rosie was all agog and chatty. "This is bigger than I thought it'd be. Not as big as Dallas, but nice. I like Cheyenne."

"The new depot is impressive," Colton said. "I read about it in one of the railroad magazines."

"It was quite the feat." Emma's father glanced over his shoulder at his passengers. "They brought in red-and-buff-colored rock from Colorado to build it. Never seen anything like it."

Emma had also been impressed by the depot the previous fall when she'd arrived for her father's wedding to Lucille. They'd had a double ceremony with Lucille's daughter, Charlotte, and their neighbor Micah Hamilton.

Her father turned the carriage down Seventeenth and headed east. Emma hoped they'd reach the house soon. She was starting to shiver.

"Do you remember Mr. and Mrs. Vogel? He's our police chief now," Lucille explained. "Mrs. Vogel used to teach your Sunday school class."

Emma easily remembered the time she'd been caught stealing liquor, and Edward Vogel had been the officer she had been given over to. "Yes, of course. Why do you ask?"

"Your house is just across the street from theirs. It's a beautiful neighborhood. Folks have worked hard to plant trees and flowering shrubs. It's already starting to bloom, what with all the warm weather we just had."

Emma wished they were having warm weather now. She couldn't hide her shivering, causing Rosie to lean closer and put her arms around Emma's shoulders.

"You're so cold, Emma."

Emma laughed, and it came out in a halted sort of gasping. "I'd forgotten just how cold it could be. When I came here for the wedding, it was still quite nice."

"Move in closer, Colton," Rosie ordered. "Help me get Emma warm."

Emma wanted to laugh all the more. They were already squeezed in tight. "I'll be fine once we're inside."

"Well, the house is just up the way." Emma's father quickened the horses' steps, and in a few minutes, he was pulling into a short, U-shaped drive. "It's not millionaire's row, but it's a whole lot nicer than some of the houses they slapped together."

Emma had to admit the Italianate-style house was all she could hope for—at least on the outside. There was a certain charm to it that was most welcoming with its small porch to the right of the front door and arched bay windows to the left.

Colton helped her down and held on to her for a moment to make certain she was able to stand. She smiled up at him in thanks, then stepped aside so he could help Rosie.

"The inside is quite lovely, and we've already managed to furnish it with things the previous owners left, as well as a few things we gathered from our ranch and the Hamiltons' old place. You should find it fairly well ordered and warm. We lit a fire in the front room before we came to pick you up."

Lucille led the way up the short brick walk between two

tall pines. Emma tried to take it all in, but uppermost on her mind was getting out of the chilly air. She could further investigate the outside of the house when it was warmer.

Once inside, Emma was immediately taken in by the woodwork. Beautiful maple framed the entryway door and those leading to the rooms at the right and left. The wood staircase immediately drew her gaze upstairs, and past this was a long hall to the back of the house.

"If you go to the right, you'll be in the main living area," Lucille explained. "To the left is the dining room." She pushed back the pocket doors to the large living room. Emma was quite pleased with the furnishings and the warmth of the room. Someone had set up a table and two chairs by one of the front windows. A chess board had been placed atop the table with the pieces set for a game. Beside that was a beautiful fireplace trimmed in white marble. Thankfully, the fire was still burning. Emma hurried to warm herself while her father added another log to the fire.

"This is just lovely." She gazed around the room at the sofa and chairs. There were lamps and tables positioned to give the best possible light and comfort.

The walls were void of paper and instead were painted in a pale wheat color. The draperies were a dark burgundy with buttery-beige sheers. On the floor was a beautiful Aubusson rug in shades of ecru and peach with hints of burgundy.

As the warmth began to thaw Emma's frozen frame, she couldn't help but sigh. "Thank you for finding this place. It seems to be everything I could want."

Her father chuckled. "Well, you've only just seen the one room."

Lucille nudged him and smiled before turning back to Emma and the others. "There's a large dining room table and chairs that were left here by the previous owners. And upstairs are four bedrooms and a smaller room that looked to have been used for storage. Your father made a good suggestion about how you might like to set it aside as an upstairs bathroom."

"That does sound nice," Emma admitted.

"We found beds for three of the rooms, but the fourth is empty." Lucille glanced over at Colton. "And we managed to get you a room at the Coopers' boardinghouse just as you requested. It's a very nice place for men only. Mrs. Cooper is a wonderful cook. I think you'll like it."

"I plan to take my meals with the ladies, but the place sounds sufficient."

"We checked around for help you might hire, Emma," Lucille continued. "I figured you'd want to arrange that yourself, but I will say that there's a woman in our congregation who is new to the area. She came here to be with her son, who owned a tailoring shop. He passed away shortly after her arrival, and she's now looking to cook for someone. She can help with cleaning as well, but her passion is the kitchen, and she's quite good. Your father and I have sampled her meals, and I'd hire her myself if I didn't already have a cook."

Emma was so weary from the trip, she didn't care if she had a cook or not. "Send her over tomorrow, if you like. For now, I'd just like to have a hot bath and rest."

"Well, you're in luck, then," her father replied. "This house has water piped into it and a heater hooked up in the downstairs bathroom to make hot water for bathing. And of course, there's electricity. You're thoroughly up to date in this house."

Emma let out a long breath. "Thank you for being so good to search for such things. I hadn't considered the details of what we'd need. I appreciate so much that we'll have piped-in water and electricity. After living with Clara and David and having neither, then moving to the city where they were available, I have to say I prefer the latter."

"You may prefer it less when you hear the price of the house," her stepmother replied. "But I took you at your word that money was of no concern."

"It's not," Colton interjected before Emma could speak. "If she didn't have enough on her own, I'd be sure and cover the cost. After all, she is family and will be allowing Rosie to live with her."

"Yes," Emma agreed. "We're all family."

Emma's father handed her the keys. "The bank has already given you access. They're managing things for the Wellingtons, as they've already left for California. The bank president will expect you to come tomorrow and handle the paperwork and other particulars."

Emma looked to Colton, who nodded. "We'll see to it."

A knock sounded at the door, and Emma's father went immediately to see who had come. It turned out to be the man with their luggage.

"I'll help your father," Colton said, leaving the three women to themselves.

Emma stepped away from the fire, finally feeling warm enough to face the rest of the tour. "Why don't you show Rosie and me to the bedrooms so we can figure out where each of us will stay?"

Lucille put her arm around Emma's shoulders. "I will do that, and then what say your father and I go to the grocers and butcher shop and pick up some things for supper? Maybe for breakfast too."

"I'd like that very much. I feel so tired that after I wash up, I'm going to take a nap. Dinner is the last thing on my mind, but I'm sure we'll all be hungry."

"Then it's settled. I'll cook us a meal. Something simple for tonight. Then we can help you make up lists of what you want, and we can go shopping tomorrow."

Emma had always liked Lucille Aldrich, even when she

was nothing more than a neighbor and, later, her mother's best friend, but at the moment, she couldn't think of another woman she loved more. The woman had incredible energy and insight, and her kindness went far beyond anything Emma deserved. No one in Cheyenne owed her much in the way of kindness. Emma had even begun to wonder if she'd made a mistake in coming to Cheyenne. With all the people she owed apologies to, it might have been smarter to just stay in Dallas.

The women gave a quick perusal of the rooms. Lucille pointed out things upstairs and commented on the various resources available. There were four bedrooms in total, with one being slightly larger and the others basically the same size. Rosie was immediately taken with the first room nearest the stairs. The walls had been papered with a print of pale pink rosebuds and twining vines.

"Oh, I like this room. It's so pretty and reminds me of my room in Texas."

"Then you should have it," Emma said, giving her a hug. "I want you to feel at home."

The larger room at the end of the hall was Emma's choice. It was clearly more masculine in style but welcoming in dark tones of green and navy blue.

"We didn't do much to decorate in any of the bedrooms, just put the beds and dressers in three of them and figured you could decide how you wanted to arrange it all later," Lucille said, capping off the upstairs visit as Colton and Rich brought their trunks upstairs.

The men waited at the top of the stairs for instructions. Rosie was quick to take charge of her brother.

"My room is over here." Rosie motioned Colton to follow her. "It looks like home."

Colton went with her, leaving Emma's father to give her a questioning look.

"I'll take the far room on the right," Emma said, suppressing a yawn.

"I'll come help you unpack what you need for your bath." Lucille motioned Papa to follow.

Once things were settled and Emma had her dressing gown and bath things, Lucille showed Emma the bathroom in a small room off the kitchen. She was about to bid Emma good-bye when there was another knock at the front of the house.

"Goodness, what now?" Emma was afraid she might never get to rest.

She followed her stepmother to the front door and was surprised to find Marybeth Vogel. She smiled at the woman, who didn't look to have aged a day since Emma saw her last.

"I thought you folks might be tired, so Edward and I wanted to invite you to supper tonight. You won't have to do a thing, just show up and eat. We'd like it if you and Rich came too, Lucille."

Lucille turned to look at Emma. "Well, whether they want to come or not, Rich and I would love to. We haven't had a nice long visit in forever. How about it Emma? I can still fix you something, if you prefer."

"No. Thank you both. I think after a nap it would be wonderful to share a meal with the Vogels. I'll let Rosie know, and maybe you could tell Colton when you drive him to the boardinghouse, Lucille."

"I'd be happy to. I think he and Rich are already in the carriage waiting for me."

Marybeth nodded and gave Emma a smile. "It's settled, then. Come about six. That'll give Edward time to get home from work and change his clothes."

"Sounds perfect." Emma glanced at the timepiece she'd pinned to her gown. "We'll see you in two hours."

Emma had to admit she felt so much better after a nap. Lucille and her father had shown Colton to the boardinghouse and promised to pick him back up in time for supper. After that, they'd gone shopping for Emma so that there would be something to eat for breakfast and lunch the next day. Emma hadn't heard them return, however, because she fell asleep almost the second her head hit the pillow.

"I'm excited to meet the neighbors." Rosie had changed into a rather wrinkled gingham gown. She frowned as she picked at the cloth. "I tried a little water to smooth out the lines like you showed me. I didn't know what else to do."

"We'll get an iron and an ironing board tomorrow, and I'll teach you how it's done, since we don't have a maid to do it for us." Emma pulled on her coat. She had told her father and Lucille that she and Rosie would just walk across the street and meet them at the Vogels'. They were picking up Colton and due back any time now.

"Do you know the Vogels very well?" Rosie asked as they made their way.

"We attended the same church, and my folks were good friends with them. They have four children, but they are younger than me and my siblings. They're good people. Like Lucille said, he's in law enforcement."

"Do you think they'll like me?" Rosie asked.

Emma glanced over at the petite young woman. She was beautiful. Inside and out. "I think they'll love you, Rosie. Just be yourself."

"Be myself? How do I do that?"

Chuckling, Emma looped her arm through Rosie's as they crossed the street. "You don't worry about impressing them or putting on airs. You just be friendly and kind. They are good Christian folks, so they believe like you believe—like I believe."

"But Colton doesn't believe like that."

"No, but Colton knows how to behave politely with others. He's had a lot of schooling in manners and etiquette because of all his business experiences."

They reached the Vogels' front door, and before Emma could knock, a young man opened the door. She figured it must be the Vogels' oldest son.

"I'm Rob," he said, opening the screen door for them. He glanced briefly at Emma. "I know you were better friends with my sister Carrie. Do you remember me?"

"I do, but you were just a very young man when I left Cheyenne. Maybe eleven years old? It's good to see you again. This is Rose Benton, my sister-in-law."

He glanced at Rosie and got a strange look on his face. It was akin to the one Colton often had when looking at Emma. "Miss Benton, I'm pleased to meet you."

"Call me Rosie. Everybody does." She grinned and looked to Emma. "Isn't that right?"

"It is indeed."

"Well, come in out of the chill. The night air is starting to feel pretty damp. Pa said it might come a rain."

Emma allowed Rosie to go first and heard the carriage pull into the drive just as her turn came. She glanced out and could see it was her father and the others.

"Perfect timing."

Once they were all assembled in the house and the coats and hats removed, Marybeth drew the other two children forward.

"Let me introduce you to Greta and Daniel." She looked at her daughter and youngest son. "This is Emma Johnson Benton and her sister-in-law, Miss Benton. They're buying the Wellington house."

"Call me Rosie." Rose stuck her hand out as she'd seen others do. Greta shook it immediately, and Daniel followed in kind.

"They were just children when I left the area. And now they're all grown up." Emma had lived an entire lifetime in the nine years she'd been gone from Cheyenne.

"Well, of course, you knew Carrie best." Mrs. Vogel looked to Rosie. "She's the oldest and a doctor now. She lives in Chicago. Greta, here, is eighteen, and Daniel is sixteen. He's already finished with his secondary classes and is heading off to college in the fall. Greta has a beau, and I believe we'll be hearing news of a wedding before the summer's out."

"Mother! You don't speak of those kinds of things with company," Greta protested.

"Why not?" Rosie asked. "Isn't it true?"

They all looked at Rosie for a moment as if to figure her out. Their confusion triggered Rose to speak up. "I'm being myself." She glanced at Emma, then back to the others. "I'm different from you. I sometimes forget, but I'm different because I died when I was born."

"What in the world are you talking about?" Greta asked. "How could you die and be born at the same time?"

Rosie didn't appear to be at all offended. "I had the cord wrapped around my neck. Three times. It choked my air, and when I was born, I wasn't alive. My mama thought I would stay dead, but I didn't. God decided to breathe into me, and I came back to life."

"What a wonderful story," Marybeth declared.

Rob stepped forward. "That is a wonderful story. God must have a very special plan for your life."

Rosie smiled and looked from person to person. "He does. But then, He has something special for you too."

"That's so true, Rosie," Marybeth said, glancing at her

husband as he came to join them. "This is my husband, Edward. He's the police chief, an elder at the church, member of the volunteer fire department, and part-time carpenter."

Rosie extended her hand once again. "Jesus was a carpenter."

"He was indeed," Edward said, taking hold of Rosie. "I'm pleased to meet all of you, but especially you."

Emma was proud of the way Rose handled herself. There was something childlike in the way she comported herself, but no one here seemed to mind. In fact, if she wasn't mistaken, Rob Vogel was rather intrigued with her.

"Dinner is ready if you are," Marybeth said. "Shall we go in?"

"Of course," Edward said, looking to the others. "We're mighty glad to have you with us."

"Did your sister take it hard that you were leaving Texas to come home?" Mrs. Vogel asked Emma.

"No, I think she's much too busy to miss me. Besides, her girls are old enough that they keep Clara occupied in their training. She intends to see they know everything about keeping a house, especially a ranch house."

"And what of your brother? He's not been back to Cheyenne since leaving years ago." Mrs. Vogel continued her questioning.

"James graduated college and settled in Boston. He married and is his father-in-law's right-hand man in a manufacturing company," Rich Johnson answered for his daughter. "I'm not sure he'll ever come back to Cheyenne. He loves the city life."

"And what is it that you do, Mr. Benton?" Edward Vogel asked as dessert was served.

Colton took the offered slice of carrot cake, then answered. "I am a lawyer by trade and education. I am also heavily involved in the railroad. My father established a line many years ago that started in Missouri and ended in Texas. He and his sister invested their inheritance and created the Missouri-Texas Railway. I serve on the board as legal counsel and handle other family investments as well."

"Sounds like you're a very busy man."

"He's always busy," Emma declared. "That's why I was especially touched that he would take time away from business to see that Rosie and I were settled here. I was told that Colton hasn't been out of Texas in years."

He chuckled. "It's true, but I felt I owed it to my deceased brother, as well as Emma and Rosie, to see them settled safely. My family is very important to me, and there are always those who would take advantage of women who seem to have no man to watch over them."

"Well, they have me," Rich declared. "And even when we are out at the ranch, I've a good number of friends here in Cheyenne who will also aid in keeping an eye on them."

"It's true. I'm one of them," Edward Vogel said, pouring himself more coffee. "We do that here in Cheyenne, look out for each other. We're like one big family."

Colton had never known people like the Vogels and Johnsons. Growing up, his father had taught him to be wary of people.

"*Everybody is after something, Colton. You must always be cautious of people and question their every motive,*" his father had told him since he was in knee pants.

Marybeth handed her husband the cream. "You can rest assured, Colton, that your sister and Emma will have a good many people looking out for them."

Colton knew the woman was sincere in her assurances. She didn't strike him as ever being pretentious. These were good people. He'd discerned that the moment he met them. Still, even good people could have bad motives. He would be vigilant and cautious, lest his sister and Emma get hurt or taken for granted.

7

After breakfast, Colton and Emma lingered at the table, drinking coffee and talking about their plans for the day. Colton thought both Emma and Rosie looked well rested and content, which pleased him greatly.

"I will say that while this doesn't yet feel like home, it is a nice house," Emma began. "I got a good night's sleep last night and feel as though I can conquer the world once again. What about you, Colton? How have you found things at the Coopers' boardinghouse?"

"Very well. They run a fine establishment. It's not home, of course, but I'm impressed with their attention to detail. It's very clean, not a bit of dust."

"Around here, that's quite a feat. The wind blows so much, and there are vast open fields and prairie. It's hard not to have dust."

"What are your plans for the day?" Colton picked up his coffee and smiled. "Rosie sounded like something's afoot."

"We were invited back to the Vogels' for a tea with some of the church ladies I grew up with. They have a sewing circle and invited Rosie and me to participate, but first they figured to have us come and get acquainted."

"And you already know these people?"

"Many of them." Emma dabbed her mouth with her napkin, then placed it beside her dish. "What about you? Do you have important matters to address today?"

"Well, after seeing the banker yesterday, I want to return and make sure that everything is set in place."

"We signed all the paperwork for the house and paid the price in full. What else could there be?"

"I want to complete setting up your bank account. I'll finish arranging for most of your money to be transferred here from Texas, or at least available to you here. It might be prudent to keep an account in Dallas as well, since you'll be traveling back and forth with Rosie. There are also some other business details that I thought I would handle for you. Fire insurance on the house, for example."

"How thoughtful. I would never have thought of such a thing."

Colton smiled. He could well imagine that most of the serious things of life had completely passed unnoticed by Emma prior to her wedding tragedy. He had to admit that he preferred this more thoughtful and reserved Emma to the woman who cared nothing for the conventions of society. Still, he hoped she wouldn't lose her joyful nature. It was something he very much loved about her. Previously, he had rarely ever seen her downcast or sad. Now as she passed her days in mourning for his brother, Colton saw her as more fragile than she'd been before.

"Are you feeling fully recovered from the injury?"

Emma seemed to consider the question for a moment. "I am. The scar will remain as a reminder, but the pain of the wound is gone. I don't suppose many women of my society can boast having been shot, but here I am."

"It was a tragic day that won't soon be forgotten."

Emma's expression softened. "I know you miss Tommy

deeply. He always felt you were the only one of his brothers who truly cared about him or understood him. Although I'm not sure even Tommy understood himself."

"I suppose I appreciated, in part, his ability to cast aside the mantle of responsibility and enjoy life. At the same time, I worried that he would forever be reckless and negligent. He trusted me to invest his money for him and to advise him on a variety of things, but when I disagreed with his plans, he was strong enough to stand up to me."

"Like when he told you we were to be married?" Emma smiled. "I'll bet you didn't think I knew about that, did you?"

Colton wasn't surprised that Tommy had told her of his disapproving of their marriage. "Tommy never was one for keeping his mouth shut."

Emma frowned. "Except about Stella. I can't help but wonder if there were others in the same situation."

"We might know in time, but personally I have no knowledge of them. I suppose in a sense I understand why he sought them out. I believe losing our mother was just too much for him. And of course, our father offered no comfort. Tommy needed our mother, and when she was taken from him, he pretty much sought love wherever he could find it. At least what he thought was love."

"I never considered that. It's all too sad."

"It hardened me. I suppose Walt and Ernest were the same, but Tommy was different. He was just eleven. Father hadn't yet overwhelmed him with a focus on business. I think our mother insisted he be allowed to be a child. In some ways, I don't think Tommy ever grew up."

"No." Emma seemed almost lost in her thoughts. "Perhaps he needed that to hold on to your mother. He often talked about how much he missed her. It was one of the reasons he didn't really care to be a father. He told me he didn't want to be anything like his father, and he didn't want to risk subjecting a child to losing a parent the way he had."

Colton felt his chest tighten. "I once found Tommy crying in his room not long after our mother died. I was eighteen and ill-equipped to be of any comfort, but I did my best. I held him and spoke to him."

"Yes, you did." Emma looked up. "It saved him."

"What do you mean?"

"He told me about it. Said you were so tender with him and promised him that you'd never leave him to fend for himself against your father and brothers. He said until that moment, he wanted to die and join his mother. He was so afraid of being without her—of not having anyone who would care whether he lived or died. But you convinced him he wouldn't be alone. That you would always be there for him. And that he could be himself with you. He could grieve with you."

"I didn't know it meant that much. I didn't know he wanted to die." Colton shook his head and ran his hand through his hair.

They fell silent for several long minutes. Colton could hear the tick of the mantel clock and knew he should probably end this conversation and go about his business. But he didn't want to leave Emma's company. Here in the quiet of her house, he felt comfortable enough to just be himself and speak his mind. Perhaps in time, he'd feel capable of telling Emma about his true feelings for her.

"Why didn't you want Tommy to marry me?"

Her question surprised him. He could hardly tell her the truth. Would she even believe him if he told her that he didn't want Tommy to marry her because he wanted to do the deed himself?

"To be quite honest, Tommy was so immature that I feared he'd make a poor husband and father. He was very self-centered in his thinking and actions. I knew he wouldn't take marriage seriously and that you would get hurt in the long run."

Emma showed no surprise at his comments. "He was never serious for long. He enjoyed himself too much to linger on obligations."

"Exactly. And a husband cannot be that way. He must always consider the needs of his wife and family. Marriage changes everything."

"How odd you should say so since you've never been married."

Colton shrugged. "But my other brothers married, and a good many friends did as well. I watched carefully how it changed their lives. Taking on the responsibility of a wife and home is one that needs serious attention."

"Do you suppose you'll ever marry?"

The longing to tell her how he felt was like nothing he'd ever known before. He studied her for a moment, losing himself in her dark-eyed gaze. He was forty years old and had only financial prosperity to show for his days on earth. Many men would find that to be enough, but Colton wanted more. . . . He wanted Emma.

"I hope so," he finally answered.

Emma smiled. "Then perhaps you'll find someone here in Cheyenne."

His nerves were about to get the best of him. He got to his feet in an abrupt fashion. "Maybe I will, but it won't happen sitting at the table." He forced a chuckle, lest she think she'd upset him. "Now, if you don't mind, I'll take my leave."

"Will you be back for lunch?" Emma, too, got to her feet.

"No, probably not. Don't worry about me. I'll see you at dinner. And you needn't walk me out."

He left her there and hurried to the front door, where he took up his hat and coat. Colton didn't even pause to put them on but left the house for fear he might say something he'd regret. He hadn't told Rosie good-bye and hoped she wouldn't be upset with him.

His insides were churning by the time he reached the bank. How was it possible that one woman could make him feel so overcome with emotions? He'd never been the type to lose himself in feelings, yet every time he was near Emma, Colton was like a schoolboy. Uncertain and confused by the sensation of love and desire that had never before been an issue. If he'd been a praying man, he might have sought divine direction, but as it was, he'd never had cause to lean in such a manner. So as usual, he'd have to face this on his own.

Emma's nerves were getting the best of her when she and Rosie joined the other women for tea at Marybeth Vogel's house. Marybeth introduced her.

"Ladies, this is Emma Johnson Benton and her sister-in-law, Rosie Benton." Marybeth moved to an older woman who looked to be in her sixties. "This is Faith Cooper, but I'm sure you remember her."

Emma indeed remembered Mrs. Cooper. She owned the boardinghouse where Colton was staying. Mrs. Cooper also attended the church Emma had grown up in.

"And this is Melody Decker," Marybeth continued.

"I remember you well, Emma."

Emma smiled. "I hope the memories aren't too terrible, Mrs. Decker. I was incorrigible as a child."

Melody laughed and shook her head. "Goodness, you were no worse than any other child. I have ten children now, ranging in age from nearly twenty to only four. I am very familiar with childish nonsense. They've all pulled some hilarious and not-so-hilarious pranks, and some have crossed lines that grieved me deeply. However, I believe in giving everyone grace."

"That's kind and greatly appreciated. I have a feeling I owe more apologies around here than I'll ever know."

"Goodness, Emma, I don't think anyone holds anything against you," Marybeth Vogel added. Her daughter joined them just then, bringing a tea cart full of goodies. "Of course, you know my daughter, Greta."

Emma thought the young lady was the spitting image of her mother. "Yes. Good to see you again."

"Hello," Rosie added, getting up to go to Greta. "May I help you?"

"Oh no, you're our guest. I will serve you." Greta took up the first of two teapots. "Would you like a cup?"

"Of course."

Marybeth continued the introductions. "This is Cynthia Armstrong. She and her husband own the big emporium in town. And this is Sarah, who is married to Bruce Cadot, and they have five boys."

Just then a knock sounded on the front door, and Marybeth went to see who it was. She returned with Lucille and her daughter, Charlotte. Emma got up to embrace her stepmother and Charlotte.

"I hope you don't feel too crowded, but once I started inviting the ladies, I just lost track," Marybeth explained. "Besides, I love having everyone here."

"No, I'm surprised to see Lucille and Charlotte, though. I know that a ride into town is one that must be planned."

"We wouldn't have missed this. Besides, there's always something we forgot to buy. Just because your father and I were here just a day ago doesn't mean we couldn't find reasons to return, even if it is a busy time at the ranch."

"I'm sure that's true enough." Emma turned back to her

hostess. "Thank you for this. I very much appreciate getting to reacquaint myself with these ladies."

"We are always happy to have an excuse to come together," Marybeth assured her.

They reclaimed their seats, and Greta served everyone while the ladies chatted and asked Emma how she was doing.

As the only one dressed in black, Emma felt a bit self-conscious. Rosie had given up mourning garb after Colton told her it was perfectly acceptable to do so. Emma wondered if everyone knew the details of her widowhood. She glanced over at Rosie, who was completely caught up in trying to balance her cup and saucer along with a dessert plate.

"It's good to see you again, Emma," Charlotte said, leaning close. "I hope you're feeling all right. If there's anything I can do for you, please let me know."

Emma was touched. "Thank you. I'm doing fine now."

"Your father must be delighted to have you back in the area," Sarah Cadot spoke above the din. The other ladies fell silent as if eager for Emma's response.

"I think he is happy I'm closer to home."

"He's beside himself," Lucille added. "When Emma wired to let us know her decision, Rich almost danced a jig. He's missed having his children close, especially after losing their mother."

Emma hadn't considered that. She'd been so caught up with her own life and enjoyment that she'd never given her father's condition any real thought. He must have been lonely after Mother died.

A clatter sounded from beside her, and Rosie shrieked when her teacup broke into pieces on the hardwood floor.

"Oh no! I'm so sorry. I'm so sorry." She hurried to try to recover the pieces.

"Nonsense," Marybeth declared. "Accidents happen

around here all the time." Greta handed her a tea towel, and the mess was soon no more.

"I'm not always very good at these things," Rosie apologized. "Emma is teaching me, but I've never been to something like this."

"What do you mean?" Greta asked, pouring her another cup of tea.

Rosie shrugged. "Remember I told you I was dead when I was born?" She looked at the other ladies and backtracked. "I was born not breathing because the cord was tight around my neck. They thought I was dead for good. I wasn't, of course." She smiled as if letting them in on a secret. "I started to breathe again, but the doctor said I would never be like normal folks."

"What in the world does *normal* mean, anyway?" Melody Decker asked.

"Exactly," Lucille agreed. "We're all different and have our various peculiarities."

Rosie shrugged. "My family kept me at home and didn't let me go to church or school. Emma's been teaching me things, though, and my Aunt Clementine taught me to memorize Bible verses. She told me about Jesus too."

"How awful that you were hidden away," Melody said with a disapproving tsk. "You are perfectly wonderful, Rosie."

"I hope it's all right, but I told Rosie she would be welcome to join the sewing circle. I've only started teaching her the past few months, but together I figure we can help her along." Emma turned and smiled at the younger woman. "Rosie is already doing quite well."

"We would love to teach Rosie everything we know," Mrs. Cooper replied. The others quickly agreed.

"Have you taught her quilting?" one of the women asked.

"What about embroidery?"

"Have you ever hooked a rug, Rosie?"

Emma had to laugh and so did Rosie. It was easy to see there would be no end of help for her beloved sister-in-law. Colton would be pleased at all the loving support Cheyenne was offering to Rosie.

"Sometimes it's hard for me," Rosie admitted. "I do have troubles from not breathing when I was born. The doctor said it makes me slower than others and not as smart. Sometimes people get . . . tired of me." She looked at Emma. "Did I say that right?"

"You did just fine, Rosie. And if you tire someone out, that's their problem, not yours. You are a wonderful young woman." The others quickly agreed.

Later, after the party broke up and the women were headed home, Melody Decker took Emma aside.

"I wonder if I might talk to you about Rosie."

Emma nodded. "Of course you can." She glanced across the room to where Rosie was regaling Lucille and Charlotte with a story about something.

"Has she ever had schooling?"

"No, none. It was a sore subject with me, but her brothers said their father never wanted her exposed to the meanness of other children. As if she could avoid it. The doctors also told the family that Rosie wouldn't ever be able to comprehend anything but the simplest instructions, but I haven't found that to be the case. I've been teaching her the alphabet and a little bit of handwriting. She's doing well."

"I can loan you some early primers to help her learn to read. We have all sorts of things at the school. I'll speak to Charlie about it."

Emma could only imagine how wonderful it would be if Rosie could read for herself. "Thank you for welcoming her. It means a lot to me to see her thrive. She meant the world to her brother Tommy—Colton too. He's the one who's come here to see us settled."

"Well, we will endeavor to make you both feel at home. And, Emma, don't let the past ruin your return. I think you'll find that most people will be willing to forgive and forget."

"I hope so. I know there are a few I definitely need to apologize to and will. Whether they accept my apology isn't something I can control. I know that."

Rosie joined them just then, along with Lucille and Charlotte. "We've been invited to church on Sunday, Emma. Can we go?"

Emma looked at her stepmother and smiled. "Of course we can. I think it will be a wonderful way for us to get better acquainted with everyone."

Rosie laughed and nodded with great enthusiasm. She reminded Emma of a little girl who'd just been promised a pony. So happy and carefree. Oh, how Emma wished she could share in that ease.

8

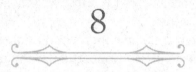

After taking a walk around town the next morning, Emma, Rosie, and Colton made their way back to the house. It was a glorious spring day, and after a light rain in the night, it seemed everything was trying to grow and bloom all at once.

"This is quite a place." Colton hadn't known exactly what to expect out of Cheyenne. "I must admit, I'm rather impressed. I can see that a lot of thought has gone into the town."

"They are certainly pushing hard for statehood." Emma opened the door to her house and ushered everyone inside. "I believe I'll open some of the windows and air out the place. Rosie, can you manage to open your bedroom window and mine?"

"Yes. I remember how you showed me. I'll go do it right now."

"Thank you."

Emma made her way into the front room and opened the window by the chess table. "Rosie and I are going to church tomorrow and would love for you to accompany us."

"So you're joining the company of the faithful?" Colton's tone was edged with sarcasm.

"There's something about nearly dying that puts things into perspective." Emma crossed the room and opened one of the other windows. "Having accepted Christ as a child and been taken to church every Sunday, I've always known what the Bible taught and what I was taught to believe. I ignored it for a long while, but after facing death, I realized that . . . well, the truth made itself known to me."

"And what truth is that?"

"That I needed a Savior." She finished with the window and turned, smiling. "I know. I know. Before you say anything, I must admit that my past feelings and thoughts about God were abominable. I allowed myself to be convinced that Christians were chained to doom and gloom in such a way as to never know any earthly happiness. I was wrong."

Colton chuckled. "It's unusual for a woman to admit such a thing."

"Ha! My mother and sister often admit to being wrong. It was the men in our family who hesitated to acknowledge their misguided notions."

Colton could easily agree with her. The men in his family never declared themselves in error unless pressed, and even then, it would be related in such a manner as to place the blame on someone else.

"I can affirm that in my own family. My father often said to never admit defeat, nor to being wrong. It makes a man look weak, and to his way of thinking, that was the worst possible offense a man could make."

"It's not easy to accept one's flaws and mistakes." Emma shrugged. "But after all I've been through these last few weeks, it's even harder to face the future based on my skills and abilities alone. I truly have nothing of myself to recommend to anyone."

"You do yourself an injustice." Colton eyed her quite seriously. "You've touched our family in a most special way. The things you've accomplished with Rose alone commend you to all."

Tears came to Emma's eyes. "I love Rosie. I loved Tommy too. But now I know that I didn't love him as a wife should love a husband."

"How do you know that?"

"Even as we made our vows, I can't say I wholly believed them or meant to keep them. I know that sounds terrible, and it is. But I wasn't sure that I would remain for better or worse. I wanted a good life—a good time. Tommy did too. We scoffed at tradition and all that came with it."

"Yet you wanted to marry. And as I recall, you told me you were the one to restrict your arrangement with Tommy unless there was a marriage."

She nodded as a single tear fell. "I did make that demand, more out of fear of what might happen if we didn't. I didn't want to find myself in Stella's position."

"And you honestly thought Tommy would do that to you?"

"I didn't know." She wiped her face with the back of her hand. "Stella proves that possibility."

Colton handed her his handkerchief. "I don't think Tommy would have ever done that to you. His relationship with you was far more serious. I'd never seen him even consider marriage before you. As much as it was understood by him, he loved you."

"I know in his way he loved me. Just as I loved him in my own way. But it wasn't enough. It wasn't right, and I keep thinking that everything happened as punishment for mocking God. I was a wretch of a person."

"But now you're not?" he asked with a grin.

"Now I'm forgiven, and while I have a lot to make up for, I'm ashamed of the way I acted. Tommy and I had no business getting married. It was purely driven by . . . well, I hope you won't find this offensive, but by Tommy's physical desire."

Colton knew his own feelings for Emma. He thought of her constantly, even dreamed of her. He could well imagine his brother feeling the same way. But Emma apparently didn't return the feelings.

"That's what I mean by not loving him the way I should have. I didn't return the passion he felt. I'm surprised to admit this to you of all people, but I just wanted to travel and see the world, and Tommy promised we could do it together. We both agreed that we should be married to do such a thing. We didn't want to hurt our families or even ruin our own reputations beyond what we'd already done."

"I never thought of either of you as having a ruined reputation."

"Perhaps not, but we walked very close to the edge of that. Yet another thing that I'm sorry for." Emma shook her head. "Tommy only wanted to please me. He told me he couldn't see himself marrying anyone else, so we might as well do the deed." She sniffed back tears and laughed. "Those were his exact words. And being the person I was then, I didn't care. I didn't believe in forever."

"And now?"

"Now, forever is all too real. I know there is more than just this life, Colton. I've no doubt whatsoever. Lying there with that bullet wound, I was terrified of death because everything I'd ever been taught came back to me."

"But there are a great many religions and mythologies, Emma. How can you be sure that Christianity points the only way to the only God?"

She frowned and considered his question. "I suppose I must take it on faith. People I love and admire have told me it's true and pointed me to the Bible as truth. I have only two choices. I can either accept it as true or regard it as a lie. I choose to accept it as true and do so through faith, which, as I recall from Ephesians chapter two, is not of myself. The grace and faith given of God is a gift—a gift I refused for a great many years."

"But now you want it?"

She nodded. "Most assuredly. I'm still quite uncertain as to how it will present itself in my life, but I know I felt immediate comfort when I sought God's forgiveness."

Colton couldn't imagine the comfort of which she spoke. He had sought comfort his entire life and was never able to find it. His father assured him it came through hard work and achievement, but then his father associated comfort with accomplishment. He had no use for religion or matters of the spirit. Colton's mother had, however. He could still remember some of her comments to him. Fleeting memories of how much each person needed God. How the human soul craved God's companionship because it had been God who had breathed life into man in the first place. That encounter left mankind always longing for more. Colton had often wondered if she was right.

"We'll leave for church around ten in the morning. We plan to walk because it's not all that far. You're quite welcome to join us." She withdrew a handkerchief from her pocket and wiped her eyes.

"Well, that does bring up another thought." Colton didn't want to commit himself to services. "You and Rosie will need to have access to a carriage. I'm certain there are places that you would prefer to drive."

"We can just rent a carriage and horse from the livery when that's needed. I have no place to keep an animal, nor anyone to care for him. I could take care of the chores myself but for now would prefer not to have that responsibility."

"You need to hire an entire staff," he reminded.

She looked dubious. "I don't know that I want to hire a bunch of people to intrude on my privacy, or on Rosie's."

"You can't very well do all the laundry, house cleaning, cooking, and gardening. That's far too much for any one or two people. You don't have to hire anyone to live in the house if you don't want to. A lot of folks these days just have people come for a few hours or for the day and leave in the evening hours."

"I know, and I have considered it. But there's a lot that Rosie wants to learn to do, and together we can see to the work. It might help us both to keep busy that way. Lucille has already suggested a woman who might cook for us, but again Rosie wants to learn to cook."

"Then let this woman teach her. You can hardly devote every minute of the day to Rosie. You need to look after yourself as well."

For some reason that brought tears to Emma's eyes once again. There was something in the way she looked, the way she opened her mouth to speak and then seemed unable to produce words, that caused Colton to do the unthinkable. He stepped forward and took her in his arms.

"I didn't mean to make you cry."

This only seemed to make matters worse. Emma broke down and sobbed against his chest. All he could do was hold her and say what he hoped were words of comfort. "You don't have to figure everything out at once. I wasn't trying to add to your burden with my comments. Take all the time you need. I only wanted you to have what you need."

She nodded but said nothing. Colton tightened his hold on her. What was he supposed to do now?

Emma had no desire to fall apart with Colton there, but her emotions were all over the place. One minute she was happy, even excited to be back in Cheyenne, and the next she was so full of remorse and regret for the past that it was far too overwhelming. She would no sooner deal with that than she'd find herself longing for something she couldn't even explain. Having Tommy ripped out of her life was what she considered it would be like to lose a limb. Nothing could make up for that loss. Perhaps she loved Tommy far more than she'd realized. For both of them there had been a certain amount of disrespect toward any established institutions and traditions. But Emma felt so different now that it was tearing her apart.

Which was why she was unable to do anything but cry in Colton's arms. She had no desire to leave. His hold was warm and gentle. He seemed to genuinely care for her. For the longest time, Emma had thought he didn't even like her.

"Things will get better in time, Emma. I promise."

But how could he promise such a thing? She didn't even know what it was that she needed. Wasn't even sure what it was she was mourning.

"Colton, leave her alone!"

Rosie's commanding voice so surprised Emma that she jumped back and regained control. "What's wrong, Rosie?" Her expression was angry, but for the life of her, Emma couldn't comprehend why Rosie was acting this way. "Colton was just being kind."

"He needs to go now." She fixed him with a stern look. "You can come with us to church tomorrow. You need to learn about God and know the truth. You would be a better person then." She took Colton by the arm. "Go on and take care of all those things you said you had to do today."

Colton appeared so surprised that he actually allowed Rosie to pull him to the door. Emma followed a few paces behind.

"I'm sure we'll be fine, Colton. Rosie and I are going to

bake cookies, so feel free to come back by after you tend to your business." He had told them earlier on their walk that he needed to get his hair cut and pick up a few things at the store.

Rosie left Colton's side and came to stand with Emma. She put her arm around Emma's shoulders. "I'll take care of Emma. You just take care of business like you always do."

Emma frowned, wondering why Rosie was so put out with her brother. He'd done nothing wrong. He'd only tried to offer comfort. Perhaps she'd ask after Colton left them.

Colton eyed his sister for a moment, then turned toward Emma and smiled. "Cookies sound wonderful. Do you have plenty of milk to go with them?"

Emma smiled. "I do. Lucille and Father made sure of it. Just come on back when you're finished. They should be ready in an hour or two." She watched Colton head down the brick walkway and waited until he was down the street a little way before turning to his sister. "What's got you all riled? I've never heard you speak to Colton or anyone else like that."

Rosie shook her head. "I just don't want him to get pushy. He likes to boss everybody around." She smiled as if it were all forgotten. "Now, what kind of cookies are we going to make?"

Rosie listened as Emma carefully instructed her regarding measuring out the ingredients for the cookies. Several times Emma stopped to show Rosie the written measurements.

"In time, I know we'll have you reading, so you might as well get used to it. I know we've gone over the numbers from one to twenty and the alphabet, so this shouldn't be too hard for you. See I've written down the recipe. *C* stands for *cup*, and this is the measuring cup that is used for the flour and sugar."

Rosie asked questions when she didn't understand but, for the most part, found Emma's directions easy to follow. Emma didn't think Rosie was unable to learn. She made Rosie feel capable and happy, not dumb as so many suggested. Emma had always been that way.

It was a good thing her brothers had let Rosie come to Cheyenne with Emma. Otherwise, she would have got on the train by herself and asked people to help her get to Cheyenne so that she could find Emma. She didn't want to live with her brothers anymore. They didn't care about her like Emma did. They never, ever told her that they loved her like Emma did. Well, once in a while Colton said the words, but Walter and Ernest never did. She was certain they didn't even like her. They thought she was a burden.

All her life, Rosie had longed for more. She wasn't allowed to be a part of the world or to go to school with the other children. She had gone to church with Aunt Clementine but was never allowed to play afterward or even attend Sunday school. She remembered waiting one day for Aunt Clementine, who was talking to the pastor, and some boys had come up and pulled her pigtail and called her names that she didn't understand. Aunt Clementine had appeared and scolded the boys fiercely before taking Rosie by the hand to make their way home.

"What's a im . . . im . . . becile?" Rosie remembered asking.

"That's someone who acts foolish or ignorantly. Why, did those boys use that word?"

"They said I was one."

"The truth is that often people call others by names that have been used for themselves. It's not the right way to act or treat others. The Bible admonishes us to love one another. Remember that, Rose."

And she had, even though there had been other occasions when she'd been called that and worse. Colton had once punched one of his friends in the mouth for calling her deranged. None of the words made much sense to Rosie. Aunt Clem had told her she was too pure and sweet to understand such obscenities. Nevertheless, Rosie knew the words weren't said with kindness. Sometimes she wondered what it was about her being slow that so offended people. It wasn't like she was trying to upset them. She only wanted to make friends, but they didn't like her. Emma was really the first outsider who had ever told Rosie she wanted to be her friend. Whenever she was in Emma's company, Rosie knew no one would hurt her. Now it was Rosie's turn to guard Emma from mean people. Even if that person was one of her brothers . . . or all of them.

"Do you remember how long we have to bake the cookies, Rosie?"

She thought back to Emma's instructions. "Fifteen minutes."

Emma smiled. "Exactly right. So check the clock we put on the table."

Rosie went to the clock and thought for a moment. "The little hand is on three, so that's the hour. The long hand is on five, and that's the minutes."

"But it's not five minutes, is it, Rosie?" Emma asked.

What was it about the time? Rosie thought hard for a moment. "When it's minutes each number . . . each number . . ." She slapped her hands against her sides. "I can't remember, Emma."

"That's all right. We only just started working on how to tell time. You're doing really great, Rosie. You remembered the hour hand. Now, some clocks, like the grandfather clock back in Texas, have little marks all the way around the face of the clock. So the first little mark at the top just to the right of the twelve is the one-minute mark. Remember?"

"Yes." Rosie nodded and started to get excited. "Each mark is a minute, and the minute hand points to the total that go with the hour."

"Yes! Very good. And each of the numbers one through twelve mark five minutes."

"But they also mark the hour, but with the little hand, right?" Rosie wanted to make sure she was remembering correctly.

"That's right." Emma smiled. "I know it's hard. You have to be able to add or even multiply to understand exactly what time it is, but I promise you that after a while you'll just look at the clock and know. You won't even think about it."

Rosie gave a sigh. "I want to know. I want to remember."

"I know you do, and it's so much fun working with you to learn."

Taking a deep breath, Rosie focused on the clock. "We practiced counting five at a time for the clock."

"That's right. So for each number we added five to figure out the minutes. The one counts as five minutes."

Rosie nodded and jumped in. "The two is ten, and the three is fifteen." She wasn't at all sure why the math worked, but Emma had assured her it did. They had spent over an hour learning to count by fives. At least, that was what Emma called it.

"In this situation, we want the cookies to bake for fifteen minutes. If you start on the five and count by fives to fifteen, what number would you land on?"

She looked at the clock. The five represented the starting place. Five minutes put them at the number six. Another five minutes made ten, and that put them at the seven. Another five . . .

"The eight. When the long hand is on the eight, then fifteen minutes have passed."

"Exactly right!" Emma was just as excited about the answer as Rosie was. They both knew it was a hard-won victory.

Emma gave her a hug. "I'm so proud of you, Rosie. You're getting better and better at figuring it out."

"But everybody else already knows this."

"They only know it because they learned it as children in school. It's frustrating that you weren't allowed to learn it when you were little, but you are learning it now and doing a good job. Don't give up."

Rosie had no intention of giving up. She was so excited about the idea of learning to read that she wanted to beg Emma to spend all her time just doing that. It was fun to learn to bake, and she wanted to know how to cook, but reading was even more important. If she could read, then she could use the Bible on her own. Just thinking about that made Rosie want to do a dance in celebration. Even if she didn't know how to dance.

That night back at the boarding house, Colton couldn't figure out what in the world had gotten into Rosie. All he had done was try to comfort Emma. Maybe it was his own fault for never showing much emotion or tenderness. His father had all but driven it out of him. He knew his lacking had turned aside women who might otherwise have agreed to seek him out as their suitor. Of course, his father hadn't encouraged such a thing. He assured Colton there was more than enough time to find a mate, and when he did, he should make certain of the most important considerations. Her financial assessment came first. She must be a woman of means, having inherited a fortune through her parents or grandparents. She needed to be high on the social registry and able to introduce him to other wealthy people who would have the potential to benefit him. It was all about the money, and Colton had allowed his father's guidance in this area. Now, however, it seemed so unimportant.

It was true that Emma had money—Benton money—but Colton would have taken an interest in her even if she'd been poor. There was just something about her that he couldn't help but be drawn to. He enjoyed everything about her, especially their discussions. But Rosie had been offended by his actions, and it still baffled him as to why.

All at once it came to mind that perhaps she was jealous. Emma had shown her such devotion, maybe Rosie was afraid that Colton would take that away. That had to be it. Rosie was just feeling overcome by worry that she might lose Emma's attention. Maybe he could reassure her that no matter what, he and Emma would always be there for her.

He leaned back in his chair and smiled. If Tommy had been here, they might have had a good laugh about it all. Colton thought again of his brother. Watching him face Stella, then seeing the life go out of Tommy's eyes was something Colton would never forget. He had been dead before he hit the floor. There were no last words or instructions. No ability to avoid the inevitable. Colton's smile faded.

And then there was Emma. The bullet grazing her without her even realizing it for the shock of what had happened to Tommy. The blood slowly oozing out across the white gown. So much blood. Colton wished he could wipe those images from his memories. Somehow, he doubted that he ever would.

9

The church services were much as Emma remembered them. The pastor was different from the one she'd known as a child. In fact, the church was changing pastors, as the pastor they'd heard today was ending his time there. Reverend Bright was to take over, and everyone seemed quite enthusiastic about the man.

The congregation had grown considerably since Emma had attended. The little white church was full to overflowing. There were already plans being drawn up to build a larger church on the same grounds. Emma supposed she would be a part of that new church. Maybe she'd even help pay for the building now that she had plenty of money. Wouldn't that be something? Tommy would have laughed but told her to do what she liked. He didn't have a problem spending money on things like that. Money had meant very little to him, except as a means to have fun.

"Sure good to see you here," her father said, coming to give her a hug outside the church.

"I sometimes wonder if Mama knows how I've changed." Emma looked heavenward. "I hope she does."

"I figure she does." He looked upward as well.

"What are you two doing gawking up into the sky at?" Charlotte Hamilton asked.

Emma lowered her gaze and smiled. "Just enjoying the day." She had little desire to explain, lest Charlotte think her odd. She noticed the man at Charlotte's side. "Micah?"

"Yes, ma'am." He smiled. "Haven't seen you in ages, Emma. Sure sorry to hear about all you went through in Texas."

Emma glanced down at the black dress she wore. Perhaps she should stop wearing mourning clothes. It only served as a reminder of what had happened. "Thank you. I must say it has been a lot to undergo."

"Well, I'm glad you were able to move back to Cheyenne. I know your pa missed having you here."

"He's got that right." Emma's father nodded. "A man ought to be able to have his family close around him."

"Emma Johnson?" a woman asked.

Emma turned and met the stern gaze of a matronly woman. She knew the woman well. She was the mother of the young man Emma had once been engaged to marry. She had broken the engagement without thought or concern to the plans being made for their wedding or to her fiancé's heart.

"Mrs. Stevens, I'm glad I ran into you." Emma decided there was no time like the present. "I owe your family a big apology."

This took the woman by surprise. "I . . . what is that, now?"

"I owe you a big apology for the way I acted in the past. I owe Thane one as well. I can't believe how thoughtless and cruel I acted. I am so very sorry. I wasn't walking with the Lord back then. In fact, I was running from Him as fast as I could. Still, it's no excuse for hurting people. I hope you'll find it in your heart to forgive me."

The older woman stared at Emma for a long moment, then looked at the others, who were trying hard to seem otherwise occupied.

"I never figured to hear those words from you, Emma." The woman straightened her shoulders. "You did cause a powerful lot of hurt. I wasn't sure my Thane was ever going to get over it, but he did. God gave him another woman to love, and she's been the best of daughters-in-law. Gave me two grandchildren as well."

Emma smiled. "I'm so glad. Thane deserves the best. He is a wonderful man."

Mrs. Stevens nodded, clearly still stunned by Emma's words. She narrowed her eyes a bit, then relaxed her expression. "I've known God to work a wonder of miracles in my life. I guess this is just one more. When I saw you, the pain came back despite the happiness God has given. I guess I let the devil get the best of me. I was all set to give you a piece of my mind, but now I find myself compelled to offer you forgiveness instead."

"Thank you. I know I don't deserve it, but I cherish it."

"This is gonna be a surprise to Thane, but I'm thinking he'll be glad to hear it too."

Emma found her heart just a little lighter. "Hopefully, I'll have a chance sometime to seek his forgiveness too."

Rosie was surprised when Robert Vogel stopped her outside of the church. She didn't know where Emma or her brother had gotten off to and wasn't at all sure how to act with this man who was very nearly a stranger.

"Rosie, I'm so glad to see you here at church. Did you enjoy yourself?"

"I did." She frowned but said nothing more. Rob seemed like a nice enough man when they'd shared dinner at his folks' house.

"I hope you liked the preaching. We've only had this pastor

for three months. I kind of thought he'd stick around a while, but maybe we'll get more time with the new one. I've heard good things about Reverend Bright."

"Have you always gone to this church?" Rosie asked.

Rob smiled and gave a nod. "I have. My ma and pa started here when they first came to Cheyenne. I was actually born in Cheyenne."

"It's a nice town. I like how cool it is at night. In Dallas, where I lived, it was always hot. Well, sometimes it got cooler. There were a couple of times when it snowed—not very much, though. Your sister told me about a time when the snow here covered up the windows."

He laughed. "It's true. We've had quite a few bad snows. And the wind is hard on us too. Blows nearly all the time, and when you combine that with the snow, you get terrible blizzards. Everyone goes inside and stays put until the storm passes."

Rosie smiled. Rob was so easy to talk to, and she really liked the way he laughed. "I had tea at your house last week. I really like your sister."

"She's very nice. I like her too. I have another sister who's older than me. Her name's Carrie. She's back east right now. My brother, Daniel, can be ornery, but he's a decent sort."

"Greta and the others didn't seem to mind my being slow. They didn't make fun of me."

Rob frowned. "Why would they make fun of you?"

"People do that sometimes because I don't think as fast as they do. They sometimes call me names. That's why my brothers made me stay home and wouldn't let me go anywhere."

"You never got to go anywhere?"

"Well, when I was younger, I went to church with my aunt Clementine. My mama died, and Aunt Clementine took care of me. There were some mean boys at church, and they called me all sorts of names. My aunt told me to pay them no attention, but I wish people wouldn't think bad of me just because I'm different."

"I think you're wonderful." He smiled and gently reached out to touch her hand. "I really like you, Rosie. I hope we can be good friends."

She couldn't contain her smile. "I'd like being your friend. You are very nice. I really like the way you laugh."

Rob grinned and started to speak again only to be interrupted by a tall dark-haired man who punched him in the arm.

"Hey, Robbie, are you going to introduce me to your friend?"

Rob didn't seem at all upset that the man had hit him, so Rosie figured they must be friends. She'd seen her brothers act that way when they were with their friends.

"Rose Benton, this is my best friend, Michael Decker. We were born on the same day in April and have been friends ever since."

"Glad to meet you, Rose Benton."

"I'm glad to meet you too." Rosie felt a little awkward but kept it to herself. Emma had told her many times that she didn't have to tell everyone everything she was thinking and feeling.

"Where's your sister?" Michael asked. "I've been looking for her."

"She was supposed to help put together the widow packages after church. I'm not sure where she's at now."

Michael shrugged. "Guess I'll go on searching." And with that he took off in the same direction from which he'd come.

"He's sweet on Greta," Rob explained. "He finished up with college early and is working with his father at the Decker School for Boys. He loves science, especially chemistry. He's really nice once you get to know him."

"He seems nice. Does your sister like him?"

"Oh yes, she's been in love with him since she was about twelve years old. I figure they'll marry before too much longer."

"My brother married Emma. It was a pretty wedding until that terrible woman killed him." She bit her lower lip. That was probably one of those things she didn't need to share with people.

"I heard about that. It must have been hard on you to lose your brother that way. Seein' it happen and all."

"It was. Tommy was so good to me. Colton is too, but Tommy was fun. He would play games with me and make me laugh when he'd tell me stories about places he'd gone. Colton said he needed to work more, but . . ." She fell silent.

"Work's important. A fella has to make a living."

His comment caused Rosie to shake her head. "Not Tommy. He was rich. He gave all his money to Emma, so now she's rich." Rosie put her hand over her mouth, then pulled it away. "Sometimes I say too much. I'm trying to learn not to be so honest."

"Never do that, Rosie." Rob took hold of her hands. "You're perfect the way you are. It's wonderful that you're honest."

"Emma thinks so too, but she said we have to be careful because sometimes what we say can cause trouble."

"I suppose that's true. The Bible does say we should guard our tongues."

"Yes! Proverbs twenty-one, twenty-three. 'Whoso keepeth his mouth and his tongue keepeth his soul from troubles.'" Rosie smiled. "I memorized that one."

"It's a good one to know."

"I had to memorize it because I can't read. But Emma's trying to teach me."

"I didn't know you couldn't read. I would be happy to help

you too. I could come over in the evenings and work with you on your reading."

"That would be nice," Rosie replied, knowing that she would truly enjoy having Rob come over and see her.

"Rosie, Emma's looking for you."

Rob dropped his hold on her hands, and Rosie looked over her shoulder to see Colton frowning. She didn't know why he was frowning, but he looked mad. She waved him over.

"Remember Rob Vogel? He's going to help me learn to read."

"Go on and see Emma," Colton said, his gaze never leaving Rob's face. "I need to have a little talk with Mr. Vogel."

Colton waited until Rosie was well out of sight before punching Rob square in the nose. "Stay away from my sister."

Vogel landed on his backside, and blood immediately poured from his nose. He grabbed his handkerchief to stave the flow but didn't bother to get up.

Colton stared down at him. "You know she's naïve and simple. You can't be sweet-talking her and taking advantage of her. She's not smart enough to know when people are taking liberties with her, but I am, and I won't tolerate anyone trying to trick her."

"I wasn't trying to trick her. I happen to like her very much, and when she said that Mrs. Benton was teaching her to read, I told her I'd be happy to help. I think she's probably smarter than you give her credit for."

"You want me to hit you again?"

Rob got to his feet and held his bleeding nose with one hand and dusted off his trousers with the other. "I didn't want you hitting me the first time." He looked Colton in the eye. "I think your sister is wonderful, and I'd like to know her better, but all of my intentions are good."

"I don't want you to have any intentions toward her. She isn't able to judge such things, and I won't have you hurting her."

"I have no desire to hurt her." Rob took a step closer. "I'm not some dandy who wants to dupe your sister and steal her innocence. You really should get to know a fella before you go judging him."

"What's going on here?" a man asked.

Colton turned on his heel ready for a fight.

It was Edward Vogel. Colton forced himself to relax, but before he could speak, Rob answered.

"Nothing's going on, Pa. We were just having a discussion."

Vogel continued to look at Colton as if to force the truth from him. Without even glancing over at his son, he continued to pry. "What happened to your nose?"

"Ran into something."

His father's lip gave just a hint of a curl. "Or someone?"

"Everything's fine, Pa. Don't make something out of nothing."

Vogel held Colton's gaze a moment longer, then nodded. "We're heading home."

"I'll be right there." Rob waited until his father walked away and then started for the front of the church.

Colton frowned. "Just leave her be."

He watched Rob go, wondering exactly what had transpired between him and Rosie. He seemed sincere enough regarding his thoughts toward her, but Colton didn't want to encourage his interest. He hoped Emma would decide to move back to Dallas, and Rosie didn't need to be caught up in the complications of romance.

As he made his way to find Emma and his sister, Colton

was troubled by what had just happened. He'd never considered that a man might show interest in Rosie. She was quite pretty with her petite frame and dark brown eyes. He could understand a man being attracted to her looks. It posed yet another set of problems. The men outnumbered the women in Cheyenne, just as they did in Texas. It wouldn't surprise him at all to find a collection of suitors vying for not only Emma's attention but Rosie's as well.

He should have known by the way Robert had acted at the dinner they'd shared that first night in Cheyenne. He was very observant of Emma and Rosie, but especially Rosie. Colton had been too tired to see that the man's interest had been more than polite tolerance.

I won't let him take advantage of Rosie. She won't recognize his toying with her emotions—doing whatever he can in order to take liberties with her. But alongside these thoughts came ribbons of guilt. Wasn't he here to take advantage of Emma? He cared about her—had lost his heart to her when he'd first met her. All of that was true, but his brothers had also sent him on a mission to win her hand in order to safeguard the family interests.

"You look upset," Emma said as he rejoined her and Rosie.

"Did you have a talk with Rob?" Rosie asked. "I told Emma that he's going to help me learn to read."

Emma met his gaze. Her brow raised slightly. "Perhaps it would be best to talk about it later . . . after lunch. Rosie and I made you something special. An apple pie. We baked it after the cookies you seemed to so enjoy last night."

Colton did his best to put on a smile. "If the two of you made it, I know I'll enjoy it. Let's go home. I'm starving."

10

All right, it's been several days since Sunday, and you're still under a black cloud." Emma fixed Colton with a look she hoped was that of a concerned friend. "Tell me what's bothering you so much."

Rosie had gone outside to gather the laundry from the lines. She was all excited because Emma had been teaching her to iron, and she wanted to show Colton how good she was at doing the job.

"I don't know what you mean."

They had finished with lunch and now sat rather leisurely in the front room. Emma shook her head. "You've been out of sorts since church. Did you not like it? Was there some reason you took offense?"

"Church was fine. In fact, I found it to be better than I expected. The sermon wasn't all focused on hell and what terrible sinners we are. Honestly, I don't know how a Christian is supposed to find any happiness at all with that hanging over his head."

"But if they accept Jesus as Savior, they don't have that hanging over their heads." Emma gave him a smile. "I know from things Tommy and you have both said that your mother was a godly woman. Surely she taught you about the joy of the Lord as well as the consequences of sin."

"Ha! You told me yourself that you didn't want to be a Christian because you were convinced they never had any fun or happiness."

"But I was a child when I believed that."

"You weren't a child when you married my brother, and you still thought that way. The only reason you changed your mind was a fear of dying."

Emma tilted her head slightly to the right and glanced at the ceiling. "I suppose that's true. I'm certainly not proud of believing that way. But I'm not too prideful to admit that I was wrong. My thoughts were selfish and self-serving. I wanted to live a life without rules or restrictions."

"And you no longer want that?"

Colton's question surprised Emma. She lowered her gaze to meet his. "I suppose there will always be a part of me that desires adventure and a good time versus a bad one. Rosie and I were talking just the other day about how we'd like to see London and the palace where the queen lives. We'd like to see some of the ancient wonders in Rome too."

His expression softened. "I didn't know that."

"I often read to Rosie, as you know. We were reading in Romans just the other day, and both of us thought it would be wondrous fun to visit Rome and see the things the apostle Paul would have seen, walk where he walked."

"I think a trip to Rome would be a great adventure."

"Would you want to come with us? That would be wonderful!" Emma couldn't contain her excitement. "Just imagine all the places we could visit. We could read about them first and figure out where all we wanted to go."

"Slow down, Emma. I only said that it sounded like a great adventure."

"I know. And I know that you aren't one for having fun, but think of Rosie. She would be absolutely over the moon."

Colton's frown momentarily silenced her. Had she made him feel bad?

"I'm sorry, Colton. I didn't mean to suggest you never want to have fun. It's just I know from Tommy and my own observations that you are very cautious and diligent about your life."

"Cautious and diligent. Hmm. Not much of a recommendation."

"Unless you're a doctor tending to the sick or a diplomat fending off war. Goodness, Colton. Those are admirable traits, and you are an admirable man. I've thought highly of you since I first met you, in part, for those very things."

"But they weren't of interest to you. You preferred Tommy's carefree spirit and desire for adventure."

It was Emma's turn to frown. For days now she felt that she'd somehow offended Colton, and now his words seemed to confirm her thoughts.

"For all that I've done to offend you, Colton, I apologize. I know the person I was, and it's already coming back to threaten my happiness. I found myself apologizing Sunday to a woman whose son I did terribly wrong."

"What was it you did to him?"

"I was engaged to marry him. I took up with someone else and broke the engagement two weeks before we were to marry. I just kept imagining myself stuck on his ranch, giving him a dozen children and never seeing the world. The man I took up with was a roving gambler who claimed to want the same things I did. He thought I was from a wealthy family and jumped the first train west after learning I wasn't. I was always glad that I didn't know Tommy had money for the longest time. I never ever wanted him to think that I cared for him because of his money." She leaned back in her chair. "It's positively awful to find out that someone only pretended to love you for your money."

For the briefest of moments, Colton's expression was one that Emma could only describe as a child being caught with his hand in the cookie jar. Then as quickly as it had come, it was gone. She decided to ignore it.

"So if church isn't putting you in a bad state of mind, what is? Has business gone bad?"

"No. I suppose . . . well, I can tell you, but I'd rather not make too much of it with Rosie. She thinks so highly of everyone she meets, and when people are kind to her, she assumes they are of good intentions."

"But you believe someone isn't of good intentions with Rosie?" Emma narrowed her eyes. "I won't stand for that."

"I found Robert Vogel talking to Rosie alone after church. He told her he wanted to help her learn to read. I don't trust him. I fear he'll take advantage of her innocent ways."

"Rob?" Emma laughed. "I don't think you have to worry about him. He's one of the most honest and trustworthy people in Cheyenne. His folks are good people, and while I haven't been here for nine years, I know from my mother's letters and later Lucille's that the Vogel family continues to be highly esteemed. Rob has proven himself over and over to have admirable qualities. I think you should get to know him before judging him so harshly."

"You haven't been around him for nine years by your own admission. He would have been a child when you left Cheyenne."

"True enough, but as I said, I've known the family for years. One of the first times I got in trouble with the law, I had to face Edward Vogel. He was firm but kind, and I always appreciated that."

"Still, a son can be very different from his father."

"I know that very well. My brother, James, is nothing like

my father. James is an intellectual, as he tells it. He studies books in all his free time. My father can barely read and would take the company of a cow over a book any day." Emma smiled. "I just think you should put your mind at ease. Rob wants to help me teach Rosie to read. He won't be alone with her. I spoke to him about it, and he would just come here after supper in the evening, and we would sit here in the front room or at the dining room table and work on teaching Rosie. You could even join us. I think it would do her a world of good if we continue her exposure to other people."

"But he's a man. I don't mind at all that you have her going to tea parties and sewing circles, but men tend toward one line of thinking."

Emma looked at him with a teasing smile. "And what would that be, Colton?"

He looked embarrassed and cast his glance toward the open window. "You aren't naïve, Emma. You know how passion and desire can build between a man and woman."

"And would that be so terrible? If Rosie were to find herself a good man like Robert Vogel and marry him, would that be the end of the world?"

"But she's not like other women."

"No, she isn't. She's better. She's kinder and more loving. She's got virtues that far outweigh the losses."

Emma got up and went to a small basket that was placed beside a chair across the room. She reached inside and pulled up a handkerchief and brought it back to Colton.

"Rosie embroidered this after just one lesson with Marybeth Vogel."

Colton took the piece and studied it a moment.

"She's better at it than I am," Emma continued. "She has taken to cooking like nothing I've ever seen. She memorizes things quickly because she can't read them. Reading would open an entire world to her. Think of how much you cherish the ability to read and then imagine if that was taken from you and you could only look on with longing."

He handed her back the embroidery. "I'm sorry. I never really thought of it that way. I never realized Rosie was capable of much until you came into our lives. Doctors told Mother and Father not to bother trying to teach her anything."

"Doctors can obviously be wrong. They didn't know what Rosie was capable of. She may be slow, and there may be some things that she'll never be able to do, but please don't try to stand in the way of her happiness."

"I don't want to stand in the way of her learning to read; I just worry that Robert Vogel isn't worthy of the trust you've placed in him."

"Then why not get to know him? Give him a chance to prove himself. And remember, Colton, someone had to do the same for you. Each man must prove himself worthy of trust and respect."

Colton seemed to consider that a moment. "I promised my mother I wouldn't let anyone hurt Rosie. I promised to look after her and care for her."

"And you have done an admirable job. But now you're the one who is threatening to hurt her. Just give it some thought and maybe invite Rob out for lunch or dinner sometime and talk about your concerns. Who knows, maybe you'll even make your first friend in Cheyenne."

"He's half my age. I don't need a boy to be my friend."

Emma shook her head and turned to put the embroidery away. "I'll take all the friends I can get, Colton. I think you should feel the same way."

Colton headed back to the boardinghouse after Rosie showed him her talent with the iron. He had no desire for his sister to work like a common house maid, but she seemed quite happy with this new skill, and he couldn't bear to hurt her feelings by suggesting such duties were beneath a Benton.

He thought about all that Emma had said and knew he was being a hypocrite. Maybe he was worried about Rob's intentions toward his sister because his own toward Emma were skewed. After all, his brothers had insisted he come here to woo her and reclaim control over all that had belonged to Tommy.

But that isn't why I want to marry her. I love her. I've loved her since I first saw her. She's everything I'm not.

Even her newfound use for religion didn't bother Colton as he once thought it might. Instead, he found her comments on faith and God to be a tender reminder of his mother. She had so often spoken of God as if He were right there with her. She spoke of having talks with Him as if He might actually listen and respond. And she believed that He did just that.

Emma's new faith stirred a sort of longing in Colton that he couldn't explain. Her presence did much the same. There was something about her that made the emptiness in his life all too evident. He had tried to fill it with businesses and education. He had enjoyed his time at the university and later studying law. He held a great appreciation for the law and its structured procedures.

He continued walking even as he passed by the boardinghouse. He had to think things through and figure out what was to be done. He would meet with some representatives from the Union Pacific tomorrow and discuss the future of their prospective railroads. The Bentons hadn't yet let it be known publicly that they were considering the sale of their railroad to a larger line. His brothers were anxious to get things concluded, however. They had plans of their own for future investments and other interests. The railroad was not without a world of problems, and those problems only grew as the line aged. The upkeep was constant, and labor forces were demanding higher wages and better working conditions. His brothers felt it was time to get rid of the railroad and eliminate the troubles that came with it. They felt there were much better places to invest their money. Walter and Ernest both had purchased property in Dallas and had great plans.

Colton had some hesitation about letting the railroad go. It was their father's legacy, something he had built with great pride to leave his four boys. He had seen a future where they would expand and invest in the various established lines, perhaps even buy out lesser railroads. But they weren't as wealthy as those who owned the larger lines. Those men were considered titans of industry, and Lawrence Benton was not listed among them. Locally he'd done well, and in Missouri, where he started, he had amassed a small fortune. But he never came close to an association of peerage with Vanderbilt, Morgan, Gould, or Hill. Father had died regretting that fact, but he still left behind a worthy financial platform for his sons.

Colton stuffed his hands into his trouser pockets and glanced around him. Cheyenne was a city just coming into its own. The biggest goal was statehood, and the citizens of Cheyenne were leading the charge. There had been multiple appeals to Washington, and all had gone unheeded. In reading various newspaper accounts, Colton believed the biggest problem was the inability of Washington politicians to truly understand the value of Wyoming. They held it as a territory, and for now, that was enough as far as the government was concerned. However, Colton knew the day was coming when all the remaining territories would be divided into states. New surges of immigration west were happening with regular occurrence, and people were pouring into the vast frontier to homestead even now.

He liked the feel of this territory pushing toward statehood and all that could be accomplished under those auspices. The fact was, it challenged him to something more. He had lived in Texas for close to twenty years. First in Houston and then Dallas, and it had never felt like home. Missouri hadn't filled him with a sense of permanency either, but he figured that had more to do with his youth than anything else.

Emma had commented on his unwillingness to leave Dallas due to business, but in truth, Colton had been afraid to travel. Afraid that his discontentment would cause him trouble, and that once he got out into the world, he might find the place he truly belonged. And then what? Leave his family? It had been hard enough to go away to school. At least with that, he was firm with himself about it being only temporary. Just as he was when deciding to accompany Emma and Rosie to Cheyenne. However, as the days passed in Cheyenne, Colton was less and less convinced that he wanted them to be temporary. Especially if he was unable to convince Emma to return to Dallas.

"Mr. Benton, I thought that was you."

Colton looked up to find Charlie Decker walking toward him. "Mr. Decker." Colton gave a tip of his hat.

"Please call me Charlie. I'm not that much older than you."

"I will, thank you. Call me Colton."

Charlie smiled and nodded. "What has you out here today, Colton?"

"I just needed a walk to clear my head and reflect."

"Time for quiet prayer. 'Prayer preserves temperance, suppresses anger, restrains pride and envy, draws down the

Holy Spirit into the soul and raises man to heaven,' so says St. Ephraim the Syrian."

"I don't believe in such a thing as saints."

Charlie chuckled. "What about prayer?"

Colton shrugged. "I'm not much on that either. My mother was a praying woman. She talked to God as if He were truly listening."

"So you believe in God, but not that He listens to us?"

A smile edged Colton's lips. "I like the way you speak your mind, Charlie."

"As a schoolmaster, I've learned that's the best way. Shall we walk together a little?"

Colton nodded and fell in step beside the man. For a while, neither said anything, but it seemed Charlie was waiting for an answer to his question.

"I do believe in God, but I've always felt that He has no reason to be concerned with me."

"And how do you figure that, Colton?"

"I suppose I equate it to the president of the United States. He exists, but I've never seen him. He's busy with his various duties and performances. He is my president as much as yours; however, he doesn't know anything about me. I'm just one of millions who live under his direction and guidance."

"You can hardly equate the God of the universe to a mere man. God is all knowing, so of course He knows you, Colton. The Bible says He's numbered the hairs on your head, and that before you were born, He knew you."

"All right, so let's say He knows me. He's the God of heaven and earth, all knowing as you say. He knows what has taken place and what is yet to come. How is it possible, then, that my prayers should matter at all to Him?"

"Because we are His children, and He loves us. He wants to hear from us, just as I want to hear from my children.

Prayer builds our faith in God. It draws us closer to Him. As we pray, we see God at work."

"But do you believe He truly hears us and answers?"

"I do." He smiled. "I've seen far too many prayers answered to think it happenstance. Were you close to your father, Colton? I only ask because . . . well, I wasn't all that close with mine for a long while. I rarely really spoke to him, nor he to me. There was a void there, and had I been willing to make it otherwise, our relationship might have been completely different. I think the same is true in our relationship with God. We should speak to Him regularly."

"And tell Him what?" Colton looked at Charlie, trying to ignore that a part of him truly wanted an answer that might change his mind.

"Everything," Charlie said, chuckling. "Tell Him everything. Your fears, your hopes, your desires, your concerns. He is pure love, Colton. That love is vast and renewing. There isn't anything you have to say that God isn't willing to hear."

Decker's words stayed with Colton long after they went their separate ways. They stayed with him well into the night, long after the boardinghouse fell silent and the boarders had fallen asleep.

Even now in the wee hours of the morning, Colton could hear Charlie urging him to tell God everything—that He would hear, that He cared.

Unable to sleep, he rose and went to the window. He sighed at the glimmer of light on the horizon.

"I want to believe. Emma believes, and it's changed her. . . . It's given her hope . . . peace." He shook his head, feeling overwhelmed. "I want to believe."

11

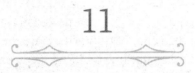

Rob, I'm glad you could work it into your schedule to help teach Rosie to read," Emma said, welcoming Rob into her house. She knew Colton was skeptical of the young man, but she felt Rob was sincere in his desire to help.

"They changed the hours they want me to be on duty. I hope that won't be a problem, but afternoons are when I'll have some free time."

Emma took his hat and put it on the side table in the entryway. "I think afternoons are fine."

He leaned closer. "And Mr. Benton is all right with this?"

"I told him I wanted to give it a try, and he begrudgingly said yes." She glanced down the hall. "Rosie doesn't know that Colton disapproves of you spending time with her. You have to understand, he's worried about her. She's spent all her life sheltered away from the world. She hasn't been allowed to go to school because of her condition."

"I understand, and it's not my desire to hurt anyone or cause trouble. The fact is, from the moment I first met Rosie, I felt something for her that I've never felt for anyone else. I've even talked to my folks about it, and they urged me to pray about it, and believe me, that's what I've been doing."

Emma had wondered about the looks she'd seen on Rob's face when he watched Rosie at church. He was in love. It seemed evident now that he'd brought it out in the open. This would complicate things with Colton. He had a hard time imagining his sister ever being able to marry and have a family of her own. Emma would have to work on him regarding that matter.

"I'll pray on it too, Rob." Emma patted his arm. She heard Rosie in the kitchen and motioned him into the dining room. "We'll be working in here. Rosie! Rob has come."

They entered the dining room just as Rosie came from the kitchen. She was dressed in a simple lavender skirt and white lacy blouse. Emma had offered to help her arrange her hair that morning. She had settled on a simple braid and left it hanging down her back, tied with a ribbon that matched her skirt. Emma thought she'd never looked quite so lovely. She glanced at Rob and saw that he was completely captivated by Rosie.

Rob stepped forward looking more than a little awkward. "It's good to see you, Rosie."

"You too. I'm really excited to learn to read. Emma has some special books that Mrs. Decker let us borrow." She held up a *McGuffey Eclectic Primer*.

Rob nodded. "I know them very well. I learned to read using these readers."

"Emma taught me the alphabet," Rosie continued. "I know how to sound out most of the letters, but sometimes I forget, and sometimes the letters have different ways to sound, so it's confusing."

"Well, hopefully it won't confuse you for long. I think you'll get through this book in no time at all, Rosie. You're very smart."

She frowned. "You shouldn't lie. I'm not smart."

Rob shook his head. "That's the lie. You are smart. People

just thought you couldn't learn, and they were wrong." He looked at Emma. "Isn't that right?"

"It is." Emma took hold of Rosie's hand. "Rosie, sometimes people misjudge situations and the people in them. Your parents and the doctors who spoke to them didn't realize how much you were going to want to learn. That's a big part of mastering any task. They judged you on other cases and situations and believed they knew best. They didn't hide you away because they didn't love you, but took the best advice offered to them and followed those instructions. They were wrong, however. You are quite capable of learning, and because you want very much to learn, I believe you will."

"I do too," Rob quickly agreed. "You just need to work at it, and we'll help you along."

Rosie smiled and gave Emma's hand a squeeze. "I'm so happy. I've prayed a long time that God would let me learn to read and be like other people."

"Just be yourself, Rosie," Rob said, pulling out a chair for her. "The rest will come in time. I'm committed to helping you learn to read. I promise I'll be here for you."

"Thank you." She took her seat and looked up at Emma. "I'm ready to start."

Rosie wasn't sure what Emma and Rob had in mind, nor what the primers would offer, but she was quickly caught up in the lessons. From time to time, Emma had her write out words that they were learning. Some of them Rosie already knew. She had been able to pick up a few words in Texas and had memorized the looks of them so that she could recognize them at a later date. Aunt Clementine had helped her memorize Scriptures, and Emma had promised they could find them in the Bible as part of their reading time. It was so exciting to imagine that one day she would be able to read the Bible for herself.

The idea of being able to understand what the printed words said was all that Rosie had ever wanted. She used to dream of it when she was younger. Sometimes Colton or Tommy would read to her and leave the book in the nursery for their next visit. Rosie would open the book and run her finger along the lines of words, wondering what they meant. She had never tired of looking at those books and imagining that she was able to read them. She had even pretended to read to her dolls, but of course it was nothing more than a recital of the story she'd heard earlier. Now, if everything went as Emma assured her it could, Rosie would be able to read books for herself.

Thank You, Heavenly Father. Please let it be true. Let me be smart enough to learn.

As their time of study continued, Rosie couldn't help but be a little distracted by Robert Vogel's presence. He was a very handsome man. Handsome like Colton, but with lighter brown-gold hair and blue eyes. She thought his blue eyes were the most beautiful she'd ever seen. They were such a rich blue that they reminded Rosie of a clear summer sky.

"All right, Rosie, let's read this page one more time," Emma instructed, "and then we'll stop for the day."

"Do we have to stop?" She looked up in question, hoping Emma might change her mind.

"Rob has to go to his job protecting the town, and you are to have a cooking lesson with Mrs. Olson."

Rosie nodded with a sigh. "I forgot about Mrs. Olson."

"Mrs. Olson from church?" Rob asked.

"Yes. Rosie and I decided to hire her on to handle the kitchen, and she heard that Rosie wanted to learn how to cook. We had been making a few things together, and Mrs. Olson said she was more than happy to teach Rosie, as she'd only ever had sons and never a daughter. She said she had all sorts of recipes that had been handed down to her from her mother and grandmother, and she didn't want them to just end with her. She's going to help Rosie write them down and keep a box of recipes for herself."

"I still need to get a recipe box," Rosie reminded her.

"Yes, we'll tend to that soon."

Rosie turned to Rob. "I'm so excited because she knows how to make pecan pie, and that is Colton's favorite. She's going to teach me to make it as soon as we can get some pecans."

Rob chuckled and leaned closer to her. His action surprised Rosie, and she pulled back. She saw the look on Rob's face. He looked upset. Was he mad at her? She reached out and touched his arm.

"I'm sorry. I didn't mean to jump. I'm not used to being close to men, except for Colton."

Rob's face relaxed. "I'm the one who's sorry, Rosie. I didn't think, and I shouldn't have startled you that way. Please forgive me. I was just going to tell you that I'm very fond of pecan pie too. Now it seems unimportant."

"No." She patted his arm. "It is important. I'm glad to know that you like pecan pie because when we make one, I'll save you a piece."

"I'd like that very much, Rosie. Thank you."

Later, after he'd gone, Rosie worked on her sewing while Emma read to her aloud. It was a wonderful book called *Little Women*. They'd already read the first volume and had now started on the second. Rosie loved the stories of the March girls and all their antics. She related best to Beth, who was very shy and delicate, and because of this stayed home from school. Beth also played the piano, and Rosie had already begun to wonder at the possibilities that might present.

"Do you think I could learn to play the piano?" Rosie asked when Emma paused to take a sip of water.

"I think you can learn to do most anything, Rosie. Of course, it is rather hard to try to take on everything at once."

Rosie knew she was already very busy each day with cooking, reading, and learning to keep house. Emma had told her that knowing how to do household chores was especially important.

"You might not always have a maid or housekeeper, and it's good to know for yourself how to lay a fire and how to make tea and do other important household duties," Emma had said.

"I sometimes feel like I was born all over again when I got to meet you. You always thought good things about me."

Emma put her glass aside. "And I always shall, Rosie. You are like a little sister to me."

"I always wanted to have a sister." Rosie had never been able to play with her brothers because they were much too rough, Aunt Clementine had told her. Sometimes Tommy would come to visit with her in the nursery, but usually their father had him busy elsewhere. It was always special when Tommy would sneak away to come and see her.

"Then it's settled. We will always be sisters."

Rosie thought about that for a moment. "Can we really make it so?"

"I married your brother, and that makes us sisters-in-law. Even though Tommy is gone, it doesn't change how I feel about you." Emma gave her a smile. Emma always had the kindest smile, and she liked to laugh. At least, she did before Tommy died. Rosie hadn't heard her laugh very much since then.

Rosie returned the smile and gave a nod. "We will always be sisters. No matter what."

"Will you be staying for supper, Mr. Benton?" Faith Cooper asked as Colton came downstairs.

"No, I'm having dinner elsewhere, but thank you for asking. I should have made it clear earlier. I know you like to have a count prior to lunch."

"It's quite all right. I know it's usually the exception when you dine with us." She reached into her apron pocket. "This just arrived before you came downstairs. I was waiting for my husband to return and bring it up."

She handed him a letter. It was from Walter. Colton took the envelope. "Thank you, I suppose I should read this before heading out."

"And I need to get back to tending supper." She departed without another word, leaving Colton to contemplate the letter.

He made his way into the front sitting room, where a couple of the boarders were occupying themselves with a game of chess.

"Evenin', Benton," one of the men said, giving him a glance.

"Good evening to you both. Just going to sit a moment and read my letter." Colton hoped the explanation would discourage further conversation. It did.

He opened the envelope and pulled the two-page letter out. Walter talked first of a meeting he and Ernest had attended regarding their plans to build an entire city block in Dallas. The details were as unimportant to Colton as Mrs. Cooper's grocery list, and so he only scanned the details. It was the second page that seemed devoted to him.

You must get Emma to marry you. There is far too much at stake, and you owe the family this sacrifice, especially since it was you who allowed Thomas to change his will. If I were able to do the deed myself, I would, knowing that without control of our own family's railroad we cannot determine the future. Now that Ernest and I have moved forward with our plans, we need to sell as soon as possible, for as much money as possible. We're leaving this matter entirely in your hands—you have our proxies—but we need for you to be swift to a conclusion. Use everything at your disposal—even threaten her relationship with Rose, if need be—but marry her before you return.

The last line was more upsetting to Colton than he'd anticipated. He didn't want Emma to ever believe that he sought her as a wife because of business. He cared too much for her to let that ever be the reason.

He folded the letter and put it in his pocket. A sense of uncertainty imposed itself upon him. How was he supposed to move forward? He truly cared for Emma and was doing his best to be there for her, to listen to her when she talked. The thing was, she wasn't always one for deep conversations. Her new trend toward sober reflections and a desire to right the wrongs of the past also tended to make her turn inward. Her boisterousness was gone. It was as if her wedding day had wiped away all the years of self-focus and playful antics. Colton supposed that was only right; she was in her late twenties, and most women her age were already married with children of their own. Still, while he enjoyed this more insightful Emma, he also found her to be more selective with sharing her thoughts.

Colton frowned. He would just have to be more open with his own thoughts, perhaps. Maybe it was time to tell her how he felt.

"Bad news, Benton?"

He looked up at the man who'd addressed him. "No, just business." He got to his feet and headed for the door.

But it wasn't just business.

On Saturday, it turned out to be such a nice day that Emma decided to take Rosie to the ranch. Emma wanted to let her experience the place where she had grown up. Rosie was always talking about horses and chickens. She had a fascination with both, and often spoke of wanting to have some chickens.

Mrs. Olson had agreed it would be easy enough to keep a few, so Emma thought she might ask her father to give up a few of his laying hens. Of course, she'd need to create a coop, but for the time being, they had a small shed with an attached one-room apartment that the previous owner had given over to the gardener. Maybe they could turn the shed portion into a coop with a little fenced area for the chickens. Emma would have to speak to the Vogels about who might be available to hire to build it. They seemed to know who was reliable and who wasn't. Maybe they could even suggest a gardener, since the grass was already green and growing.

The trip to the Johnson ranch was quite a distance, and even though things were much more settled in the area, there was still the occasional outlaw or ruffian who caused problems. Because of this, Emma asked Colton to come with them. He readily agreed, much to her surprise.

"What else do I have to do on such a fine Saturday?" he had replied.

Now as they approached the ranch, Emma's joy was replaced by a wave of regret. She had been here the previous September for her father's wedding and even stayed in her childhood room. Initially, when Emma had heard about her

149

father remarrying, she'd felt indifferent to the matter. Traveling back for the wedding was done more for Tommy than for herself.

She had wanted to give Tommy time with his dying father, for one thing. Lawrence Benton had a bad heart that was progressively getting worse. The doctor had told his sons that it was just a matter of time. Tommy wanted to avoid his father's death bed all together, but Emma had told him of her regret regarding her mother and encouraged him to do otherwise. They could still have plenty of fun together. And in a way, she had hoped facing his father would mature him a bit more.

She had become engaged thinking Tommy would be less inclined to going out on the town and flirting with other women, but apparently that hadn't been the case. After all, there had been Stella. She pushed that thought aside. Tommy's infidelity hurt her terribly, but she didn't want to think about it. He was gone, and there was no sense holding his sins against him.

The trip to Cheyenne the previous year had come on a whim, but in the back of her mind, Emma had been somewhat troubled at the idea of her father taking another wife. Her mother hadn't even been gone a year. How could he consider such a thing? Truthfully, a part of her had hoped to change her father's mind about marrying their neighbor. But from the moment she'd arrived and met Lucille Aldrich again, Emma had found an unexpected comfort in the woman. She'd been her mother's best friend, and Emma could still call to mind times when they had shared canning and roundup. The two women had been inseparable, helping each other until both were weary enough to drop. They shared stories and laughter in a way that Emma envied.

"This is so beautiful," Rosie said, craning her neck to take in everything at once.

"It represents a lot of hard work. When we first arrived, there wasn't any house or other buildings." Emma remembered it as if it were yesterday.

"Where did you live?"

"We had the wagon, of course, and my father bought a large tent. We lived in that all summer, and by winter we had a very small cabin. It wasn't much, as I recall, but it suited and got us through. Those early years were pretty hard."

"I can't imagine bringing my family to such a wild, open place." Colton shifted in the seat beside her but kept his focus on handling the team of horses they'd rented for the carriage.

He'd said very little up until now. Rosie had been so excited to talk to him about her studies and all that Mrs. Olson was teaching her that no one else could quite get a word in. Emma noticed that as he listened, he seemed almost in disbelief. A couple of times he had muttered under his breath, but Emma wasn't sure what he'd said.

"It was certainly wild. There were still problems with the Indians, and my mother feared for our lives. Not just because of that, but snakes were plentiful, and wild animals too. Mama worried terribly about rabies."

"What is that?" Rosie asked.

"It's a disease that animals can get and pass on to people," Emma explained. "It's deadly, although now they have a treatment that helps if you get it quickly enough."

"Did you ever see Indians?"

"I saw Indians in town, but never here at the ranch. I think they were as afraid of us as we were of them."

"Why were you afraid of them? Were they bad?"

"Some were very aggressive and didn't like us coming to buy up the land. Land that they had been hunting and living on for years before our arrival in the west. There was a very bad war between the Indians and soldiers several hundred miles from here just a little over ten years ago, so people are still rather fearful of what might come.

"Just pull over there, Colton," Emma directed. She barely waited until he stopped before she jumped down unassisted.

Just then, her father came from the house. "I saw the dust and knew someone was heading our way but never imagined it was you. What are you doing here?" He gave her a powerful hug.

"Rosie wanted to see horses and chickens, and I could think of no better place to bring her than the ranch. I hope you don't mind us showing up unannounced, but I could hardly telephone to let you know."

Her father laughed and left her side to help Rosie down from the wagon. "You're all very welcome here. Colton, good to see you again."

"Thank you, Mr. Johnson. Good to see you too."

"Emma!" Lucille called as she came from the house. "What a wonderful surprise." She quickly joined them and hugged Emma and Rosie at the same time. "Are you hungry? Your father has just come in for lunch. I do hope you'll join us."

"Do you have plenty? We did bring a cake that Rosie helped to make. Mrs. Olson assured me that this is one of her finest recipes. It's a spice cake."

"With frosting," Rosie added.

Lucille gave Rosie's face a gentle touch. "How wonderful. Dessert is always welcome."

Her father joined in at this. "I'll say. My sweet tooth would just as soon have dessert and nothing else. However, Lucille made some corn bread and ham steaks that might make me reconsider."

Lucille laughed. "I fried potatoes, as well, and baked some beans with molasses. It's Rich's favorite. There's plenty of food. Come on inside and wash up."

"Colton and I will unhitch these horses and be right in," Emma's father said, already getting to work.

Emma made her way toward the house with her stepmother, linking arms with her and Rosie. "It's just so good to have you here. I've hoped you'd come out sometime. Even prayed for it." Lucille seemed genuinely delighted by the turn of events. Emma hadn't really thought of their visit being all that special.

"Look! Chickens!" Rosie left Lucille's side and headed toward the cottonwoods, where a few dozen chickens were pecking at the earth.

"She's taken on a strange fascination for poultry," Emma said, laughing. "I told her we would see if you could spare a few for us. I'll still need to build a coop for them, but Rosie is quite excited to take on their care and harvest their eggs."

"Of course we can spare some. I think that would be a wonderful thing for Rosie. She can learn to watch over another living thing. It's the best thing for a person to do."

"She's doing so well, Lucille. She's learning so much so fast. It brought tears to my eyes to see how eager she was to read. When I think of all the lost years, it breaks my heart." Emma knew she meant it for more than just Rosie. Her own wasted time weighed heavy on her.

"Then don't think on that. The past is the past, and mistakes were made, but you're helping to right them now." It was as if Lucille understood perfectly that Emma spoke for herself as well as her friend. "Rosie is going to be just fine. You've opened a whole new world to her."

Emma watched as Rosie approached the chickens, laughing as they skittered away from her. It didn't stop her from continuing to seek their company.

Lucille put her hand to her mouth. "Rosie, come on to the house. Later we'll take them some feed, and they'll soon enough be your friends."

Rosie pulled up the hem of her calico dress and came at a run. She laughed all the way and gave a little twirl when she reached Emma and Lucille.

"I know ladies aren't supposed to run," she told them rather breathlessly, "but today I don't want to be a lady. I want to have fun."

Emma laughed. "Then that's exactly what we'll do. Besides, today is my birthday."

"It is," Lucille said, nodding. "We have a cake now that you've brought one, and we can celebrate in grand order."

"How old are you, Emma?" Rosie asked, still panting from her run.

"Twenty-eight." She didn't bother to add that she felt Tommy's death had added a decade or two on to her years. She had spent the first twenty-seven years of her life being a child at heart, but now she felt suddenly old. It was hard to think about most of her friends being married now with several children.

12

On April the nineteenth, the entire neighborhood and half of Cheyenne was invited to come and celebrate the birthday of Robert Vogel and Michael Decker at the Vogel residence. April had been unseasonably warm and perfectly suited for the party to be held outdoors, so multiple tables were set up to accommodate all of the food, and friends and family turned out en masse.

To Emma's surprise, her stepmother and father had driven in for the party, bringing with them one of her father's long-time workers. Gary Price was nearly sixty and lame in one leg. Papa had kept him on out of sympathy for the man. Old cowboys had nowhere to go once they were no longer able to do the hard work required of them. Gary, however, continued to earn his keep in whatever way he could and was more family than employee.

"I was thinking about your desire for chickens," her father told her as they climbed down from their wagon. "Tomorrow, Gary and I are going to build you a proper coop and chicken yard. We even brought a passel of hens for you to get started with."

"I don't know what to say. That's wonderful. Thank you."

Emma gave him a hug and kissed his cheek. "I do have the shed out back with its small apartment attached. The previous owners used it for the gardener. As you can see, I'm going to need to hire one soon."

Her father drew her aside. "That's another reason I brought Gary. He's a hard worker, but ranch life is agreeing less and less with him. I think he'd be good for you to have around here as a gardener. I trust him with my life, and it might put Colton's mind at ease when he heads back to Texas to know the two of you gals have someone watching over you."

"Do you think Gary would be willing to help with the yard and shrubs?" Emma knew old cowboys could be quite prideful. It might be beneath the old man to help with gardening work.

"I think if you were the one to ask him, maybe emphasize that having him around would make you feel safer, then he would say yes and save himself embarrassment. He's always had a soft spot for you."

"Then I'll do it."

Gary came to join them just then, and Emma surprised the older man by giving him a hearty embrace and kiss on the cheek. "Gary, I haven't seen you in such a long time. You were on a trip for Papa when I came back last September, and the other day you were busy elsewhere."

"I was indeed, but it's mighty good to be here now. You're all grown up."

She laughed and patted his shoulder. "I was all grown up nine years ago when I left for Texas. Oh, but it's good to see you. I remember all those wonderful stories you used to tell me."

"I've got a bunch more, right up here," he said, thumping his head.

"I will certainly look forward to that." She looked back to her father. "Where are you staying?"

"We put Gary up at the hotel, and we figured to stay with you, if you don't mind."

"Of course. I would have Gary, too, but I've only got one extra bed." Emma looked apologetically at the man.

"Now, that's not a problem. I even told Rich that I could sleep outside in a bedroll, but he said no. Civilized neighborhoods might frown on that."

Emma laughed. "It wasn't that long ago that many of these folks were living in tents. I don't see that they should have room to criticize, but I'm glad Papa chose a nice place for you."

"It's good to spoil a man now and then," her father declared. "We're gonna unload the things we brought, including the chickens. Then Gary's gonna take the wagon to the livery and himself to the hotel. He'll join us tomorrow to work on settling the chickens."

"That sounds wonderful. We can just put the chickens in the garden shed for now." Emma looked around for Rosie, then remembered she'd gone to the Vogels' to help Marybeth with setting up for the party. "Rosie will be beside herself with delight."

When Emma and her folks were finally ready to head to the party, the Vogels' yard was already full of people. They even found that Colton had gone there first rather than come to the house.

"I figured you and Rosie would already be here," he told her, looking around at all the people. "Where is Rosie?"

"She wanted to help Mrs. Vogel set things up for the party."

Colton frowned. "Do you think it was wise to let her go alone?"

"Relax, Colton. She's in good hands with Marybeth. The woman adores Rosie, and they enjoy each other's company."

He looked skeptical, but Emma didn't give him time to brood. "My folks brought us chickens, and tomorrow morning Papa and Mr. Price are going to build us a proper coop and chicken yard. You should come and help. I'll be fixing breakfast, so come early."

"Ranch style early or city life early?" He grinned and shrugged. "There's about a two-hour difference."

Emma chuckled. "Let's go with the city life. My father seldom gets to ease into the morning. He and Lucille deserve a leisurely time before setting to work."

"Emma, Mr. Benton, how good you could make it." Marybeth moved to where they stood. "Where are your folks? Did they come?"

"They did. I thought they were still here with us, but apparently, they're already mingling in the crowd. This is quite the grand party."

Marybeth nodded and turned to see the bulk of her guests. "I would never have been ready on time if not for Rosie and Greta's help. Those girls are so organized. They had the food table set up and dishes and silver in place before I could even ask them to see to it."

"I'm so glad. I would have come to help as well, but you assured me you didn't need anyone else." Emma wondered if Marybeth had just been polite.

"We really didn't, and besides, it gave me time to be with Rosie and hear about her reading lessons. I understand she's progressing quite nicely."

"She is. She's so eager to learn. The primers that Mrs. Decker lent me are perfect for the job. I'm no proper teacher, but things are going quite well."

"I'm glad to hear it. Mr. Benton," she said, turning to Colton, "how are you finding your time in Cheyenne?"

"Good," he admitted. "I'm enjoying myself more than I expected to. The town is quite enthusiastic about the prospects of statehood."

"Yes, although I daresay we aren't getting the attention

of Washington. They're far too consumed with the upcoming land rush in Oklahoma. They anticipate thousands and thousands of people will participate. No doubt it will be quite the ordeal."

"Free land is always going to attract a certain kind of man," Colton replied, shaking his head. "The real challenge will be setting up an actual place to live within the six-month requirement."

"Especially since so many of the people they expect to race for the claims are poor immigrants," Emma added. "I read about that just a few days ago in the paper."

"I also read that the town fathers here are inviting those who lose out on Oklahoma to come to Wyoming," Colton shared. "Though I don't think a rush of new settlers is exactly what is needed. Crime would almost be certain to rise."

Marybeth glanced up as someone called her name. It was her husband. She gave him a wave and then took hold of Emma's arm. "Come with me. I have a surprise."

"A surprise?"

Emma allowed Marybeth to lead her through the mass of people to where the food tables were assembled. There she found Melody Decker, along with her son Michael and Rob Vogel. Rosie was standing just to Rob's side.

"We thought we would include you and Melody in the birthday celebration. I learned from your stepmother that you had a birthday on the thirteenth of April. You should have told us, Emma. That's also Melody's birthday."

Emma was more than a little surprised. "I don't know what to say. It's very kind of you."

"I was just as surprised." Mrs. Decker took hold of Marybeth's arm. "But leave it to my dear friend to pass along such kindness."

"Well, since folks were coming to have a party, we figured the more the merrier. Happy birthday!"

Several other voices joined in. "Happy birthday!"

"I knew about the surprise, Emma." Rosie came to her side and gave her a hug. "I know we celebrated at your father's ranch, but Marybeth said it was all right to celebrate more than once."

Emma glanced around at all the happy faces. "Well, I can hardly complain."

Colton handed her a small box. "You caught me off guard with the first celebration, but Rosie apprised me of this one, and I was able to secure you a gift."

"You shouldn't have." Emma opened the box and gasped. Inside, nestled down in folds of black velvet, was a diamond-and-ruby broach. "Oh, you really shouldn't have done this."

Colton shrugged, and Rosie frowned. She turned to her brother and shook her head. "You shouldn't buy expensive gifts for Emma. She's not your wife."

Hours later as the party wound down, Emma announced that she was going to head home. Her stepmother and father were caught up discussing cattle with several of their friends, and she encouraged them to stay on and enjoy themselves.

She kissed her father on the cheek. "The front door will be open, just lock up when you come in for the night."

"I'll walk you back," Colton told her. "Just let me find Rosie."

They located her helping to wash dishes. She was so happy, and Colton didn't have the heart to demand she join them.

"I can walk her back when she's ready to come home," Rob offered.

Colton had watched him throughout the evening with Rosie. He was very considerate of her and never overstepped the bounds of decency.

"I think that would be wonderful, Colton," Emma whispered. "It will give Rosie a feeling of independence."

If it hadn't been for the fact that Colton wanted to talk to Emma alone, he might have found a reason to say no, but instead, he nodded. "Thank you, Vogel. That would be fine." He offered Emma his arm. "Shall we?"

"Of course."

They walked at a leisurely pace, leaving the revelry behind them as they made their way to the house.

"Would you like to come in for some coffee?"

"Yes, I'd like to come in for a few moments to talk, but no coffee. I'm still quite full even though I ate hours ago."

They made their way inside, and Emma turned on the front room lights. "It was quite the party. I think most of Cheyenne was there." She took a seat in the rocking chair and sighed. "I'm glad to just sit and relax a bit. Tomorrow will certainly be very busy, so I plan to go to bed early. What did you want to talk to me about?"

Colton sat on the sofa and leaned forward. "I hope you weren't offended by my gift this evening. Rosie made it clear that she thought it was inappropriate, and I was worried that I might have made you uncomfortable."

"Not at all." Emma fingered the broach that she'd pinned to her dress. "I thought it was quite special. I was really touched by it, in fact. Thank you."

"I thought it only right. You deserve beautiful things. I know Tommy was always lavishing them on you."

"He did. That is certainly true. I was always telling him to stop. I didn't want anyone thinking I was with him for the fancy baubles and gowns. I told him you and your brothers were going to think very poorly of me, but he didn't care. He said, 'I want to deck you out in a way that will make everyone stop and look.'" Emma laughed. "He said his friends were going to be so envious, because he'd . . ." She fell silent as her cheeks reddened. "It's not important. I'm not that woman anymore."

"But you are an amazing woman, and were even then."

Emma nodded. "I just want to be done with the old Emma and all her hurtful attitudes and actions. Though I still find myself wanting to have a good time. I loved the party tonight. The people were happy and full of life, and I felt truly cared about."

"You are cared about, Emma."

"Oh, I know. My father loves me; there's no doubt about that. My stepmother has turned out to be a surprising influence in my life, and I can honestly say that she loves me as well. And of course, I know Rosie loves me."

"And I love you."

He hadn't meant to speak the words aloud, but now that he had, he watched to see what Emma's reaction might be. She looked at him for a long moment and then smiled.

"That's good of you, Colton. I know you care. I'm your sister-in-law."

"It isn't that, Emma. I had no intention of telling you this tonight, but . . ." He tried to organize his thoughts so that he wouldn't make a fool of himself. "From the time Tommy first brought you home to meet me, I was . . . well, for lack of a better word, I was dumbstruck."

She said nothing, so Colton hurried to continue. "I never believed in love at first sight, but it happened to me with you. There was something about you that spoke to my soul. I wanted to take you aside and tell you how I felt. I wanted to woo you, but you were with Tommy, and I couldn't intrude on that. He was my brother, and I would never hurt him by betraying him that way.

"I honestly figured he'd play out his time with you and then be off to someone else. Then after a bit of time, I could seek you out for myself. But instead, he really loved you—at least in the manner of love you both chose."

She shook her head. "I don't know what to say."

"I know, and I'm not trying to cause you further grief. But I wonder if you could think about a future with me. We wouldn't have to marry right away, but I can't go on not being honest with you. I overheard Rosie speaking to someone at the party about how much she hates lies, and I knew that I was living a lie. I came with you two to Cheyenne because I couldn't bear the idea of letting you get away. I saw the way the men looked at you tonight, and it worried me. I figured if I didn't say something soon, you might well take up with one of them. I need you to know that I care about you . . . that I love you, and I always will."

13

Emma found sleep impossible that night. She tossed and turned and dozed a little from time to time, but never found restful sleep. Colton's declaration of love had totally taken her by surprise. Looking back on when she first met him, she had thought his standoffish behavior was due to his dislike of her. Now she knew it was because he had feelings for her. It was admirable that he didn't act on them or challenge Tommy's place in her life, but at the same time, it was a strange feeling to imagine him desiring her for himself.

When dawn finally lit the horizon, Emma gave up trying to sleep. She sat on the edge of her bed, contemplating all that Colton had said. He was obviously of a mind for them to marry.

The thought complicated things more than just a little bit. Emma had finally gotten used to the idea that she would live in Cheyenne—that this, and not Dallas, would be her home for the rest of her days. She had figured that in time she might remarry. The thought of having a family of her own appealed more and more. She wasn't even entirely sure why. Dealing with Clara's brood had been difficult, but there was also the tenderness she observed. Her sister adored her children. She had once told Emma that they were everything wonderful about her and David. All the goodness of their love was given life in their children. The idea touched Emma in a way she couldn't explain. It was always there for her to see, but until now, she hadn't appreciated it. Perhaps in settling her adventurous spirit, she had come to see what was truly important in life.

Then there was the possibility of Rosie marrying Robert Vogel, and if not him, then perhaps someone else. She was a lovely young woman with a great amount of love to give. Rosie certainly didn't need to spend the rest of her life keeping Emma company.

But marrying another of the Benton brothers wasn't at all what Emma had in mind. Now having him here in Cheyenne really served to confuse matters. She couldn't imagine having him around and not wondering what he was thinking or planning. Every time she looked at him, she'd know that he was in love with her and wanted to marry her.

"But I'm not even out of mourning," she murmured to herself. Perhaps she should be. After all, she didn't feel like a wife lost in sorrow.

She got up and went to the armoire her stepmother had found for her, but instead of reaching for one of her black gowns, she chose a brown skirt and white blouse. It was nothing overly ornate, but definitely symbolized Emma putting aside her mourning.

Would that say too much to Colton? She wasn't yet ready to urge him on in his feelings. She placed the skirt and blouse on the end of her bed and stood back. She didn't want to give Colton—nor any other man—the wrong idea. She wasn't looking to find a beau or mate. She hadn't even come to terms with the past. There was still so much yet undone.

She sank onto the bed and lightly fingered the lace-edged collar of the blouse. Tommy had been gone for almost three months. She knew what he'd say. He would have condemned her decision to wear black in the first place. He would have told her life was too short to go around in mourning clothes.

Thinking of mourning clothes, Emma couldn't help but remember Stella Mikkelson all dressed in black, a heavy veil hiding her tear-filled eyes. Poor woman. How she must have suffered. She must have been so afraid. Emma had never held a grudge or felt the slightest bit of anger toward her. The fact was the entire situation still didn't seem real.

Emma remembered it all so clearly, as if it had been yesterday. Stella walking toward them, stopping and pulling back her veil. Then she raised the gun at Tommy. Emma had been facing Tommy, but Stella's actions had caused her to look away. Stella's expression was one of absolute heartbreak. This was a woman who had loved and trusted, only to realize her feelings were all one-sided.

And now she was dead, as well as Tommy. Emma wondered if someone was mourning her. Perhaps her parents? Maybe siblings?

Getting to her feet, Emma gently rehung the skirt and blouse in the wardrobe, then took up one of the black gowns. She would hide in the shadows a little longer. She would wear black for Stella as much as for Tommy. There was no sense in encouraging any man to show her extra attention.

After she finished with her hair, Emma made her way downstairs. Mrs. Olson had Saturday and Sunday off, so Emma would be responsible for getting the meal and coffee going. She added wood to the stove and soon had a nice fire going. Checking the coffee box, she measured out beans and ground them before getting the pot and filling it with water. Once the coffee was on the stove, Emma turned her attention to breakfast. They were going to work hard this morning, so she wanted to make a hardy meal.

"I thought I heard someone down here," Lucille said, coming into the kitchen. "Do you have an extra apron?"

"The ladies from the sewing circle made me new ones. They're in the third drawer down." Emma pointed.

Lucille retrieved an apron and tied it on. "What can I do to help?"

"I was thinking that flapjacks, scrambled eggs, and maybe ham instead of bacon would be filling and keep the fellas going until lunch."

"Sounds perfect. Would you like me to handle the eggs and ham while you make the flapjacks?"

"That would work well. I just got the coffee on."

"I told Rich to sleep in a little longer. We told Gary he didn't need to show up until seven."

Emma smiled. "I was hoping all of you would stay in bed and get a little extra sleep."

"We women aren't always able to take the extra time when it's afforded us, are we?" Lucille smiled. "You're up awfully early yourself."

"I know. I couldn't sleep."

"What had you so restless?"

Emma went to the cupboard for flour. She didn't feel like sharing her confusion with Lucille. "I suppose just all the excitement of yesterday. The party and all. I had a good time. I hope you did too."

"I did. I was a little concerned that perhaps you would have a difficult time. I know you've been worried about running across people you offended. Did that happen?"

"There were some there that I thought I should probably say something to, but after the first couple of people told me they couldn't remember what I'd done, I stopped. Maybe it's not a good idea to bring up the past. Maybe most folks aren't as grudge-holding as I figured them to be."

Her stepmother nodded. "Maybe not. Maybe let them be

the ones to bring it up. That way if it's weighing them down or troubling them, they'll be able to come to you."

"But the Bible says in Matthew five that if you bring your gift to the altar and then remember that your brother has something against you, you should leave the gift and go be reconciled to them. I think there are a lot of folks out there who have a right to hold something against me."

"Having the right to hold something against you and actually doing it are two different things. I know people who might have wronged me in the past, but I let go of my right to demand retribution. Maybe others have, too, and don't hold anything against you."

"Maybe, but I'd like to know for sure. I thought about talking to Reverend Bright about it. Maybe I could offer an apology at church. You know, make a public confession." Emma shook her head. "I just don't know who I've offended . . . well, I know some, but others are less obvious."

Lucille came and put her arm around Emma's shoulders. "Pray about it and trust God to direct. Your heart is yielded to Him, and your desire is to be reconciled. God will guide you to the right people, at the right time. Then you can apologize or whatever you feel is right to do. Don't let your contrition get bogged down in guilt. So often guilt just festers into anger or weighs you down in regret. It makes you ineffective."

"Thank you. I know you're right. I will commit this to more prayer."

"Good. Now let's get busy. Those fellas are going to show up soon and expect to be fed."

Colton made his way to Emma's house wondering, as he had throughout the night, what she might be thinking or feeling. He hadn't meant to just blurt out his feelings to her the night before. Once said, it was all he wanted to talk about. It was clear Emma didn't share his desire to discuss, however.

She hadn't expected his declaration. He knew that much. He could see it in her eyes. She'd been a widow just three months, and in normal circumstances, no decent man would approach with intentions of marriage. He felt bad for having put that weight on her shoulders. He blamed his brothers and their constant push for him to secure the majority stock for the family railroad. Colton felt certain that Emma would listen to whatever advice he gave her regarding the railroad sale, but his brothers were far more skeptical. Up until now it hadn't been that urgent, but after his meeting with the Union Pacific, things were starting to move forward with new momentum. He would definitely need to discuss the railroad with Emma as soon as possible.

Colton knew she was more practical now, more mature. Once he explained a matter, she would make good choices. But why should Walter and Ernest believe that? She hadn't been that way when she was being courted by Tommy. The twosome had been irresponsible most of the time. Tommy even more than Emma.

When Colton reached Emma's house, he saw Rich and Gary were already standing in discussion out near the garden shed. Colton made his way over to them, cutting across the backyard area.

"Morning, Colton. Gary and I were just figuring out what we need to do first." Rich grinned. "We both agreed . . . breakfast." He slapped Colton on the back. "The ladies should just about have everything ready. They were cooking up a storm when we came out here twenty minutes ago."

Colton gave each man a nod. He didn't have much in the way of work clothes, so he'd chosen his oldest pair of trousers and shirt. His hat and jacket were newer, but he could put the coat aside for the manual labor part of his day. It had been a long time since Colton had worked with his hands in such a fashion. When he'd been young, his father had insisted on the boys getting an education so as to benefit the business of running the Benton empire. Physical labor was for servants and staff. Colton had trained in law, Walter in banking and finance, and Ernest in government and politics. Tommy was the only one to disappoint. Father had sent him off to higher education with a focus on business investments, but Tommy had no interest whatsoever. He would have been far happier breaking horses or learning to rope. He loved animals and had even told the family at one point that he intended to have his own horse farm where he could breed thoroughbreds for racing. At least that was something acceptable in the upper-class society his father enjoyed.

"Come and get it," Lucille called from the back door.

Rich laughed. "Don't have to tell me twice."

They sat down to breakfast and marveled at the feast created by Emma, Lucille, and Rosie. Rosie seemed happier than usual, and Colton wondered if that was in part due to Mr. Vogel's attention. When he'd headed back to the boarding-house last night, he found them sitting on the porch talking about something as if they were old friends. It had bothered him to wonder once again if Rob was taking advantage of his sister, but he kept hearing Emma's words of assurance that Robert Vogel was a man of good report. Still, Colton had no intention of letting the man get too close to Rosie.

"Colton, you've been here about a month now. When do you plan to return home?" Rich asked him. The question was one Colton didn't have an answer for.

"I hadn't really thought about it, sir. I've been meeting with a variety of railroad people. I've been eager to learn what plans the UP has for their future around here. For example, they've decided that with the large number of families settling to the south of the many Union Pacific tracks, they're going to build a viaduct over the tracks to connect the south side settlement with town."

"What's a viaduct?" Rosie asked.

"It's a road that will go over the railroad tracks on a bridge-like structure," Colton explained. "They also plan for the streetcar line to expand and go to the south as well."

Emma offered him a plate of flapjacks. "I read in the newspaper that the streetcar line is about to be completed from Capitol Avenue to Lake Minnehaha."

Colton took the platter and added a couple of the cakes to his plate before passing it to his right. "They seem to be expanding the streetcar in all directions." He had come to enjoy this casual style of family dining. Back in Texas, there had always been someone to serve him.

"We've definitely seen this place grow over the years, haven't we, Lucille?" Rich said, shaking his head. "Hard to believe there was hardly anything here twenty years ago."

"It's true. I remember thinking then that we'd come to the end of the world," Emma said, laughing.

"It's always been an ambitious little town," Lucille admitted. "I remember when they put in some very fine dress stores not long after the town was established. They carried Worth gowns in one of them. I don't know where they thought the women out here were going to wear them, but ladies bought them just the same. At least, the very wealthy ladies did."

"Of course, those fancy European noblemen all wanted to have their own ranches out here. They set up those big ranches and hired folks to live there and care for them, at least until the Great Die-Up." Rich referenced the horrible winter of 1886 and '87. Thousands upon thousand of livestock had died in the Cheyenne area alone. "After that, a great many of them pulled out."

"Takes a tough man to stand up to the weather out here."

Lucille chuckled. "My Frank used to say that all the time, and now I hear it from Rich."

"Well, it's true. This ain't the place for those fancy dudes and their dreams of ridin' the range. A fella has to work hard to make a go of it out here."

The talk continued, and the question of how long Colton planned to stay was soon forgotten, just as he'd hoped it might be when he brought up the subject of plans for the city's future.

When the men moved outside, the conversation was only about the chicken coop and the decision to attach it to the far side of the garden tool shed.

"The other side has the little apartment, so no sense building the coop on that side," Rich said, already starting to walk off the space needed for the coop. "I think this will be just right. Once the building is in place, we can attach the fence post to the wall of the coop and bring it out about ten feet. We'll dig a trench to put the fence a little ways into and stake it down. That will keep the critters from trying to dig under to get to the chickens."

Rich and Gary had obviously worked together on more than one occasion. Colton was impressed at the way they seemed to read each other's minds as they worked to put together a frame for the addition. Rich took Colton in hand and had him hold the newly built wall frame in place while he and Gary nailed it to the shed. Little by little, the coop took shape.

"We'll build some nesting boxes and roosts," Rich said, grabbing a two-by-four. "Once we have the roof on. Gary, you might as well start working on it. We're going to slant it to the back, that way the snow will slide right off the back with the push of a broom. Won't be hard for the gals to keep up with in the winter."

Winter. When he'd first come north, Colton had hoped

they'd be moved back to Dallas by wintertime. Now, however, he'd been considering the benefits of staying in Cheyenne. It seemed with each passing day he was becoming more and more invested in the city, and Emma and Rosie certainly seemed content here.

They continued the work. They were nearly finished when Emma announced it was time for lunch. At her father's bidding, she came out to see what they'd accomplished.

"It's looks really great. You men are quite the team." She smiled at them all and kissed her father's cheek. "I am so glad you decided to do this."

"After lunch, we'll get the fence in place to quarter off your chicken yard. I saw that your neighbors let their flock run around free, but yours need to learn their home first. Get them settled and penned in. After a while, they'll be okay to let out. It won't take any time at all."

Colton helped Rich collect the tools while Emma took Gary aside to talk. He caught bits and pieces of the conversation. It seemed she wondered if he'd like to have a job taking care of her yard and overseeing the place.

In a hushed whisper that Colton could barely hear, she told the older man that she'd feel so much safer if she had someone around who she knew she could trust.

"Let me show you the apartment here. It's not much at all, just a large room, but the last owners fixed it up nicely." She led him into the room, and Colton found himself staring after them.

"I didn't know she didn't feel safe."

"She's helping me out," Rich said in a low voice. He motioned for Colton to follow him. Once they were nearly back to the house, Rich explained. "Gary's an old cowhand, and his body isn't letting him do his job anymore. I've offered to let him sit around and just fill space, but he won't abide such laziness. Insists that he can pull his weight, but he's becoming a liability. He's always adored Emma, and if she makes it clear to him that he's needed here, then I think he'll be willing to give up the ranch and come help her. The duties will be much less difficult and definitely not so dangerous if he slips up."

Colton glanced back at the building, where Emma and Gary Price were just coming out. She looked happy and gave the man a hug. "Looks like she talked him into it."

"She has a way of winnin' folks over."

"She's a good woman. I saw that the first time Tommy brought her home. She was so patient with Rosie. She treated her like she was no different from anybody else."

Rich nodded as Colton met his eyes. "She's finally come around to right thinkin'. Her mama always said she would in time. It's taken a long while, but I think my Emma is ready to settle down and live a life that's pleasin' to the Lord."

Later that afternoon, Rosie oversaw her chickens while Emma said good-bye to her family. Gary Price had agreed to come and live with her but headed back to the ranch with the others to retrieve his things.

"I don't have much, Miss Emma, but what I have is dear to me. I'll ride back in tomorrow and get settled."

"Tomorrow is soon enough. I can't fault you for wanting your things around you." She waved to them as her father put the horses in motion.

"We should be home by dark," Lucille called back. "So don't worry about us."

Emma gave a wave. "I'll try not to worry." She didn't say it loud enough for her family to hear. She also didn't bring up the fact that the paper carried a story about a man being attacked by Indians only about twelve miles to the west of the ranch. The man could have been telling a tall tale, but the account mentioned the editor witnessed the horse that had taken several arrows in the attack.

She headed back to the house, exhausted from the long day and still confused by everything that Colton had said. There'd been no chance for the two of them to discuss the matter, but now that they were alone, she felt almost certain he would say something.

Hoping not to give him much of a chance, she went straight into the house and into the kitchen. There were plenty of leftovers for supper, so she couldn't even occupy herself by cooking.

"Rosie seems pretty happy," Colton said, joining her in the kitchen.

"The chickens will become special friends for her. They were for me when I was young." Emma put away a few things that had been left out from their earlier preparations. "She's already started naming them."

Colton chuckled and turned. "What good is it to name them? They won't come when they're called."

"No, but the more time she spends with them, the more they'll know her and come whenever they see her. Especially when they know she's the source of food. Naming them is more for her benefit than theirs." Emma wiped down the countertop. "Will you be staying for dinner?"

"No."

Emma startled when Colton spoke. He was standing right behind her now. She turned, pressing her back against the cabinet and counter. She looked up into his eyes.

"You're, uh, welcome to stay."

"I want to stay, but I think I should go. You know how I feel, and I want you to have some time to consider what I've said without me being here to further complicate matters. I care so much about you, Emma."

His look was almost pleading, as if begging her to understand. She gave only the slightest nod, knowing that if she tried to speak it would be all muddled and confused, because that was how she felt.

"I just want to say . . . well . . ." He stopped speaking altogether and took her in his arms, pressing his lips to hers. Emma could scarcely draw breath. Tommy had kissed her a hundred times, but never like this. Never with the passion and desire that she, too, felt in that moment.

And then as quickly as he'd begun the kiss, Colton stopped and pulled back.

"I'm sorry if I surprised you, but I'm not sorry that I did that." He left her then.

Emma stood there unable to move for several moments. She heard his boot steps as he passed through the dining room and down the hall. She heard the screen door open and close, and only then did she draw in a gasping breath.

She touched her lips, still not able to reason all that had happened. Colton's kiss had ignited something deep within her. Something completely unexpected. It was like coming awake after a long sleep. Coming awake to a world she'd never known existed.

She wasn't sorry that he'd kissed her. She was sorry that he had stopped.

14

It was the busy season for the ranch, and Emma knew she'd see very little of her father and Lucille. With that in mind, she planned ways for her and Rosie to keep busy at their own place. Rosie was more than content with her chickens and Rob Vogel's daily visits to help with reading. Emma had bowed out altogether with the reading lessons, knowing that Rob was fully capable of teaching Rosie. She knew they were caught up in each other's company, as well, and felt like she was in the way.

She had a certain longing for the happiness that she saw in Rosie. Emma wasn't entirely sure she could ever be that carefree. She had seen too much and experienced the ugliness of a life lived in self-indulgence and irresponsibility. Rosie was innocent of all of that. Maybe having been sheltered all of her life was a blessing that none of them quite appreciated.

Emma focused on the gardens and yard. She planted flower starts and seeds near the front porch and spoke often with Gary about plans for planting some additional trees. After twenty years, it was impressive to see how much of a difference trees were making in the town. Most of the women belonged to the Cheyenne Arbor Society, which focused hard on the beautification of Cheyenne through trees. Just the year before, Cheyenne had passed an Arbor Day Law and pledged to celebrate Arbor Day every April to note the importance of planting new saplings in their territory. Emma was impressed with the short but well attended celebration they'd had at the end of the previous month. Cheyenneites knew well the importance of beautifying their town.

Uppermost on her mind, however, was Colton and his feelings for her and, frankly, her own growing feelings for him. Knowing how he cared for her, Emma had allowed herself to consider a life with Colton. The thoughts that came to mind weren't at all unappealing. Colton Benton was a handsome and thoughtful man. He was highly intelligent, and she truly admired that about him. When he was interested in a topic, he did whatever was necessary to learn about it and better understand. He'd spent numerous days over the last month with representatives from the Union Pacific regarding their desires to expand their lines north and even south, and often spoke of what he'd learned over supper. She had no idea to what degree he was involved, but it kept him busy enough that she'd not seen that much of him lately.

That was why it was so surprising when Colton showed up an hour later for lunch. Emma hadn't really planned anything at all. Rosie was spending the day with Marybeth and Rob. The threesome were painting and papering the Vogels' upstairs, and Rosie was so excited to participate that Emma didn't have the heart to tell her no. Not that she really had any reason to refuse her. Colton was less than pleased, however, to hear about the activities.

"I don't like that she's doing common laborer jobs."

Emma looked up from slicing bread. She had decided to make sandwiches, since Colton's surprise arrival. "But she enjoys participating in just about everything. Your family kept her from experiencing much of anything, and now she's making up for lost time."

"We would have kept her from common labor even if the circumstances of her birth had been different. You weren't raised with a staff to care for you as we were."

"That's true." Emma tried not to think of the fact that she was alone with Colton in the same room where he'd given her their first kiss. "But there's nothing wrong with working and working hard. You helped to build a chicken coop and set up fence. It didn't hurt you a bit." She smiled and went back to slicing bread.

"That's different. I'm a man. Men are often called to participate in a variety of tasks that are often assigned to common workers."

"My point is, that it doesn't hurt either men or women to try their hand at a variety of jobs. Rosie is happy. She's blooming just like the flowers around here. I've known her a short time, but you've been with her a lifetime. Wouldn't you agree that she's happier than ever before?"

Again, she glanced up to catch Colton's serious expression. He drew a deep breath and let it go. "She is happier. Smarter too."

"She enjoys learning, and I've no desire to take that away from her. Whether it's reading, sewing, or painting a room."

"It's taking me some time to adjust to this new Rosie."

Emma stacked the slices of bread and put them on a plate. Next, she went to the icebox and took out the leftover ham, butter, and roasted pears. She brought this to the table, then went back for plates, silverware, and napkins.

"She's not just happy; she feels she has a life worth value. Everyone needs to feel that way. Would you like coffee or something else?"

"Coffee is fine."

"Good." Emma went to the stove, where she'd put the leftover brew from breakfast. "I doubt it's all that hot, but it is warm. I could heat the stove more and get it hot."

"No, it's fine as it is. I really don't care. Water would serve me just as well. I didn't come here with lunch in mind."

Emma poured him a cup of coffee and then set it in front of him. "Then what did you have in mind?"

Colton looked anxious, and rather than answer immediately, he picked up two slices of bread and began to slather butter on each piece. "I . . . wanted to make sure you were both doing all right. I know I haven't been around a lot. At least, not as much as I maybe should have been."

Emma took a seat at the small kitchen table opposite Colton. She took a slice of bread and a piece of the ham. Without bothering to butter the bread, she plopped the piece of ham on top and cut the whole thing in half.

"Would you like me to offer grace?" she asked.

Colton nodded and bowed his head. Emma wondered how things were going for him spiritually speaking.

"Father, we thank You for this food and ask Your blessing on us as we seek You. In Jesus's name, amen."

"Amen," he murmured.

Emma took that opportunity to ask about his beliefs. "So have you come to any further conclusions about God?"

"No. I have listened more carefully to Reverend Bright's sermons. I definitely have a deeper desire to understand," he admitted. He glanced around. "Where is Mrs. Olson?"

"She had a doctor's appointment. Her knee has been bothering her, and she wanted to have the doctor check it out."

"It's probably nothing more than old age." With that, he took a bite and completed his sandwich.

"Yes, I'm sure you're right, but if it offers her comfort to seek the doctor's opinion, I think it's a good idea. Besides, he might have some medication that can help. They're always coming up with something new. The newspaper is constantly advertising a variety of tonics."

"Usually made up of alcohol or opium in some arrangement or another. People can't stop old age with a tonic or pill."

"True enough." Emma spooned a cold pear onto her plate. She wanted to talk about Colton's feelings for her, and at the same time, she wanted to avoid it. She certainly wasn't ready to pledge undying devotion to him, yet she couldn't help but think that she should at least address the matter. But before she could figure out what to say, Colton spoke up.

"There's something that we should discuss. I've not said anything until now, because . . . well, it wasn't all that important."

Emma figured he meant to discuss their feelings for each other. She nodded and put aside her spoon. She wasn't certain she could eat and listen to him pledge his love for her.

Colton took a sip of coffee, then pushed it aside. "As you know, I've been in meetings with various railroad officials."

Emma was disappointed that he brought up business rather than their kiss. "Yes, I know that very well."

"The fact is, we have been talking about selling our railroad to one of the larger lines. We were approached by the Southern Pacific first. Our plan was to arrange things and sell by autumn or sooner, but now the Union Pacific is aware of our desire to sell. They have approached us to consider selling to them."

"I don't understand the desire to sell in the first place. This is your family's legacy. Your father worked hard to build this railroad so that you would always have something of him to hand down to your children and their children."

Colton nodded. "I'm well aware of that. However, the upkeep that goes along with the railroad is costly and cuts deeply into the profits. The responsibility and potential for problems is growing with each passing year. My brothers and I feel that we could sell the railroad and reinvest the money in other things and do just as well, if not better.

"The Southern Pacific Railroad has been buying up smaller Texas railroads for many years. They've bought them all across the southwest and elsewhere and brought them, quite successfully, under their management. They could do the same with ours and benefit greatly. However, the Union Pacific also is of a mind to buy our railroad. You might not be familiar with our line, but it runs from Missouri to Houston. The UP already has track in Missouri, and incorporating our line will give them a greater benefit in reaching the Gulf."

"I don't think it's a good idea. This is something that seemed quite important to your father," Emma replied before biting into her sandwich. She began chewing and noted the look on Colton's face was one of surprise.

"Father is dead, but even before he passed away, the possibility was discussed. It isn't something we've decided without great consideration. We weighed the good and the bad."

Emma swallowed and dabbed her mouth. "It seems that I should take interest in this and learn for myself what is most beneficial."

Colton's expression suggested confusion. "Why would you want to thwart our efforts? We certainly aren't looking to cause harm. You know nothing about railroads. Until earlier this year, your only real knowledge of such matters was traveling on them to those wonderful destinations you longed to see."

His tone took on a hint of sarcasm, and Emma didn't intend to stand for that. "I might have been focused on having a good time, but that doesn't mean I was without understanding of good investments. Tommy and I talked more than once about reasonable risks and investing money wisely."

Colton tossed his napkin down. "Ha! My brother knew

very little about such things. Believe me. We tried to educate him. Father sent him to college to learn about business investments, but he returned home a miserable failure."

Emma knew that her response had upset him, but she didn't care. "Tommy was smarter than any of you gave him credit for. He was bored with college because he already understood the world of finances and investments. If any of you had bothered to ask his opinion, you might have realized that. Just because classroom lectures and testing didn't suit him didn't mean he wasn't brilliant. How do you suppose he made all of that money investing? You credited yourself for handling his affairs, but he had other accounts that you knew nothing of."

"How do you know?" he questioned, raising his voice.

"He told me!" Emma matched his volume. "I didn't bother to know more about it, but Tommy fully understood and took advantage of it. You might recall I had a visitor come to see me at the house before we left Dallas. He was a lawyer Tommy had used in addition to you."

Colton was more than a little agitated. "I find this hard to believe."

"I'm sorry, Colton. I'm not trying to stand in the way of plans that you and your brothers have made. I just want to be informed and see for myself that it's the wisest plan to make. I owe it to Rosie, if for no other reason. I want the money to last and support her."

"Rosie is my sister, not yours."

Emma leaned back in her chair. "Rosie is her own person. She's fully capable of making decisions for herself. She may have started out slow, but she's running full steam ahead. Just like your trains."

Colton got to his feet. "This is ridiculous. My brothers were afraid you might try to do something like this."

"I'm not doing anything," Emma countered and got to her

feet too. "That's my whole point. I just don't think we should do anything yet. What's the hurry? As you just pointed out, two major railroads want to purchase your railroad—our railroad. Shouldn't we investigate a little further and at the very least see who is willing to pay the most for it?"

She was right. Colton knew he should calm down and just admit it. His brothers were the ones pushing for this sale, and while Colton could see problems in the future, he knew their greed was really the only reason for rushing the transaction.

"I should go."

As he exited the house, thunder rumbled. Colton looked to the skies and noted the heavy black clouds moving in. They matched his mood. He would have much preferred discussing his future with Emma, rather than the railroad. The railroad had always been a thorn in his side. He'd never cared for the business, nor his father's devotion to it. Here it was once again causing trouble for him.

No, I'm causing trouble for myself. I'm the one who got upset. Emma did nothing but ask questions. Good questions, and yet I acted the cad.

Colton made his way down the street with no destination in mind. The wind picked up, and lightning flashed. Wherever he was going, he needed to get inside soon. He turned and headed for the nearest restaurant. He was still hungry.

He barely made it inside when the rain began to pour in a deluge. The lightning and thunder increased, causing the electrical lights to flicker. The storm outside matched the one in his soul.

"Table for one?" a man asked.

"Yes, it's just me." And if he wasn't careful, it might remain that way for the rest of his life.

15

Colton awoke the next morning knowing that he needed to apologize to Emma. He had let his frustrations get the best of him. His brothers' demands that he get Emma to marry him so that he could control Tommy's stock, along with the fact that he knew he'd need to return to Texas soon, was making Colton's life a misery. He didn't want to leave Cheyenne and Emma. Thoughts of Texas didn't even matter.

At ten o'clock he found himself at the Cheyenne Depot. He'd received a proposal from the Union Pacific officials related to purchasing the family railroad. After talking with Emma, Colton knew he would have to stall. They couldn't sell without her approval. Colton figured he could delay them by explaining he would have to return to Texas and discuss the matter with his brothers. Even though he knew they wouldn't care who bought the line so long as the price was the best they could procure and they could get their money soon.

"Mr. Benton." A young man waved him down. "I was just coming to deliver this telegram to you. My good luck to find you here at the depot." The runner handed him the telegram.

Colton flipped the man a coin despite the fact that he'd

not had to do much of anything and walked away to have a little privacy. The telegram was from his brothers.

News? Marry Emma quickly and return home. Must have her stock. R.R. sale imperative.

He crumpled the telegram and stuffed it in his pocket. They must be getting quite desperate. Colton knew that their need of cash was critical in order to secure contractors since most of their money was tied up in other investments. He had thought of just making them a loan from his own assets, but he'd never felt all that good about their construction plans and hesitated to get involved.

Colton glanced down the long hall to where he had planned to discuss his need to return to Texas with the UP officials. It could wait. He headed outside and made his way back down the street toward Emma's neighborhood. He needed to talk to her and make things right. That was far more important at this point than anything else.

The storm from the day before had damaged some of the roofs and businesses, and there was a fair amount of cleanup being done as he passed Sixteenth Street on his way to Seventeenth. The opinion of Mr. Cooper was that it was a straight wind rather than a tornado, but either way there was work to be done. The Coopers' house had sustained some heavy hail, and the roof had suffered, as well as two upstairs windows. Colton prayed Emma's house had been without harm.

He approached her yard and saw her outside talking to Gary Price and pointing toward the roof. He glanced up but didn't see anything of importance. She noticed him then and gave a wave. Apparently, he was welcome to join them and did.

"We've taken some damage," Emma declared as Colton

drew closer. "Gary says it's not all that bad, but he intends to take care of it right away."

"It won't be all that difficult," the older man assured.

Colton nodded. "Is there anything I can help with?"

"No, young fella, I can take care of it just fine." He turned to Emma. "I'll need to get some supplies."

"We have an account at the Armstrongs' Emporium. They should have everything you need. If you don't want to wait for them to deliver it, feel free to rent a wagon from Abney's Livery Stable."

"Yes, Miss Emma. I'll see to it. You don't worry a bit about it. We're sittin' pretty good compared to some folks." He tipped his hat and headed off across the yard.

"He's been such a godsend." Emma watched as Price moved off down the street. "I don't know what I'd do without him." Emma started for the house.

"I came to apologize."

She glanced over her shoulder. "I'm sorry too. I didn't mean to get so upset, and I certainly didn't mean to imply that I knew more about the railroad than you. I prayed about it last night and want you to know that I will agree to whatever you think is best."

She led the way into the house through the front door. "Why don't you have a seat, and I'll put on some coffee? Unless you'd rather have tea?"

"No, I don't need either one. Please just come and sit with me for a bit. I want to better explain."

"Can I take your coat? It's quite warm today, and I certainly don't need you to stand on formalities and suffer the heat."

Colton smiled and unbuttoned his coat.

Emma reached up to help him remove it. "I've opened all the windows, so at least we'll have a breeze." She draped his coat on a chair by the entryway and then took a seat in the rocking chair. "I've always been partial to rockers, even when I was young." She ran her hands down the arms of the chair. "This one belonged to my mother, and sometimes I can still see her sitting in it, rocking and crocheting or knitting. I didn't appreciate the memory before, but now it's quite dear."

Taking a seat on the sofa, Colton remembered his own mother in her rocker. "My mother preferred her rocker to any other chair in the house. Sounds like our mothers would have agreed over that."

Emma folded her hands. "So, when will you need me to sign the paperwork on the sale of the railroad?"

"Well, you weren't the only one to reconsider things. I received a proposal from the UP and figure I should have my brothers review it and then present a counteroffer to the Southern Pacific. As you said, it should be sold to the highest bidder to benefit the family as much as possible."

"You'll be heading back to Texas soon?"

He couldn't very well tell her that he didn't want to go back to Texas at all, especially without her. Having had a fight with her the day before, Colton had hardly slept last night, and this morning it had been uppermost on his mind to apologize for his attitude. Now that he was back in her company, he wanted only to make everything right.

"First, I want to make sure that you are in agreement with the idea of selling. We didn't arrive at this idea without a great deal of thought, and I didn't fully share that fact with you. Walter and Ernest are always talking to other financial and investment-minded men. There are signs of economic problems on the horizon. They may well pass without any issue or hardship, but if not, then we believe railroads will suffer a good deal.

"I know you read the newspaper and probably already know from your family that the agricultural market has been depressed for years, and, of course, the Great Die-Up caused even more problems. Those two things have lessened a great deal of shipping on the railroad. Everything is funneling down to create problems not only for America but other places that have depended on us to send food and animals. Meanwhile, there have been quite a few smaller railroads that have gone bankrupt or been forced to sell out. My brothers and I feel that before we find ourselves in that situation, we would rather part with the railroad on our terms."

"I agree. I didn't know about all of the economic issues, but I do know that you are very astute when it comes to the law and financial responsibility. Since inheriting, however, I have tried to read reports in the newspaper and listen to what's going on around me. I want to be cautious and wise when it comes to managing what Tommy left to me."

"As a woman with a substantial portfolio of investments and large bank account, you should be mindful of the things you do. I feel bad that I didn't offer you more information before just making demands." He paused and drew a deep breath. "As you know, I care deeply about you. I don't want things like this to come between us."

Emma met his gaze, and Colton lost himself in her dark brown eyes. He longed to take her in his arms and kiss her, to persuade her to marry him that very day so that they might never need to be apart again.

At the sound of the screen door opening, Colton straightened. Rosie entered the front room with a huge smile on her face.

"Rob is going to teach me to ride a horse," she told Emma. "We need to buy me a riding skirt." She noticed Colton and sobered. "I want to learn to ride."

"That's a great idea, Rosie," Colton said, trying to sound as if he completely agreed. He didn't, but he wasn't about to admit that. Though he did have to admit that Rosie was becoming more and more capable of deciding these things for herself.

She smiled again. "I am so excited. When can we go to the store, Emma?"

"I could take you after I finish talking with Emma," Colton offered. "You and I haven't had time alone for a while now. Taking you shopping and getting lunch together might be fun."

"I'd like that." Rosie very nearly danced over to where Colton sat and bent to kiss him. "I'll go get ready."

"You do that, Rosie." He smiled up at her, eager for her to leave him alone with Emma. "Take your time getting ready."

She headed toward the door. "Is this your coat, Colton?"

"Yes. Why?"

"There's a stain on the collar. I'll go clean it for you."

Colton figured that would work well to keep her occupied a little longer so that he could discuss his feelings with Emma. "Thank you. That's very considerate."

She took up the coat and left Colton and Emma alone once more. Colton felt he should press the matter quickly before he lost the opportunity.

"Emma, have you thought about what I said?"

"You mean that you love me?" She shifted in her chair. "I've thought of little else."

"And what did you conclude?"

She gave a light laugh. "I don't think I've concluded anything. You took me by surprise."

"But are you . . . do you think you could care for me?" Colton very nearly found himself praying she would say yes. Lately his thoughts turned more and more to spiritual matters. Would the God of the universe help his cause in matters of the heart?

"I already care for you a great deal. I believe in speaking frankly, so I will say that it's quite possible my feelings for you could turn easily into love. But I haven't truly allowed myself to consider the outcome of that. This is all very new to me, as I'm sure you understand."

"Yes, though it's not new to me. I've cared about you for well over a year. It was more than a little difficult to ignore my feelings for you, but my love for Tommy held me in check. Tommy's gone now, and there's no reason to deny my heart any longer. I would make you a good husband, Emma."

He stood and walked to where she sat. Pulling Emma upward into his arms, Colton held her close for several silent seconds. "I love you, Emma. I want you to be my wife."

Pulling back just a bit, Colton met her gaze. Lowering his lips slowly to hers, he hesitated only a moment before kissing her. If she resisted him, he would drop his hold and give her more time. He'd taken their first kiss without warning. This time he would let her decide. She pulled his head toward hers in answer.

The kiss was sweet, and more than Colton could have hoped for. Emma clearly wasn't opposed to the idea of their love.

"Let her go!"

Rosie's words came out like a battle cry, causing Colton to pull away to the side. Still, he held on to Emma. "What's wrong?"

"I said to let her go." It was clear Rosie was angry.

"I don't understand why you are yelling at me. What has you so riled up?"

She didn't answer him but went to Emma instead. "Don't let him kiss you. He's only doing it because Walter and Ernest sent him here to marry you."

Emma looked at him and then back to Rosie. "What are you saying?"

"I heard my brothers talking before we came to Cheyenne. Walter and Ernest want Colton to marry you."

"Wait a minute, Rosie. They might have felt that way, but I already cared about Emma." Colton could see the by the look on Emma's face that she was starting to doubt him.

She backed away, edging around the rocking chair until she stood behind it. "What's going on?"

"Rosie, that's not why I kissed Emma. What our brothers want isn't important to me."

Rosie shook her head. "They want the railroad, Emma. They need your stock. I don't know why, but here. Look at this."

Colton felt his heart sink as Rosie handed over the crumpled telegram. "I read it." Rosie glanced at Colton as if daring him to deny what it said. "I don't know the last word, but the others will show you what I say is true."

Emma took it and studied it a moment. When she looked up to face Colton, her expression was one of disbelief . . . betrayal. "Is this true? Are you courting me so you can get my railroad stock? I already told you I would approve whatever sale you wanted to make."

"But you have Tommy's money too," Rosie said. "Walter and Ernest want everything, and they want Colton to marry you so that everything stays in the family. I heard them talking before we came to Wyoming. They said I was a burden."

"It would seem we are both burdens to the Benton brothers."

"Now, Emma, it's not that way. Hear me out. My brothers did push me to court you and marry you to keep Tommy's inheritance in the family. But that is not why I've pursued you. I was absolutely truthful about my feelings for you. I've loved you since I first laid eyes on you."

"You didn't even know me. How could you love me?" Emma shook her head. "Get out."

"Emma, please, you must allow me to explain."

"Go now."

Colton could see he was getting nowhere. He looked at Rosie. "You know that I don't lie."

"But you didn't tell the truth either. Isn't that the same thing as a lie?"

He was defeated and knew that there was no possibility of convincing Emma of his regard for her. Not with that telegram and Rosie relaying all that she had heard.

"I'll go, Emma. But promise me that after you calm down, you'll let me explain."

Emma shook her head. "I don't want to ever see you again. Just go."

It was impossible to tell exactly what Colton was thinking, but Emma no longer trusted him to speak the truth. She looked down once again at the telegram and felt her heart break into a thousand little pieces. She had believed him. She had thought him worthy of her confidence, and all this time he'd merely been after her money and stocks.

Rosie led him out, and through the open window, Emma could hear them talking on the porch. "You did a bad thing, Colton."

"But I didn't, Rosie. Walter and Ernest have their ideas for getting things done, but it wasn't my plan. You know me, Rosie. I wouldn't marry someone without love. That's why I've never married. I haven't found that love until now."

Emma came around the rocker and felt her knees grow weak. She sat for fear of fainting.

"If you weren't doing what Walter and Ernest wanted, then why did they send you a telegram?"

"It's not what it seems, Rosie. They do want me to sell the railroad, and Emma agreed we could do that. Look, I really do have feelings for her. I love her." Colton sounded desperately sincere.

"Emma is a good person, and I won't let you hurt her. You should never have kissed her."

"No, you should never have kissed me," Emma murmured, tears filling her eyes.

She had just begun to believe that they might have a future together. She had been especially touched that he'd come to apologize for his behavior the day before. Emma shook her head and closed her eyes. The Benton men seemed to have a special affinity for betrayal.

The conversation between Rosie and Colton ended, and Emma heard Rosie return to the house. She glanced up to find the young woman watching her from the foyer.

"I'm sorry, Emma. Colton was wrong to hurt you like that."

"I'll be fine, Rosie." She forced a smile and got to her feet. "I suppose this means we need to go shopping ourselves to get you that split skirt."

"You don't have to," Rosie said, coming to Emma. "I know he hurt your feelings. He hurt mine too. I was hoping he wasn't going to listen to Walter and Ernest. They're mean and don't care who they hurt."

Emma patted her arm. "I just want to forget about them all. Shopping will be a good way to put my mind on something else. Let me go change my clothes, and we'll head out." She dabbed her eyes with the back of her sleeve and got her emotions under control.

Rosie gave her a hug, and it was nearly Emma's undoing. She gave Rosie a squeeze, then pulled away and hurried upstairs before she burst into tears. For all the pain Tommy's betrayal had caused her, why was it that Colton's hurt so much more?

16

Two weeks passed with Colton coming to see Rosie and Emma making herself scarce. She couldn't bear to dwell on his betrayal and knew she'd fall apart if forced to speak to Colton. She had been unable to sleep or eat much after learning the truth. Every day she hoped Rosie would come and tell her that Colton was heading back to Texas, but at the same time she feared that if he did, Colton would insist on taking Rosie with him.

Emma knew she couldn't allow that to happen. Rosie and Rob were in love, and she fully expected Rob to ask for Rosie's hand in marriage. They seemed perfectly suited to each other despite Rosie being a little older.

When Reverend Bright came calling that Tuesday morning, Emma was thankfully the only one at home. She had refused to go to church the last two weeks in order to avoid Colton and knew that sooner or later someone would come to check on her. Thankfully, her folks were busy at the ranch and hadn't been attending either, or they would have been demanding answers. She had instructed Rosie just to tell folks she was under the weather, which she was as far as her emotions were concerned.

"Reverend Bright, please come in," Emma said, welcoming the man. "I'll put on the kettle for tea."

"No need to serve refreshments, Mrs. Benton. I've just come from one of my other parishioners, and believe me, I couldn't drink another cup of anything."

"Well then, let's just enjoy the morning. Perhaps here on the porch." She motioned to the arrangement of chairs.

"Perfect." He went to be seated, and Emma followed.

"I thought since I was already in the neighborhood, it would be good to stop by and see how you were doing. You've not been at church lately."

"I know. I've just not been feeling up to coming." She shifted her gaze to the Vogel house, where she knew Rosie was busy helping Marybeth with a project. Hopefully, she'd stay put and give Emma a chance to speak privately with the reverend.

"I hope you are now a little better?"

Emma nodded and gave him a smile. "Yes, of course. I do have to say that I've very much enjoyed your teachings."

"Thank you. Someone told me you've been gone from Cheyenne for nine years. Have you found it much changed?"

"I have. Things are vastly different, and there are so many more people. When I was a child, you could walk about town and recognize most of the people passing by. Now that's not the case. But I'm happy to be back in Cheyenne." Emma took the white wicker chair opposite him. She arranged her black gown, then looked up with a smile. "I've actually planned to come speak with you. First, to welcome you to the church, and second, to get your advice."

"Advice about what?"

She twisted her hands together. "It's a long story, but I'll make it brief. We moved to Cheyenne when I was a young girl. I've known most of the Methodist congregation since then. For a time, I even attended school in town and stayed with one of the teachers during the week. I'm afraid I wasn't an obedient child. In fact, I was rather wild and earned a reputation around town that . . . well, wasn't very good."

"I see. And how did this wild spirit play out?" The older man's expression was quite serious, but there was an undeniable kindness in his gaze.

"I was always getting in trouble. Some of it I was put up to by my brother and his friends. I could have said no, but I enjoyed impressing them. Some of it was my own ideas. Some of it was played out for adventure and a sense of excitement. With other things, I'm not sure why I did what I did. I was often rude, sometimes insensitive, and other times downright mean. A lot of times I didn't even get caught at my misdeeds but should have."

"Sounds like most children, especially boys. You mentioned being influenced by your brother and his friends. Sounds like you were a bit of a tomboy."

"I was that. When growing up on a ranch, girls must work just as hard as the boys, and the influence of being genteel and ladylike suffers. Not that my mother didn't do her best to instill proper behavior in both my older sister and me. When my teacher tired of trying to keep me out of trouble, she refused to let me stay with her, and I returned home. My mother schooled me after that, but I was still finding ways to cause problems." Emma paused and shook her head. "I left here when I was eighteen and had just broken the heart of one man and gotten duped by another. I didn't return until last fall when my father married Lucille Aldrich. I was afraid to come back."

"Afraid that people would want retribution?"

"Yes, I suppose. I don't know if you know my story, but last January I married Tommy Benton in Dallas. He was the brother of Colton and Rosie. He was killed while we were still at the altar. A woman he had wronged shot him. When they were wrestling the gun from her as she tried to kill herself, it went off, and the bullet hit me. The entire situation was life-altering for me. That silly, frivolous, and rather heartless girl grew up overnight in a hospital bed. I turned to God and made my peace with Him. Now I want to make peace with the people I wronged."

"That's admirable and not without a little difficulty, I'm sure."

Emma leaned back and did her best to relax. "I want to make sure I do what's right. I know there are people who surely hold things against me. I don't know who all that might be, and a good many things I did . . . well, I've forgotten them. When I encounter someone and they bring it up, I'm quick to seek their forgiveness and apologize for my behavior. And with some of them, I've brought up the past and asked their pardon."

"And have they been willing to give it?"

"Yes, to my amazement. I once jilted a man to whom I was engaged. I saw his mother at church, and her anger toward me was evident. I asked forgiveness even though I knew I didn't deserve it. When I think of him now, it pierces my heart. Later, I encountered the man himself. We talked briefly, and I told him how sorry I was. That my treatment of him was appalling, and I was praying that he could forgive me. He did and already had. He said God had completely blessed him with a wife and family that he cherished more than his own life. He could see God had given him a much truer love than what we had. I was so happy to hear that. Especially knowing my own choices led me to sorrow."

"And repentance," the minister injected.

"Yes, that's certainly true. Seeking forgiveness hasn't been easy, but then there are times when some don't even remember my horrid deeds."

"So they've forgotten just as you have." The older man

smiled. "Mrs. Benton, it sounds to me as if you are truly contrite for all your wrongdoing. If you're looking for absolution, you surely know God has given it. Christ died for your sins as well as mine and those of the folks you offended."

"I know that . . . at least in my heart. I just keep thinking I could do something more."

"As I understand it, you've inherited quite a bit of money. Why not use some of it to help folks around the area, or at least make their lives better. You could buy property and create a park or benefit the park already in place. There are all sorts of things you might do. Perhaps start an orphanage or a clinic for doctors to care for the poor who can't afford a doctor."

"Those are wonderful ideas. I don't know why I never thought about it. I do plan to give money to help with the church construction. I'll speak with . . ." She fell silent. She'd nearly said she'd speak with Colton about it.

"Then I'll be on my way. It was a pleasure to talk with you, Mrs. Benton. My advice to you is to stand ready to offer your sincere apologies, but otherwise let your actions prove your change of heart. Words are easy to offer, actions not so much. Pray for guidance, and God will direct your steps. He is all about reconciliation among His children."

Emma stood. "Thank you, Reverend Bright. I appreciate your thoughts on the matter."

When Mrs. Olson called lunch a couple hours later, Emma was still contemplating what she might do to show generosity to the people of Cheyenne.

"Are you eating alone today?" Mrs. Olson questioned, bringing her a plate.

"Yes. Gary's gone to the ranch to fetch milk and other things my father had for us, and Rosie's across the street. I'm guessing she'll eat with the Vogels. You may certainly join me." She really didn't want company but also didn't want to be rude.

"Actually, I have some shopping to do and was going to take my leave for an hour or so, if that's all right."

"Absolutely. Take your time, Mrs. Olson."

The cook removed her apron and headed back to the kitchen without another word. Emma looked down at her plate and sighed.

She sampled the roasted pork and potatoes, but nothing tasted very good to her. Why did life have to be so difficult? Why were people like Colton allowed to hurt her like he had? She thought then of the way she'd treated Thane and some of the other people in her life. They could accuse her of the same kinds of betrayal.

She put aside her fork. Perhaps God had allowed this to happen to teach her a lesson—to show her the pain and suffering she'd caused.

"Forgive me, Lord. I know You have, but I feel so overcome by all of this. I want to be forgiven, however, so show me what to do."

Colton wanted to be forgiven as well. Perhaps he was even telling the truth about his feelings. He'd been quite adamant with Rosie, and as he said, Emma had never known him to lie. He was confident enough in himself to speak his mind and to face the consequences or challenges that might come from that.

Emma put her face in her hands. It was all so confusing and frustrating. Cheyenne was supposed to be a new start, so why did it feel like she was drowning in the same old problems?

A knock sounded at the front door, and Emma slowly got to her feet. What if it was Colton? She wasn't ready to talk to him. She glanced down the hall as the front screen door opened.

"Emma, it's your father!" Rich Johnson's bellowing voice filled the house.

"Well, this is unexpected." Emma stepped into the hall to greet him. She found Lucille following behind.

"We decided to drive back into town with Gary. Had some shopping to see to and thought we'd say hello."

"Do you want to stay the night? I can arrange things in the guest room."

"No, we need to get right back. We're commencing to get ready for roundup. Cows calved early, and the boys are itchin' to get it all tended to."

Emma hugged her father and forced a smile. "Well, I was just having lunch. Why don't you come and eat with me?"

"I have a meeting to attend, but I'm sure Lucille would enjoy that."

Her stepmother smiled. "I would indeed." She embraced Emma. "I want to hear all about what's been going on."

Emma looked away. It was going to be a long day.

"I have to say, I was surprised by your invitation to lunch, or should I say your insistence that you needed to meet with me," Rich told Colton.

"When I saw you folks ride into town, I thought maybe God was helping me out. I mean it was—"

"Are you ready to order?" a waiter asked them, interrupting Colton.

"Yeah," Rich answered. "Bring me a steak—rare—and fried potatoes. Black coffee."

The waiter looked at Colton. He nodded, knowing that nothing had tasted good since his fight with Emma. "I'll have the same."

The man left them to their discussion, but Colton wasn't at all sure where to start. He looked at the table and said nothing. It was Rich who finally broke the silence.

"You seem mighty troubled about something, son. Why not just tell me?"

Colton looked up and heaved a sigh. "I was just wondering where to start."

Rich laughed. "Start at the beginning. I'm figuring this probably involves Emma."

"Yes." Colton straightened. "To be quite blunt, from the moment I first met her, I loved her. I never even believed such a thing was possible. I said nothing because she was my brother's girl. I didn't want to do anything to interfere with their plans. Not only that but I was much too settled and . . . lackluster for Emma. She was full of life and excitement. Tommy was too. They seemed a perfect match.

"Added to that, my father's heart was giving out, and I was focused on handling all the legal details of the family business. I did my best to ignore my feelings and forget about Emma. Then Tommy got killed, and Emma and Rosie wanted to move up here to Cheyenne, and the thought of losing Emma was far more troubling to me than leaving business undone in Texas and pursuing her."

"So what's the problem? She seems to like your company well enough. If you're asking my permission to court her, you have it. Not that you need it."

"No, it's far more complicated. After Tommy died, Emma inherited a great deal of money and other things. Tommy left everything he owned to her, which made Emma the majority stockholder in our family railroad. This happened because my father and his sister had gone into making the railroad together. They were equal partners, and when my aunt died, she was partial to Tommy and left him all her shares. Then when our father died, Tommy inherited one-fourth of his stock. Tommy always left the business dealings to me, so our brothers, while jealous of the value he now owned, weren't worried about the situation."

"But now that Emma holds the stock, they are?" Rich leaned back in his chair. "That does cause problems."

"They came up with what they thought was the perfect solution. They insisted I come to Cheyenne and get Emma to marry me so we could retain ownership of the stock. Rosie overheard them haranguing me about it, saying I owed it to the family. But that wasn't why I came to Cheyenne. I couldn't bear the idea of Emma leaving my life. I came to convince her that I loved her and wanted to marry her for real.

"Then the other day I got a telegram from my brothers pressing me to marry Emma and get the stock secured quickly. I left it in my pocket, and Rosie found it and showed it to Emma. She believed the worst of me, and now she won't speak to me. She makes sure to be absent any time I'm around. Mr. Johnson, I love your daughter. I'm not playing her false, I promise you."

Rich shook his head. "You've got yourself in a pretty good mess."

"Rosie doesn't even believe me. How can I hope to convince Emma?"

"And you thought I could help?" He gave a laugh. "Emma hasn't listened to me since she was knee-high to a grasshopper. She's not going to start now."

"She might. She's changed. Watching Tommy die, nearly dying herself, it changed her heart. She's gotten right with God."

"What about you, son? You get right with God? Seems to me you can't move forward with Emma until you square that away."

Colton shook his head. "I want to. Last week when the reverend talked about Matthew ten, verse twenty-eight, it chilled me to the bone. 'And fear not them which kill the body, but are not able to kill the soul: but rather fear him which is able to destroy both soul and body in hell.' I remember my mother sharing verses, and that was one of them. I wanted to go forward when there was an altar call, but I was afraid Emma would think it was just for show."

"Do you believe God sent Jesus to die for your sins, son?"

"I do now. I remember a time when I believed it as a child, but I let my father convince me otherwise."

"Do you believe Jesus rose again from the dead?

"Yes. Yes, I do."

"Romans ten, verse nine says, 'That if thou shalt confess with thy mouth the Lord Jesus, and shalt believe in thine heart that God hath raised him from the dead, thou shalt be saved.' John three, verse sixteen says, 'For God so loved the world, that he gave his only begotten Son, that whosoever believeth in him should not perish, but have everlasting life.'" He paused and gave Colton a smile. "That's about the extent of my memorized Bible verses, but the point is, God loves you and wants you to be saved and gave us Jesus in order to do it. You've accepted that it's true and have confessed to me that you want to be saved. Therefore, you now belong to God."

"I don't have to do anything else? Perform some sort of deeds?"

"If you had to do that, you'd be saving yourself instead of God saving you. You can't work your way into salvation. There's nothing you can do to save yourself, Colton. We Christians follow in baptism and fellowship, communion and such, but at the very heart of the matter is one thing: accept Jesus as Lord and be saved."

"I do." Colton leaned back and felt a weight lift off his shoulders. "But now what?"

"Now the hard part begins. Satan will do what he can to rob you of your peace and joy in Christ. He'll do what he can to convince you that God's salvation isn't that simple. Oh, we encourage Christians to pray and read their Bible daily, to get baptized and tithe. We encourage them to do good works for God. But those things won't save you. Only Jesus saves."

"How can you be sure of that, Mr. Johnson? Seems much too simple a solution for something that keeps a soul out of hell."

"Are you familiar with the crucifixion—when they nailed Jesus to the cross?"

"I am."

"Remember one of the malefactors who hung on a cross beside Jesus who asked Jesus to save him, and Jesus told him He would? Told the man he'd be with Jesus that very day in paradise. He was condemned to die and had no hope but Jesus. And Jesus was enough."

Colton slowly nodded. "I see what you mean."

Just then, the waiter brought their food. Colton felt his stomach rumble at the delicious smell wafting up from the plate.

"Mr. Johnson, Mr. Benton, would you mind if I joined you for a moment?"

Colton looked up to find Robert Vogel. He glanced over at Rich, who was already nodding.

"It's fine by me, Rob. Is the town keeping the peace?"

"For the most part," Rob replied, taking off his hat. "I hate to interrupt, but I need to speak with Mr. Benton. And you're welcome to stay too, Mr. Johnson. I don't want to interrupt your meal."

"What can I do for you, Mr. Vogel?" Colton asked.

Rob gave a hesitant smile. "I want to ask permission to marry your sister."

Colton hadn't expected that at all. He knew the young man was sweet on Rosie but had worried he wanted only to toy with her affections. He hadn't expected him to want to propose marriage. Apparently, the man was as honorable as Emma suggested.

"Isn't this kind of quick? I mean, you've only known her a couple of months."

"I knew from the first moment I laid eyes on her that she was the one for me. I know that might sound impossible, but I knew it from the very start."

Colton felt a tightening in his chest. He glanced at Rich, who was smiling. He couldn't very well tell Rob that he didn't believe in such things after just telling Rich that was how he felt about his daughter.

"Rosie doesn't have a dowry. She's not going to bring a big inheritance into the marriage."

"I don't care about that, Mr. Benton. I love her. I can't imagine my life without her. I want to take care of her and provide for her. I have a small savings, enough that we can get a place of our own. My job is good, and the town much calmer than when my father took the same job twenty years ago."

"You know that Rosie isn't like other women. She'll never be able to do a lot of things, and the things she does do, she might do much slower than others."

Rob smiled. "She's more driven to accomplish things than anybody I know. But the fact is, we can't all be good at everything. My pa is good at building things out of wood, but I make a mess of it every time. I am good, however, at tearing apart a gun and putting it back together. I've given thought to becoming a gunsmith. I just seem to understand how to handle them. It doesn't matter if Rosie's good at everything so long as she's happy. And I intend to do what I can to make her happy."

Colton couldn't deny the young man's sincerity, nor could he fault his answers. He knew what it was to love someone so much that it didn't matter what they had or what they could do.

"I promise you, Mr. Benton, I'll always put her first and take good care of her and anybody else who comes along. I know you and I haven't sat down and had long talks about life or gotten to know each other as well as maybe you'd like, but that will come in time. If you let me marry Rosie, we'll be family, and you'll always be an important part of our lives."

"Have you prayed about it, Rob?"

"I have. I've been doing nothing but praying about it since I first met Rosie." He grinned, and Colton had never seen a happier expression on anyone's face. "I'm praying right now."

Rich snorted a laugh, and Colton had to chuckle as well. "Then you have my permission to ask Rosie for her hand."

For a moment his response took Rob by surprise. It took Colton by surprise as well. He'd never figured to give his sister's hand to anyone, and now here he was, agreeing to let a stranger marry her.

He looked at Rich and shook his head. "Now if I can just figure out how to convince Emma that I am just as sincere in my feelings for her."

17

Emma had been most uncomfortable sitting next to Colton at church, and now that he was coming home with them for lunch, she was even more dismayed. It had been raining all week, and her mood matched the heavy skies overhead. She hated nursing hurt feelings but still wasn't sure what to do about anything.

She'd said very little to Colton aside from offering him a nod and a "Good morning." She didn't want to get caught up in conversation or to revisit the situation of his brothers wanting him to marry her. She had come to the conclusion that she would sign over all of her railroad stock to Rosie, and maybe then Colton and his brothers would leave her alone. The only problem was that she didn't even want to discuss that much. She was afraid to talk to Colton. Afraid her feelings might get the best of her. Instead, she planned to see a lawyer as soon as possible and let him arrange everything.

Some people might think her hasty to make such a choice, but she'd been thinking about this even before learning the truth. The railroad was a family legacy, and no one ever expected that the youngest brother would die so young. Just as no one had expected Rosie to be so capable. After much consideration, Emma felt it was only right that Rosie should have the stocks, or the money from the sale of them, and her mother's jewelry. That way she'd never be dependent upon her brothers for her future. Emma hadn't yet discussed the matter with Rosie but figured perhaps once Colton left after lunch, she'd have an opportunity to explain it to her. She could just bring it up over lunch, but she wanted to let Rosie know first.

"You can sit and read the newspaper," Rosie told Colton as they entered the house. "Emma and I will get lunch."

Emma and Rosie had cooked a pork roast and other things on Saturday and only needed to warm them up for Sunday luncheon. Maybe once she helped Rosie put it together, Emma could make her excuses and get something later. Rosie anticipated her, however, and made it clear that she expected Emma to join them.

"You didn't have any breakfast, and I know you must be hungry. Colton won't say or do anything bad. I won't stand for it. We'll put him on the other side of the table away from you."

Emma didn't want to argue. She was tired of the entire matter. She gave Rosie a nod and tied on an apron. Surely, she could endure one meal.

They worked together as they often did to get things ready. Rosie no longer had need to ask so many questions and went to her duties without concern. Emma might have offered something of praise, but she didn't feel much like speaking. There was something about just knowing she'd have to face Colton over the luncheon table that wearied her.

When they finally sat down to dinner, she let Colton and Rosie talk about whatever topic they chose. She would eat with them and then quickly leave to find solace in her bedroom away from Colton's presence. Maybe then she'd feel some relief. But she doubted it.

Why did this have to hurt so much? How had he come to mean so much to her in such a short time? She hadn't even been a widow six months, and yet she'd allowed herself to be kissed by Colton twice. She allowed his passion to become her own.

She thought of Tommy and all that they had planned to do, but thoughts of those things were already fading away. They certainly no longer held her interest as they once had. In having faced death, Emma could say that most of those things now seemed unimportant, even ridiculous. Why had they acted so childishly?

"These new potatoes and creamed peas are the best I've ever had," Colton said, giving both ladies a big smile. "I don't know who is responsible, but they're really good."

"Emma made them," Rosie offered. "She learned it from her mama. I wish our mother could have taught me to cook."

Colton chuckled. "I'm not sure our mother knew how. She was raised in a very well-to-do family with more servants than you could count. I think the main things she was taught to do were sing, play the piano, and embroider."

"I think I'd like to learn to play the piano. Emma said we could get one if I was serious. I have so many things I want to learn, though, that I figured we should probably wait."

Emma kept her eyes on the food. She picked up a dinner roll and tore a piece from it. She popped it into her mouth, hardly tasting it as Rosie began on another topic.

"Rob and I are going for a walk this afternoon. After that we're going to have a riding lesson. He's been teaching me about the saddle and telling me stories about when he was a boy learning to ride. I'm so excited. I want to have my own horse someday."

"Goodness, Rosie, it would seem you want to do everything at once," Colton chided.

"I feel like there's just so much to learn. I don't even know for sure what I like and don't like since I'm just trying a lot of things for the first time. The other day I learned how to put up wallpaper."

"But a lady doesn't usually have to do that for herself. You can hire someone to come and put the wallpaper up in your house. You would just pick out what you wanted them to put up and then let someone else do the work."

"What fun is that?" Rosie asked, pouring herself a glass of lemonade. "I like doing things for myself."

Emma wanted to laugh at the look on Colton's face. When he glanced at her, she quickly lowered her gaze back to her plate. The Bentons never had to fend for themselves. She had grown up in a family who didn't rely much on servants to do their chores. Papa had always had a team of cowboys to help with the herd and a foreman to watch over those men, but he was quite capable of doing most things for himself. Mama had always taken care of the house, even though she did have a hired cook to help during calving season. She and Clara were also responsible for the household duties, garden, and chores like milking and gathering eggs. Emma had helped hang wallpaper when she was twelve and Mama had wanted to spruce up her bedroom. They settled on a flower print, and together, the three of them mastered the work. There were certainly no hired paperhangers.

Things got quiet, and Emma glanced up to find Rosie frowning at her. She knew Rosie had tried to get her to cheer up. She hadn't mentioned the incident with Colton and the telegram, as if it were already dealt with and had no further influence. That was Rosie's way. She was usually very quick to drop a matter and move on. It was one of her childlike charms.

"Colton, I think it's time for you to go back to Texas. You're still making Emma sad."

Emma's eyes widened. She hadn't expected that. She

returned her focus to the food and hoped that the matter would resolve itself. She had no desire to get caught up in the conversation.

"I would love to help Emma not be sad," Colton said. "But, Rosie, she won't talk to me. You can't work things out with someone unless they'll talk to you."

"You lied to her, Colton. That hurt her feelings."

"I didn't lie to her at all. You heard our brothers encourage me to come to Cheyenne so that I could talk Emma into marrying me. You saw the telegram they sent, and I could even show you letters from them demanding I get Emma to marry me, but I never agreed to that. I didn't come here to deceive Emma."

"They sent letters too?" Rosie shook her head. "Walter and Ernest only care about money. They don't know how Emma feels. They never care about anybody but themselves. Aunt Clementine used to say that, and it's true."

Emma kept her head bowed. She was so embarrassed that she wanted to run from the room. How dare Colton talk about her as if she wasn't even there. Tommy had once told her that the only thing that really mattered to his brothers and father was money and the railroad. She had to admit she had seen Colton as the exception. He cared deeply about Rose and her comfort. He was also kind to the staff, although he didn't offer to alleviate their burdens like Tommy might. She had once seen Tommy help the old gardener trim trees and carry away branches. None of the other Benton men would have done that. Still, Colton had helped her father and Gary with building the chicken coop. She supposed a lot of his hesitation might be a lack of knowledge as to how the work needed to be done. He'd never been taught such things, so how could she fault him for not doing them?

"If Emma would allow me to speak with her about all of

this, I feel we could come to an understanding. I hate that things got out of hand."

"I think that you should just go home. You hurt Emma's feelings, and there's nothing you can do to make it better."

"I can tell her the entire story. The whole truth of what happened in Texas and why I came here. See, what you don't know, Rosie, is that I fell in love with Emma way back when Tommy first brought her to meet us all. Do you remember that day?"

"I do. Emma brought me flowers."

"That's right. As I recall they were hothouse roses. Pink ones."

Rosie's voice took on an excited tone. "Yes! Yes, they were pink, and they matched my favorite dress."

"I remember. Emma was very kind to bring them, and as I recall, the two of you sat together and talked for a long time while Tommy was busy with Father."

"We did. Emma asked me to tell her about my life. Nobody had ever done that before."

Emma remembered that moment quite well. Tommy had told her that Rosie was rather shy and would probably say very little to her. However, when Emma started asking her simple questions, Rosie seemed more than happy to give answers, and by the time Tommy returned, Rosie was telling Emma all about her routine as the only Benton female.

"Emma, do you remember the first time you read to me?"

She still didn't want to get involved in the conversation but found she had no choice. She drew a deep breath and looked up. "I remember it very well, Rosie. It was just about this time last year."

"Yes! I love it when you read to me." She looked at Colton. "She still reads to me, but someday I'll be able to read to her."

"I feel confident you will, Rosie."

Emma thought she would leave them to discuss the matter

further. She scooted her chair back, but Rosie commanded her to stay.

"Don't leave, Emma. Colton, you go ahead and tell Emma what you want to say. That's only fair, Emma."

She was surprised at the impromptu reprimand but nodded. "Very well. Say what you like."

"I want first to apologize for not bringing this matter to your attention when Walter and Ernest first brought it up. I think hearing that Tommy had left you everything was so shocking to them and their plans for the future that they worried they would have much to forfeit. The fact is, however, I told you the truth. I've loved you since I met you. I spent a great deal of time doing everything in my power not to think about you. Even though I wasn't a religious man then, I knew it was wrong to covet my brother's wife-to-be. But it was impossible to ignore my feelings once Tommy was dead. When I saw the bloodstain on your wedding gown, I wanted only to scoop you up in my arms and rush you to the hospital. I couldn't bear the idea that you might die."

His words seemed sincere, and Emma wanted to believe him. Thinking of him caring for her even back before the wedding did perhaps explain the reason for his behavior. But coming to Cheyenne to pursue her was the problem. Not his feelings from last year.

As if reading her thoughts, Colton continued. "I came to Cheyenne because I couldn't stand the idea of losing you, of living without you in my daily life. I used Rosie as an excuse to come, even though I knew the two of you would be just fine. You were coming home, after all. I had no reason to doubt that you'd have plenty of people who would come alongside you to assist you in every way possible. And that's exactly what happened. But so long as Rosie was with you, I knew I could come as well, and no one would question my decision. But I didn't come here because Walter and Ernest insisted I do so. Just as my decision to remain here has nothing to do with them or the railroad. I've made up my mind to make Cheyenne my home so that I might convince you of my sincerity."

"I'm glad you're going to stay." Rosie's entire expression lit up. "I want you to be here. But you should have told her the truth, Colton."

"I should have." Colton's gaze pierced through the armor Emma had secured around her heart. Why did he have to stir feelings within her? Why couldn't she just accept his apology and send him on his way?

"I'm very sorry for not telling you everything, Emma. But please believe me, my desire to marry you has nothing, *nothing* at all to do with my brothers or the railroad or anything else. I love you, and that's the only reason I asked you to marry me."

"I believe him now, Emma." Rosie's simple way of stating her facts always amused Emma. Even now it was as if because Rosie believed, she expected that Emma should as well. "Colton doesn't lie. I think Walter and Ernest were wrong for trying to make him marry you, but since Colton really loves you, it would be all right. I know you love him, or it wouldn't hurt your heart so much."

Emma got to her feet. "Enough. I don't want to talk about this anymore."

"But do you forgive Colton?" Rosie asked.

Her own desires for forgiveness left her little choice. She looked at Colton and squared her shoulders. "I forgive you, but I do not trust you."

"She said she forgives him." Rosie had enjoyed the long walk she and Rob took out toward the lake. It wasn't all that far, and many other people were either riding or walking toward the same destination. It seemed a perfect thing to do on a Sunday afternoon.

"That's a start," Rob replied, patting her arm. "We'll have to keep praying for them."

"Oh yes." Rosie had been praying most fervently for Emma and Colton. Frankly, from the first time she'd heard her brothers talk about them marrying, Rosie had thought she'd like that very much. However, she wanted them to marry for love, not money. After talking with Colton the last couple of weeks, Rosie was convinced of his feelings for Emma. He really did love her. The only problem now would be convincing Emma that she, too, loved Colton. And of that, Rosie was certain. As she had said, Emma wouldn't be so hurt by all that had happened if not for her feelings running deep.

"Colton has changed a lot, and he plans to stay here in Cheyenne. He told me he prays now," Rosie said, looking to Rob. "He said he put his trust in Jesus."

"I heard that too. It's a wonderful thing."

"Yes. No one in my family went to church except Aunt Clementine. Well, my mama did. I remember Colton saying that she did, and that she talked about God. I wish I could have known her. Your mama is so special, and I like to think mine was like that."

"I imagine she was." Rob took hold of her hand.

"What was it like having your mama around all the time?" Rosie had often tried to imagine. She had known Aunt Clementine's presence, but even then, she had spent more time alone in the nursery than anything else. It had been a very lonely existence.

"My mother is always doing things for us or other people, making treats or clothes or fixing up something. She was always busy, but not too busy to stop and listen when we needed her to. She was always there for us and made sure we knew we were loved."

"How'd she do that?" Rosie had started to imagine the possibility of being a wife and mother one day, but she knew nothing about either job. Maybe she'd have a talk with Rob's mother about it.

"She'd tell us every day that she loved us. And she'd show us. There were times when one of us would get hurt, and she'd dry our tears and clean us up. All the while, she'd tell us stories about when she was a girl. It took our minds from our woes. And she was always so patient when she taught us things."

"Like you're patient with me when we read." She looked up at him and smiled. "You're not like my brothers. They have no patience."

"Rosie, you're easy to teach, and no patience is required. I think a lot of things in life will come instinctually to you."

"What does that word mean?"

"*Instinctually*? It means you'll just know what to do when it's required of you."

"I wouldn't know how to be a mother," Rosie said, not really meaning to speak the words aloud. She looked at Rob and shook her head. "I was just thinking that. . . . You don't have to say anything."

Rob raised her hand to his lips and pressed a kiss across her knuckles. "I want to hear all about what you're thinking. I want to know everything. I love you, Rosie."

It was the first time he'd said those words to her, and Rosie couldn't help but stop and look at him quite seriously. "I love you, Rob." She frowned a moment. "Is it all right that I said that?"

Rob laughed, and after a quick glance around, he gave her a quick embrace. "It's very right, Rosie. It's very, very right."

18

On Thursday, Emma and Rosie joined some of the other ladies from the Methodist church at Marybeth Vogel's house. They were meeting to plan a bake sale that would be held at the Firemen's Tournament. The festivities would be held on the ninth and tenth of July in lieu of an Independence Day celebration. It was most unusual that the city wouldn't be celebrating the Fourth in grand style, but not only was the tournament of great importance, but the Union Pacific was also to hold ceremonies celebrating the laying of a cornerstone for the new shops. The city fathers felt certain that celebrating Independence Day as well as hosting the Firemen's Tournament for Wyoming and Northern Colorado would be far too taxing on the city. After all, many businesses had plans to close down, and the town was expecting to receive some five thousand additional people.

The ladies of the Methodist church figured this would be a perfect opportunity to host a huge bake sale. It was to be bigger than any they'd ever held before. The money they made would be added to the church's building fund, and everyone was encouraged to work hard and bake more than ever before. It reminded Emma that she wanted to make a substantial gift to the church. Unfortunately, that would require talking to Colton about what needed to be done. Her local bank account had plenty of money for daily living, but not the kind of money she hoped to give the building fund.

"We want to organize the various things everyone will make," Marybeth Vogel began after the ladies had taken a seat in her large front room. The day was quite warm, and many of the ladies had already begun to fan themselves. Emma hadn't even considered bringing a fan and felt most uncomfortable. Of course, she still wore black mourning with long sleeves and a high neck. If anything had convinced her it was time to leave off with such traditions, it was the heat.

"Who among you would like to make cookies?" Marybeth asked.

Rosie's hand shot up along with most of the other women's. Marybeth smiled. "What say we all agree to bring five dozen cookies each. If you want to make more, that would be fine, but I'm hoping some of you will agree to bake other things like breads, dinner rolls, hand pies, and cakes. I've no doubt that everything will sell quickly. It's roundup season, and every ranch around here has extra cowboys. This along with the hundreds of firemen who are coming will make for a quick sale. In the past, the men have swooped in and bought up everything before noon, so whatever you're planning to make, just keep in mind we cannot make too much. Since I first got involved in these bake sales for the church building fund, I've never seen anything left over."

"I'll be happy to make hand pies," Melody Decker declared. "I'll get the children helping with it. We have the ovens at the school as well as the house. I think between me and my brood, we can promise to make ten dozen and at least as many cookies."

"Oh goodness," Mrs. Cooper said, shaking her head. "That

would be wonderful. I figure I can get my kitchen girl to help me bake loaves of bread. We'll pledge at least eight loaves and five dozen cookies."

Other women chimed in, with Marybeth doing her best to write down the information. Everyone was eagerly talking at once.

Rosie leaned over to Emma. "What should we promise to make?"

Emma smiled. "What would you like for us to make?"

"Well, I think we can make a lot of cookies. You can afford to buy extra ingredients, right?"

"Of course. Whatever we need, I'll arrange it."

Rosie nodded with great enthusiasm. "Some people can't afford to bake a lot, but we can. Let's make lots of cookies and get Mrs. Olson to make those little frosted cakes she makes sometimes. They're so good."

"I agree they are. They're kind of delicate though." Emma imagined a big burly cowboy grabbing Mrs. Olson's lighter-than-air cakes and plopping them into his mouth two at time.

"Can we make a lot of different kinds of cookies, Emma?"

Rosie's excitement over the idea of making dozens and dozens of cookies in a hot kitchen made Emma want to laugh out loud. She remembered how, as a child, such suggestions only brought to mind the discomfort of the work to come. For Rosie, it was all pure joy.

Oh, Lord, I want to have a joyful heart like Rosie. A heart of giving and love.

"We can make as many kinds of cookies as we can figure out how to make. Out at the ranch, there's a tin box with old recipes my mama used to make. We can ride out there tomorrow, look them over, and copy down the ones we want to make."

Rosie gave Emma a hug. "This is going to be so much fun."

"Marybeth?" Sarah Cadot spoke up.

"Yes, Sarah?"

The other ladies quieted.

"What about making candy? I know it's harder to do in the heat of summer, but I got a nice sized shipment of maple syrup from my sister. I could make up a bunch of maple candy and keep it cool in the cellar until the tournament celebration."

"Oh, that sounds heavenly. I remember how popular that new fudge candy and divinity was at our Christmas sale," Marybeth replied.

"We'll make a whole bunch of cookies. Too many to even count," Rosie declared. "And we're going to ask Mrs. Olson if she'll help teach us to make some little cakes. She makes them so good."

Thinking of something Rosie had said, Emma had an idea. "And if anyone has plenty of time on their hands and not enough supplies, I'd be happy to contribute the needed baking goods. Coming up with supplies is easier for me right now than it might be for others."

"That's so generous of you, Emma. Thank you!" Marybeth was quite excited by this announcement. "I know that's often a hindrance of mine, as we've been coming up with money to send Daniel back east to college. Some of you other ladies have your own financial limits. Don't let your pride stand in the way. Please take advantage of this offer from Emma since it's all going to the church."

Again the room grew noisy with chatter as the women began figuring what they would make and need. Emma felt a sense of connection that she'd never felt before. These sales had been going on as long as Cheyenne had existed. The Methodist women were good at holding bake sales several times a year to raise money for the building fund, but Emma hadn't cared much about them . . . until now.

As the discussions continued and the afternoon wore on,

Greta called Rosie to her side, and together they arranged and served refreshments. Emma had never been so glad for a glass of iced lemonade in her life. She felt as if she could down the contents in just a couple of big gulps, but forced herself to be more ladylike.

By the time the ladies started departing for home, Emma had enjoyed two glasses of the cold drink and was on her third when Melody Decker approached.

"I love your idea of providing supplies for the women who don't have the money to donate such things themselves. That was positively brilliant. I wish I'd thought of it."

"I feel quite inadequate at times, but since I inherited this money, I might as well use it to better things around me."

"Oh, I agree. I grew up knowing poverty at times. My da worked for one railroad or another, and we always managed but never had a great deal to show for it. When I married Charlie, I married into banking money and was surprised at how my days of counting pennies were no longer needed." She laughed. "And it's a good thing too. With ten children, there's always something to purchase, mend, or make. When I get that brood to work making cookies and hand pies, we'll have enough to feed half of Cheyenne."

"Ten children. I can't even begin to imagine. I don't know that I would be much good with that many to watch over, but I would like to have a family one day."

"God is good to teach you what you need to know as you go along. My mother died when I was young, and I didn't really have an example to learn by. I found, however, that by seeking the Bible, I learned a great deal. I also learned to humble myself and ask the women around me for help. They're all so good to lend a hand or show you the way. I used to rely a lot on a woman we called Granny Taylor. She was like a grandmother to everyone. She's passed on now, but oh, that woman was pure love."

"My mother was that way," Emma said, looking at the floor. "Only thing is, I didn't appreciate it at the time. I wasted a lot of years."

Melody took hold of her hand, and Emma couldn't help but face her. "Emma, if there's one thing I know God can do, it's restoration. He won't give you back the years with your mother, but He will restore your heart and give you something else. You have a lot of people around you who knew your mother well. Your stepmother, for instance. I know she would be happy to help you in every way if you just reach out to her."

Emma nodded. "I know that you're right. Lucille is a treasure, to be sure, and she knows stories about my mother that will help me to remember her. She can also tell me about the years I spent away from her."

"Exactly."

"What an excellent meeting," Marybeth said, coming to join them after all the other ladies had gone. "Those who couldn't make it in told me at church on Sunday what they would like to make. Sounds like we'll need a dozen or more tables to hold it all."

"We have plenty of tables at the school you can borrow, and what we don't have, the fellas can make. You know how they are. Just give them a task, and they'll find a way to master it."

"It's true." Marybeth reached out to touch Emma's arm. "I really was touched at your offer. I know several women who didn't come today who can't afford to spare extra supplies. I'll let them know that you donated supplies if they would be willing to do the labor. I know they'll want to join in. I'll even arrange with Edward to see to it that they have plenty of wood or coal for their stoves."

"Rosie was more excited about this than just about anything else. Of course, she's excited about most things that involve a new challenge or way that she can help. Mrs. Olson has been so good to help her learn things in the kitchen."

Marybeth glanced over her shoulder before turning back to Emma. "You know that Rob has lost his heart to her. He plans to ask for her hand."

Emma had anticipated that he would but had no idea of how Colton would react. "I didn't know, but I think it's wonderful. He cares for her so tenderly and never loses his temper with her. I only hope he can convince her brother."

"He already has." Marybeth exchanged a conspiratorial look with Melody and then back to Emma. "Rob sought him out one day and told him how he felt. Your father was there at the time. Rob said having him there gave him extra courage." She chuckled. "I would have liked to have been a fly on the wall."

"Rob has already spoken to Colton?" Emma was surprised Colton gave Rosie's hand to Rob after the way he had spoken out against the young man.

"Yes. He made it clear to Rob that Rosie has no inheritance, so if he was marrying her for money, he should know there wasn't going to be any. What Colton doesn't realize is that such things mean very little to Rob. He's industrious and will earn whatever they need. But from the moment he laid eyes on Rosie, he's spoken of little else. He lost his heart at first sight of that girl."

It touched Emma deeply to hear of Colton's change of heart. He loved Rosie dearly, and his willingness to let Rob marry her was proof that he wanted only her happiness.

"Don't say anything to Rob, but I plan for Rosie to have plenty. I've made up my mind that she deserves a cut of the family inheritance. Tommy got more than his share because of his aunt, and I plan for that to go to Rosie. She'll be quite wealthy."

"Oh my." Marybeth's eyes widened a bit. "Maybe don't tell

anyone else just yet. If Colton and his brothers know that their sister is to be rich, they may be less inclined to let her go." She shook her head. "I know that sounded ungracious. Forgive me. I just don't want anything to happen that will cause trouble for Rob and Rosie. They are so perfect together, and I very much want her for a daughter-in-law."

"I understand. I think maybe you're right. I'll hold off. The Bentons plan to sell their railroad. I can go ahead and let that happen and set the money aside for Rosie. Maybe give it to them as a wedding present."

"Yes, do that rather than give it to her now. Please. I just have a feeling it will only complicate matters for them. Better that they be wed and face it together than separately."

Melody nodded. "I agree. Money can cause the worst of problems. Men will say and do almost anything for it."

"You don't think Rob would—" Marybeth started, but Melody put her hand up.

"Not Rob. The Benton brothers."

"She's right. I've told you both enough for you to know that money is the thing they love most." Emma paused. "At least it is with Walter and Ernest. I think perhaps that though it might have been taught to Colton that way, he's different from his brothers. Tommy was too. Although Tommy loved the adventure and lavish lifestyle that money could buy."

"It sounds like you've had a change of heart regarding Colton in the last few weeks."

Emma realized she was defending the man she had accused of greed and deception. "I suppose I have, although until just now, I hadn't realized. He is different, and he's made his peace with God, so I must allow for that as well. Still, I think it's best to wait until Rosie and Rob are married to give her the money. Who can tell what it might stir up."

"But I didn't think the federal government was interested in Wyoming statehood at this point," Colton said as he stood talking with other men in a special reserved room at one of the men's clubs.

After hearing that Colton planned to make Cheyenne his home, Charlie Decker had invited him to join the important gathering. Colton hardly knew any of the several dozen men but figured it would be wise to get to know them. These were the men who would make things happen in Cheyenne, and he wanted to be among them.

"The government might not be ready for Wyoming statehood," Charlie replied, "but the men and women of Wyoming are. Tell us no, and we just get all the more muleheaded."

"It's true," Henry Hay, cattleman and banker, declared. "We're going to be a state, and that's all there is to say about that. Should have been one ten years ago, but we'll settle for this year or next."

The men nodded and gave their unanimous agreement.

"Mr. Benton, we're glad to have you join our group. I'm Elwood Mead, territorial engineer." The small-built man extended his hand to Colton. They shook hands, and he continued. "I am even now at work to write up a system by which water will be controlled in this state. I say *state*, for we most assuredly will become one."

"Yes, yes!" another man affirmed.

"Colton, this is Governor Warren. He has fought long and hard to bring us to statehood." Charlie Decker made the introduction.

"Governor Warren, I'm pleased to meet you."

"As am I you, Mr. Benton. We always need educated men in our pursuit of statehood. I'm pleased to hear you intend to make Cheyenne your home. I believe you're a lawyer and railroad owner, are you not?"

"I am," Colton replied, eyeing the older man with the

full, bushy mustache. This was a man who got things done. He exuded confidence and strength, two qualities Colton prized most highly.

"I am a railroad man myself, as well as the owner of a livestock company and electric company, to name a few. Now as governor of this territory, I am seeking able-bodied, intelligent men to come alongside and fight to see this territory to statehood. This town was once considered too rough to tame. It was figured that the entire place would disappear off the map and be nothing more than a water stop within five years of the railroad pushing west, but we proved them wrong.

"When I arrived in this town, it was little more than a settlement of covered wagons and tents, but I was determined, as were many of these fine fellows, to see Cheyenne become something more than a camp town, and it has. We have a fine city and impressive territory. My question to you is, Will you join us in supporting the push for statehood?"

Colton appreciated the man's straight-to-the point enthusiasm. "I would like very much to be a part of this territory achieving statehood. That's why I came tonight. When Mr. Decker apprised me of what was happening, I found it intriguing, and I would love to hear more."

"Governor, we're ready for you to speak," a younger man interrupted.

Warren smiled and gave Colton a nod. "In time you shall hear all that there is to tell."

19

I t's such a surprise to see you both," Lucille said, hugging Emma and then Rosie. "What brings you to the ranch to brighten my day?"

"We've come for my mother's recipe box. We attended the Methodist church ladies' meeting yesterday and talked about the bake sale for the Firemen's Tournament. Rosie has it in mind to make as many different kinds of cookies as is humanly possible." Emma chuckled. "I can't even begin to imagine what we'll come up with, but I've already put Gary to work setting up an outdoor kitchen."

"What a marvelous idea. It's much too hot to be doing all that baking indoors. I plan to make a few things myself. Of course, we're already pretty busy, and I'll start cooking for roundup next week. I hope to get ahead of things. We're starting in on the twenty-fourth and will have over fifty men to feed. If you and Rosie are free, I could sure use the help."

"We could come for a couple of days. Of course, we've pledged a great many baked goods to the sale, so we'll have to have time to take care of that."

"We plan to be finished up by the twenty-eighth. It might be wishful thinking since we've added so many animals this year, but that's why we hired extra men. We're combining everything with Charlotte and Micah's animals, as well as ours."

"I think it will be a lot of fun, Emma. I've never been to a roundup," Rosie declared.

Emma smiled. "Then we'll be here on the twenty-fourth."

"I'll put fresh bedding in your room and Clara's so that you and Rosie can stay here and not have to go back and forth."

"Oh, this will be so much fun!" Rosie's excitement was contagious.

"I hope you still feel that way after we're done," Emma said, knowing roundup would be like nothing Rosie had ever experienced. "For now, however, we've come so that I can take a look through Mama's recipe box. I told Rosie there were a lot of cookie recipes we could use in there."

"I know just where the box is. We put it on the top shelf in one of the kitchen cupboards. That way it would be easily available." Lucille headed for the kitchen, and Emma and Rosie followed. "You ought to take it home with you. After all, your mother would want you to have it."

"I had thought about that. Clara copied down the recipes that she wanted in a journal, and when she wants to make something, she gets the book out and finds what she needs. Of course, after all this time, she's got most of them memorized."

Lucille grabbed a stool and placed it in front of the cabinet. She opened the door and pointed to the small tin box. "I'll let you get them."

Emma did just that and went to the kitchen table with the box in hand. She and Rosie sat down and immediately began to go through the recipes. A flood of memories came back to Emma. She could see her mother in the kitchen laboring over her creations. There were recipes here that had been given by her mother's mother and grandmother. A legacy

passed down from mother to daughter for multiple genera-
tions. It made Emma feel a much-needed connection with
her mother.

"Oh, look here. Do you remember this gingersnap recipe
my mother used to make?" Emma handed it up to Lucille.

The older woman glanced at it a moment. "I do. I remember her gingerbread as well. It was so moist and flavorful.
We used to get together and bake. Do you remember that?"

Emma nodded. "I do. I remember hearing you and Mama
laughing and talking. I didn't appreciate it and wanted to
escape as fast as possible. Clara was always happy to be
involved, but not me." She looked at Rosie and shook her
head. "I lost a great deal in not seeing value in my mother's
teachings."

"I wish I could have known my mother," Rosie replied.
"Colton said she didn't cook because she always had servants, but I would have liked to have talked to her and heard
her stories. I'd give anything if I could do that now."

Emma easily recalled the camaraderie of ranch wives that
took place in this kitchen. "I would too."

They continued to pore over the recipes, and when it was
time for lunch, Lucille never said a word but instead readied
the meal on her own. Emma was so absorbed in reading
recipes to Rosie and telling her any story or thoughts that
came to mind regarding them that when Lucille called them
to come to the dining room, Emma wasn't sure why she
wanted them there.

Seeing the table set with a variety of things to eat, Emma
gave a glance at the large grandfather clock. "Goodness, I
didn't realize it was lunchtime already."

"You girls were having such a good time. I loved hearing the stories you told, Emma. It brought back so many
memories."

"I was surprised to remember so much." Emma took a seat at the table beside Rosie.

"Smells mighty good in here," Emma's father declared as he bounded in from the kitchen. "I see someone's been going over recipes."

"Hello, Papa," Emma said as he came to give her a hug. "Rosie and I are going to be baking for the church sale, and I wanted to get some of Mama's old recipes."

"Well, I just got back from helping bring in some of the herd. I suppose Lucille told you we're going to start branding on the twenty-fourth? We've been riding over half the state bringing in our cattle. Thankfully, Lucille thought to fence off big pastures last year. We can gradually work the cattle down and separate them out to get our counts and see what's what."

"We're going to come help," Rosie piped up. "And stay here at the ranch."

A big smile spread across the man's face. "Well, that's just fine. I'm happy to have you both. We'll get Rosie ropin', and Emma can brand."

Emma laughed. "I've done it before. I remember you making me do it a few years in a row. You said I needed to know every aspect of ranching as I might one day need to help my husband."

Her father nodded. "It didn't hurt you any, did it?"

"No. I didn't like the smell of burnt hair and flesh, but I could do it again if I had to."

"I don't want to learn to brand," Rosie said in a most serious tone. "I don't want to hurt the babies."

"Then you don't have to, Rosie girl." Emma's father tucked a napkin into the neck of his shirt. "It'll be nice just to have a few pretty gals here. Makes the fellas work harder when they know the ladies are watching."

Colton knocked at Emma's front door and waited for her to answer. When no one came after several minutes, he knocked again. Still nothing.

He heard noises coming from the backyard and made his way around the house. The chickens were contentedly pecking the ground in their pen, and Gary Price was busy putting something together not far from the backside of the house.

"Mr. Price, how are you, sir?" Colton asked as the man noticed him and straightened.

"Mr. Benton. I'm doing good. Busy as a beaver, but good."

"I knocked on the front door, but no one came."

"Emma and Rosie went to the ranch, and Mrs. Olson is shopping. What can I do for you?"

"Emma and Rosie went alone? There wasn't a man to drive them or keep watch?"

Gary chuckled. "Emma can manage for herself. She has a brand-new rifle and knows how to use it. If anyone or thing causes her grief, she'll be able to fend for herself and Rosie. Besides, the soldiers are out that way on some sort of maneuvers. It was in the newspaper."

Colton didn't like the idea of them being miles from the city on their own. There were still occasional conflicts with Indians. If he and Emma were on speaking terms, he might have explained his feelings on the matter.

Gary started sawing a piece of lumber. He clearly wasn't concerned about the ladies, and Colton did his best to let go of his fears.

"Looks like you're busy building again." Colton couldn't help but wonder about the situation.

"Putting together a summer kitchen. The gals plan to do a lot of baking for the church sale, and Emma didn't want to heat up the house. I'm building them a place to take care of business out here."

"If I weren't heading to a meeting, I'd offer to help. Maybe if you're still at it this afternoon, I can lend you a hand."

"I'll still be at it. You come on back, and I'll put you to work." Gary finished sawing and straightened. "If you'll pardon me for now, though, I've got to get back to it."

Colton nodded. "I'll see you later."

He started walking toward the depot, where he was scheduled to meet with men from the Union Pacific. They were presenting their final offer to purchase the Bentons' railroad. Colton knew they would accept the offer. They had already been negotiating the cash and stock options, and he felt certain they could get no better deal. His brothers agreed.

He hoped, prayed even, that Emma would agree to the terms and conditions. He wasn't all that sure his prayers were heard. He was so new at all this faith and Bible stuff that he couldn't help but feel rather adrift. Was he praying the right way? He remembered his mother would pray as if talking to God like a friend. She would bow her head, close her eyes, and just pour out her heart regarding her needs, desires, and concerns. She was always thanking God for one thing or another, and thinking of that now made Colton smile. His mother had always stressed being thankful.

"We have it so much easier than others," she had told him more than once. *"We should always take time to thank God for His generosity to us."*

As a new Christian, Colton could understand the sense of that. Having known a life of abundance, he was grateful. Here in Cheyenne and back in Dallas, he had observed poverty. He'd seen many in need and had even donated to some of the causes to aid the poor. His brothers had thought it ridiculous.

"Let the poor work and make their way as we did." Colton could hear them saying that even now. They didn't understand

or bother to consider that they had been born to wealth and luxury, and hard work had never been put upon them.

And hopefully never would be, but the economy had started showing signs of problems. Colton was grateful for an education that allowed him wisdom in catching hold of signs that suggested trouble. His real concern was to protect Emma from loss, as well as himself. His brothers could fend for themselves as they always had.

The meeting with the UP went well, and Colton had to admit they had come up with a better offer than he'd originally thought they would make. He shook hands and agreed to sign all the paperwork on Monday. He had his brothers' proxies and hoped that Emma was still of a mind to cooperate with the sale. He planned to talk to her that evening.

It was hard to believe they were giving up the railroad, and yet Colton felt as his brothers did that there were other investments that might be more worthy of their consideration. He still didn't know the extent of Tommy's other investments. Emma had indicated that he had taken it upon himself to invest in quite a few other things. Colton was eager to see if those choices had paid off. Perhaps in time, he could earn Emma's trust. He could still hear her saying that she forgave him but didn't trust him. How could he blame her? And yet it troubled him deeply to have lost her faith in him.

He hurried back to the boardinghouse and changed into his work clothes. These were the same older pieces that he'd worn to help build the chicken coop. He had to admit his life had taken on a different turn when he moved to Cheyenne. And he could also allow that he enjoyed the changes. He wouldn't want to have to work at a physical job every day, but lending a hand now and then had been beneficial in more ways than one.

Together, Gary and Colton worked on the outdoor kitchen until Emma and Rosie returned from the ranch. The ladies came to see how things were going, and both were surprised to find Colton helping and the kitchen mostly built.

Rosie gave him a big hug and immediately began to talk about the Johnsons' roundup. "Emma and I are going to go and stay for several days and help. I'm going to help cook and clean up, and Emma too. There are going to be about fifty cowboys to feed, and they're going to brand the calves and do other things. I'm so excited to see it all."

"Well, that will be something completely different for you to experience." Colton glanced at Emma, who was still inspecting their work on her outdoor kitchen.

"I think it will be fun."

Emma gave an unexpected laugh. "I told her that it's hot, dirty work that never seems to end. You fall into your bed each night exhausted and praying that morning won't come too soon." She straightened from her inspection and turned to meet Colton's gaze. "She'll learn soon enough. Life isn't always what you expect."

"It's going to be fun." Rosie headed for the back door. Colton noticed a tin box in her hands. "I'm going in to show Mrs. Olson our new recipes." She slipped into the house, leaving Colton and Emma alone, since Gary had also disappeared from the group.

"I'm glad I have a moment to talk to you. Would you consider going to dinner with me tonight? I have a great deal of business to discuss with you. I met with the Union Pacific officials today and have their final proposal. They'd like us to meet with them on Monday and sign the papers of transfer."

Emma's expression sobered. "Why do we need to go out

to dinner? We could discuss it here. I'm sure Mrs. Olson has already started supper and has included the both of us."

"I'd just like some time alone with you, Emma. Please?"

She seemed to consider this a moment. "I suppose we can go to dinner. What time?"

He pulled out his pocket watch and did his best not to appear too excited. "I'll come for you at six. Will that be acceptable?" He closed the lid of the watch and returned it to his pocket before allowing himself to look at her again. "That will give me time to get cleaned up."

Emma's stoic expression did nothing to reassure him. "Very well. I'll look for you at six."

"Thank you, Emma. I promise to be on my best behavior." He smiled, hoping it might lighten the mood.

She shook her head. "I still think we could manage it all here, but if this is what you want, then I'll come."

"I promise you we'll have a wonderful evening."

She gave him an odd look as her eyes narrowed. "You shouldn't promise things that might well be out of your control."

Colton said nothing. Gary soon rejoined them, and Emma spoke to him about the kitchen while Colton gathered his things.

"I can come by tomorrow, Mr. Price. I have nothing planned."

"We've worked side by side enough now that you should just call me Gary. I'd be happy for the help."

"Good. I should be able to get here first thing."

"Just come for breakfast at seven, Colton." Emma offered him a hint of a smile.

Colton gave Emma a nod. "I'll pick you up at six tonight." He didn't wait for her reply but kept on walking in case she changed her mind.

He was halfway back to the boardinghouse when it dawned

on him that he should get Emma some flowers. It was a rather bold move, but he knew she enjoyed them and hadn't had any since those he and Rosie had brought her in the hospital. He wasn't used to going downtown in such a slovenly manner, but there wasn't time to go home and change. The flower shop would close by five.

At the florist's, Colton quickly selected some pink roses, just as Emma had given Rosie the first time they met. He remembered her commenting on how much she liked pink roses and hoped she had been sincere in her statement. As he made his way from the shop, he was surprised to hear someone call his name. He turned and found Edward Vogel.

"Mr. Vogel. How nice to see you again."

"Mr. Benton." Vogel smiled. "I've been meaning to come see you. I wanted to thank you for giving Rob permission to marry your sister. I know that meant a lot to them both."

"I appreciated that he would ask. I know I wasn't overly kind to him when I first met him, but . . . well, I guess you could say God's been changing my heart about a lot of things and people."

"He has a way of doing that when we give ourselves up to Him."

"It's all new to me. My mother, who passed away when I was young, was a Christian, but my father was decidedly not. He had turned me pretty much against religion, but I guess God wanted something more from me."

Vogel chuckled. "Indeed. I have to say in all my years of following Him, God still manages to surprise me on occasion. I think, however, you'll find that walking with Him is far better than walking without Him."

"I feel at a complete loss sometimes. Short of going to church, I really don't know what else to do."

"Praying and studying the Bible has helped me most. There's a group of us men who meet to study God's Word on Saturday mornings. We meet at various places. Tomorrow we'll be at my house. Why don't you come?"

Colton glanced away. "Truth is, I don't own a Bible."

"That's easy enough to resolve. Come with me."

Vogel glanced to his right and then left before crossing the road. Across the street was Armstrongs' Emporium, and that was where he seemed to be headed. Colton had no choice but to follow him.

"I want to buy you a Bible," Vogel said as they went inside the store. "Armstrongs' carries a nice selection."

"You don't need to do that. I can buy my own."

Vogel reached the counter where the Bibles were displayed. "I know you can, but I want to do this. You're soon to be family, and it would be my honor to purchase you your first Bible."

A clerk came to join them. "How can I help you gentlemen?" she asked.

"I'd like to see that Bible with the black leather binding," Vogel said. He turned and smiled. "Just wait until you start reading. We're studying in Luke, and tomorrow we're ready for the story of the prodigal son. You've heard that one before, haven't you?"

Colton could only smile. "I've heard of it. Never read it."

Vogel nodded and opened the Bible the clerk had handed him. "It's all right here."

Rosie had watched Colton and Emma earlier from the upstairs window. She couldn't hear what they had said, but at least they were talking. She had been thinking about ways to get them to open up to each other, and one thing that came to mind was to give them plenty of time alone.

After Colton left, Rosie watched as Emma spoke with

Gary. They seemed to measure something out, and after a while Emma finally started back for the house. Rosie hurried downstairs and came into the kitchen just as Emma came in from the mudroom.

"Mrs. Olson," Emma said, removing her sunbonnet, "Colton and I won't be here for supper. I'm sorry I couldn't give you more warning. Some business matters have come up, and Colton feels they would best be discussed over supper elsewhere."

"That's quite all right. I made a big roast, and it should take you through tomorrow."

"I'm glad you're going to dinner with Colton," Rosie said, trying to think about each word before she spoke. She didn't want to mess things up by saying the wrong thing. "I hate it when we talk about business at our meals. My father and brothers always did that, and it was so boring for Tommy and me."

Emma smiled. "I can understand that. I remember a few of those dinners with your father and brothers. We should make a rule to never talk business at the table."

Rosie nodded, but already she was trying to think of what other encouragement she could offer. "I'm glad you wore your old dress out to the ranch. It's pretty dirty now. Would you like me to help you clean up?"

"I suppose I do look a sight. It's probably too late to take a bath and wash my hair."

Rosie looked at the clock. The hour hand was on four and the minute hand on the six. She smiled. "It's just four thirty. I can get your bath ready while you gather your things. You'll feel so much better afterward since it's been so hot. I can lay out clean clothes for you while you bathe."

Emma nodded. "That sounds too good to pass up. "Would that be all right with you, Mrs. Olson? I wouldn't want us to be in the way since the bathing room is just off the kitchen."

"It's perfectly fine. I have everything under control here. I can help Rosie prepare the bathwater."

Rosie was already headed for the bathroom. She imagined Emma all cleaned and dressed up meeting Colton for supper.

Lord, I want them to be friends again. More than friends, if possible. I never want to lose Emma as my sister, and I want Colton to stay here in Wyoming, like he says he's going to do, but he might not want to stay if Emma doesn't like him again. He's different now, and he wants to know more about You. Please help him.

20

Emma glanced at the clock as it chimed six. She was nervous about going to supper with Colton. So many thoughts went through her mind. She had been praying about the things God would have her do. She knew that Colton cared about her—could believe that he loved her as he said. She was even coming to terms with her own feelings for him. But why hadn't he just been honest with her? He could have just told her what his brothers wanted him to do.

She thought of his brothers pressuring him to marry her to get back the railroad stocks and other things Tommy had inherited. She had already resolved that the family heirlooms, jewelry, and the railroad stock value would go to Rosie, but she would keep other things. Like Tommy's investment in a San Francisco shipping firm. He had been so enthusiastic about that particular deal. He had promised Emma they would sail and see the world. The thought of his excitement brought a smile to her face. Maybe someday she would still see the world on one of Tommy's ships. Maybe after she saw Rosie married and endowed with her inheritance, Emma would just quietly slip away and keep those plans.

A knock sounded on the front door, and Emma drew in

a deep breath. She went to the door and opened it. Colton had chosen a navy blue suit and looked quite resplendent. He smiled and tipped his hat before presenting her with a bouquet of pink roses.

"Oh my." She was taken completely by surprise. This was supposed to be a business meeting, not a courtship. "Thank you."

She took the bouquet and without thinking drew them to her face to breathe in the sweet scent. She glanced up over the flowers to find Colton watching her in the way he often did. She recognized the passion in his eyes. It caused her breath to catch.

"Let me put these in water."

"I can do it for you, Emma." Rosie swept into the foyer and took the bouquet. "Hello, brother." She stood on tiptoe to kiss his cheek.

Colton smiled and kissed the top of her head. "I'll have Emma back in a couple of hours."

A couple of hours? The thought of such a long time in Colton's company made her knees weaken along with her resolve. What was she supposed to say to him for two hours? They would discuss business of course, but then what?

"Have a wonderful dinner," Rosie said, giving Emma a side hug. "Try to just relax and enjoy the evening."

Emma heard her words but felt certain relaxing in Colton's company would be quite impossible. Especially if he started looking at her with that same impassioned gaze.

"I hope you don't mind if we walk. I was going to rent a buggy, but it's such a beautiful night, and the restaurant is just a few blocks away."

"Walking is fine with me." Emma checked to make sure her hat was straight, then drew on her gloves. "Let's be on our way."

She moved out the door past Colton, not even bothering

to wait for him as she made her way down the walk. She felt her breath quicken and did her best to calm her anxious mind. It was just one dinner. One evening.

"You look beautiful in that green gown. I'm so glad to see you've stopped wearing mourning. Tommy would have hated for you to wear black."

"I know. I thought of that every time I donned it. He would have shredded all those gowns and told me to dress in all the beautiful clothes he bought me for my trousseau. Keeping that in mind, I decided to put mourning aside."

"I'm glad." He sighed, and Emma took it as a sign of sorrow.

"I know you miss him." Emma didn't so much as glance at Colton. "Tommy said you were the only one who ever bothered to spend time with him, especially once you became adults. Tommy said at times you were the best of friends. That must have been hard to lose."

"It was. Finalizing the railroad business today only served to remind me of him. I also thought a lot about things you have said in the past about our father's hard work to leave this legacy."

"Yet you're certain selling is the right thing to do?"

Colton offered her his arm as they crossed the street. Emma took hold of him and waited for him to answer. After half a block, he did.

"I feel confident it's the right thing to do. There are things going on in the economy that give me pause. I've heard of more than a half dozen small railroads going bankrupt, and it concerns me that such a thing could come our way as the large railroads become stronger and stronger. None of us wanted to be railroad barons, nor to be steeped in the upkeep and regulations. The sale will provide much-needed income for the projects that Walter and Ernest feel compelled to accomplish and will make you a very wealthy woman."

"I'm already a wealthy woman. I have no great needs. When the sale is done, I shall have that money put into a separate account until I decide what I want to do with it."

"You should invest it as soon as possible so that you can continue to have a flow of income. I can share with you several investments of which I intend to take advantage."

"Thank you. I'm sure that will be helpful. One thing I'm certain of is that I want to contribute to the church's building fund. I want to make a substantial contribution, in fact. I was meaning to speak to you about it."

"I can manage all of that for you. How much did you have in mind?"

"Whatever remaining amount they need to fulfill the plan. I want them to be able to build the church the way they want it and have all that is needed. My folks have helped with bake sales and fundraisers since we first met for services in the schoolhouse. I want to see this church completed in grand order."

"I want to help as well. I'll talk to Reverend Bright and find out what is still needed and take care of it for you—for us."

"Thank you."

They continued to walk, but Emma had no idea of where they were going. She focused on the way ahead and did her best not to think of the man who held her arm so confidently.

After a long time of silence, Colton cleared his throat. "I really am sorry, Emma. I never meant for you to get hurt by my not telling you about Walter and Ernest. I'm sorry, too, that Rosie overheard their conversations. They weren't very kind toward her. They've never cared about her the way I do. The way you do."

Thoughts of Rosie always made Emma smile. "I love her as a little sister. I want to ensure that nothing, and no one, hurts her, yet I know that isn't realistic in life. There's always something that will come along to cause us pain."

"And I deeply regret that I was the one who caused it for you."

Emma knew it wasn't fair to continue to close her heart to him. "I'd rather you be honest with me, Colton. I always felt I had that with you. You completely fooled me, and it makes me skittish to think of trusting you again."

"I know I should have said something about my brothers, but Emma, I didn't fool you. I love you more than I've ever loved anyone. I don't even know what to do with myself. You're on my mind constantly. I wake up, and you're my first thought. I go to sleep at night, and it's your face I think of."

She hadn't anticipated his words of love but marveled at how they touched her heart. Still, there was so much doubt. She'd done her best in life to avoid feeling too deeply, caring too much. Emma Johnson was known for having a good time and taking nothing seriously. But Emma Johnson had died on the day of her wedding. At least that part of her had. She no longer felt the need to run from one thing to another looking for something that she couldn't even explain. Coming to an understanding of God had changed everything.

"I will do anything you ask to prove myself to you. I want only to be worthy of your love and to share my life with you, Emma." He stopped walking and turned her to face him. "I will sign any papers you like that protect the inheritance you have. If that will prove to you that I truly love you—not the stocks or the money you received from Tommy—I will gladly do it. There are legal means to ensure that everything remains in your protection, even after we marry."

"Not *if* we marry?" Emma found that amusing. "You're terribly sure of yourself."

The fact that he was willing to go to such lengths spoke volumes to Emma. The Bentons were known to cherish money above all, but Tommy hadn't cared one whit about such things. Now Emma could see that Colton was willing to cast it all aside . . . for her.

He reached up to put his hands on either side of her face. "Emma, I will never marry anyone but you. I cannot ever love another. You've completely captured my heart. Please, please tell me that I might have a chance to convince you of my sincerity and win your heart."

Emma swallowed the lump in her throat. His words consumed her, but even more so, the truth of it was written in his eyes. In that moment, she felt that if she didn't give this romance a chance, she might never know what it was to love and truly be loved.

"You know we have rules here about public displays of affection."

The man's voice caused Emma to jump. She turned and found Edward Vogel grinning. Her heart was nearly pounding out of her chest, and all she could do was shake her head.

"I'm sorry. I didn't mean to frighten you, Emma." He looked to Colton. "Nor you. Please forgive me."

"I never wanted to punch a lawman in the nose more than I want to right now," Colton said quite seriously.

Emma worried momentarily that there would be a fight between the two men, but she heard Chief Vogel laugh, and Colton joined in. Relief washed over her.

"We got a bit caught up in the moment," Emma admitted. "I'm afraid I'm causing trouble in Cheyenne once again."

Chief Vogel laughed all the more. "Oh, Emma, I used to get such a laugh out of your antics. I think a lot of folks did. You were a wild one, but such a sweet thing. We used to converse among the deputies as to what outrageous thing you might try next. I think some even bet on it."

She felt her cheeks grow hot and looked at the ground to calm her nerves. "It's rather humiliating to imagine anyone taking bets on what act of disobedience I might try next."

"Well, you've proven yourself a changed woman," Chief Vogel assured. "I think most everyone I know is glad to have you back."

She drew in a deep breath to steady her nerves. "I'd like to think that's so."

"Then think it. You've grown up a lot in the last nine years, Emma. God's working on you just the same as He's working on the rest of us. None of us achieve the perfection of Jesus, but we keep aiming for that. He's the only one we need to concern ourselves with. Keep your eyes on Him, and you'll do just fine." He paused, and Emma glanced up to see him fix his gaze on Colton.

"You do right by our Emma, or you'll have me to answer to."

"Yes, sir. You and her pa. I wouldn't want to challenge either one of you."

"It's a good thing you feel that way. Now, I'll see you in the morning. Seven sharp."

"Yes, sir."

Colton didn't hesitate, and Emma wondered what was going on between him and the chief of police.

"I'll be on my way." He tipped his hat at Emma and gave Colton a nod.

Once he was gone, Emma couldn't help but heave a sigh of relief. "I thought I was bound for the jailhouse once again."

Colton laughed and took hold of her arm. "I thought we both were. Let's keep moving so that he won't have any reason to do that again."

A couple of hours later, Emma invited Colton to sit on the porch. She was amazed at how comfortable she was with him now. He'd talked for part of dinner about the negotiations with the Union Pacific and all that they'd agreed to. She was pleased to hear what her share of the sale would entail. Rosie was going to be a very wealthy woman. She didn't tell Colton her plans. She wanted to respect Marybeth's request to say nothing for the time being. There was still concern that if he knew, he might not allow Rosie and Rob to marry. Emma hated that she felt that way. She wanted to trust Colton, but it would take a little time. Time that she had also agreed to give him.

"Thank you for this evening. I had a wonderful time just talking to you and hearing about your life," Colton said as they sat in the darkness.

Emma had turned on the front room lights so a muted glow could be had on the porch. She could just make out Colton's face. He was quite handsome. Where Tommy had had boyish charm and a roguish air about him, Colton was refined sophistication and ease. He knew what he wanted out of life and wasn't afraid to risk it all to have it.

I'm a part of what he wants. The thought met no resistance in her heart.

They heard Rosie's giggle before they spotted her with Rob crossing the street. He was saying something to her in a hushed voice, and she was laughing gleefully. As they drew closer, Rob spied Emma and Colton on the porch and pointed them out to Rosie.

"I'm so glad you two are speaking again," Rosie said, nearly dancing her way up the walk. "I have something to show you . . . to tell you."

Emma knew without a doubt what Rosie would say next. She couldn't help but smile and turned to Colton, who was also looking quite pleased.

"Rob asked me to marry him, and I said yes!" She laughed and gave a twirl. "Look at my ring." She extended her hand, but it was hard to see in the dim lighting.

"Why don't we go inside and have a better look. We can celebrate too." Emma got to her feet and looked at Colton. She wondered if there would be any negative comment or trouble. He had given Rob permission to marry his sister, but he might have had a change of heart.

"I think that's a wonderful idea," Colton said, jumping up. "Rosie, I couldn't be happier for you."

She laughed and ran into his arms. "I couldn't be happier either. My life is the very best."

Emma couldn't help but feel the young woman's joy spill over and engulf them all. Rosie had endured so much in her short life. People had all but locked her away in a cage. They had decided from the start that she would be a terrible burden, a worthless and troublesome curse.

They had been so very wrong.

21

After Sunday services, where Rob and Rosie announced their engagement, Emma invited Rob's family and hers to come back to her house for lunch. Colton had never been one to enjoy family gatherings, but with the Johnsons and the Vogels, it was quite different from the affairs his own family had endured.

These were people who enjoyed a lot of laughter and love. Colton watched their interactions and thought of how different his own life might have been if his family had been like theirs. Instead of money directing their conversations and time, the men enjoyed discussions about their families and hobbies. They talked about God and the things they were learning in the Bible. Colton had thoroughly enjoyed his time the previous day learning about the various elements of the prodigal son. He saw himself in the elder son, angry and frustrated that the younger son had demanded his inheritance and left to live his life in a reckless manner. The oldest son had remained faithfully at work, doing his father's bidding, just as Colton had. He'd missed out on so many of the things Tommy had experienced and enjoyed, but in the end those things had, in essence, killed him. Colton hadn't even realized his anger toward his younger brother until this study. He was able to talk to these men and listen to them share similar feelings.

Realizing his feelings about Tommy was difficult, though. Tommy's love of life and refusal to live by rules had gotten him killed. Yet his death had allowed Colton to break free of certain self-imposed chains regarding his feelings for Emma. It created a mixture of guilt, regret, and hesitancy about the future. Did he deserve to enjoy a life with Emma when it had come at the cost of his brother?

He hadn't shared all of this with the men in the group, but mentioned enough of it that they offered counsel that had met a certain need. Edward Vogel seemed to understand a great deal more than Colton expected. He had even told Colton about the house he lived in and how it had come to him because of the death of a good friend. For years he felt too guilty and regretful to truly enjoy it, but finally, he came to see that such feelings couldn't bring back his friend.

Just as Colton's feelings couldn't bring back his brother.

Without a doubt, Tommy would have wanted Colton to live his life and to love Emma. Tommy would want her cared for, because Colton had little doubt that he had truly loved Emma. It was this thought that helped him to put aside guilt. Tommy was beyond caring, but Emma needed love and support, and Colton intended to give her both in generous quantities.

With the weather so pleasant, they had set up tables and chairs in the backyard not far from the summer kitchen. Everyone was quite impressed with what Colton and Gary had created.

"I sure couldn't have finished it off as quick as I did without Colton's help. For being a city boy, he can handle himself well enough," Gary told the gathering.

"That's good to hear," Rich Johnson declared. "Maybe he can come out and help with the roundup."

"I think I'd be better at attempting to juggle than rope and ride," Colton mused. Everyone laughed.

Rich laughed more than anyone else. "I'm pretty sure we could teach a smart fella like you."

"I'm afraid Colton is leaving tomorrow after we sign papers with the Union Pacific." Emma glanced at Colton and smiled. "He is selling his family's railroad to the UP and then has to journey to Dallas and give his brothers the news and documents."

"But he's coming back," Rosie announced in her boisterous way. "He's going to live in Cheyenne."

"I shouldn't need more than a month or so to straighten everything out."

"You'll come back in time for the wedding and give me away, won't you?" Rosie said, turning a concerned look on Colton.

"I'll never give you away, Rosie," Colton replied sternly. Then as she began to frown, he added, "I'll share you with Rob, but I'll never let you go all together. You're my only sister, and I want very much for us to remain close."

She smiled and then laughed. "We will always be close, Colton. Nothing will change that."

"I'm glad you feel that way, because I intend to make Cheyenne my home. Hopefully, we'll be able to see each other often."

Rosie clapped her hands. "I'm so happy. I was praying you'd stay here. You're happier here."

"It'll be great to have family all around us," Rob interjected. "Ma has always taught us the importance of family. She lost her ma and pa when she was young. I hope we can all be close."

Everyone murmured their agreement, and even Colton

felt a warmth of unity that he'd not experienced before. Family had always been important to him, but it was tied together with financial stability, business associations, and social standings. These people held together out of pure love for one another. There was no expectation of performance or increasing the family coffers.

"So, you two have decided to get married in September?" Lucille questioned.

Rob answered before Rosie could speak. "Yes. We figured September first. It's the first Sunday, and that gives us a couple of months to prepare. We need to find a house of our own and make plans for the wedding."

"Don't forget you'll have lots of help," Marybeth Vogel spoke up. "I can't imagine anything happier than working with you to plan a wedding and reception."

"We don't need anything fancy," Rob said, looking to Rosie. She nodded. "Rosie and I talked about it, and we just want a simple ceremony after church. We can have a big party afterward, if you like."

"That sounds perfect. We can hold a big celebration at our place, if you want," Marybeth told her son.

Colton found himself envious as discussion about the party continued. He'd like very much for them to be talking about his and Emma's wedding reception.

"Emma," Rosie interrupted, "I want you to stand with me. You're my sister and dearest friend."

Emma appeared genuinely touched. "Of course I'll stand with you Rosie. I'm so happy for you and Rob." She glanced at Rob. "I think you've found yourself a wonderful man to marry. The two of you are going to be ever so happy."

"So long as you put Jesus at the center of your marriage," Rich Johnson added. "I can't stress that enough. When things go wrong or you bicker and fight, looking to Jesus will get you through."

"It's so true," Marybeth and Edward said in unison. They glanced at each other and laughed. It seemed they were of one mind.

Talk continued, and mention was made of a couple houses for sale nearby. Colton figured to offer the couple a house as a wedding present. He had more money than he knew what to do with anyway and would have even more after tomorrow. He didn't want to bring up such a thing in the company of everyone, however, and figured he'd wait until later to discuss it. Since he needed to figure out a place of his own to live, maybe he'd just set out seeing houses on the pretense of buying one for himself.

"I'd like to see some houses too," he finally said. "Perhaps I could accompany you and Rosie as you make your search. I'm going to need some place to live."

Rob gave him a smile. "That would be great, Mr. Benton."

"Call me Colton. We're about to become family."

"Thanks, Colton. I think it'd be good to have you along on the search. Pa, it'd be good for you to look things over too. You're good to spot problems."

"None of the places around here are all that old. Some were built with better materials than others, to be sure, but I'd be happy to do what I can."

When lunch was concluded, Rosie and Rob announced their desire to go for a horseback ride. Rob said that Rosie had taken to it like she did most things, and he felt she was going to be a fine horsewoman.

Once again, Colton marveled at the thought of his sister's accomplishments. She had overcome so much. It was still obvious that she worked at a slower pace than others when it came to details like reading and math. Maybe she always would, but the important thing was she was learning every day and doing quite well.

Emma convinced her stepmother and father that they

didn't need to help with clean up. "I have everything under control. Gary and Colton will manage the tables and chairs, and I can get the dishes."

"I'll stay and help you," Marybeth said.

"No, I'll help her after Gary and I get the chairs and table back in the house," Colton said, getting to his feet. "You go enjoy the afternoon with your family."

"They'll probably all have something else to do. Greta was already busy with the Deckers, and Daniel mentioned fishing." She tousled her son's brown hair. "Of course, fresh fish for supper sounds just fine by me."

"Hopefully, I'll catch a whole string." The sixteen-year-old got to his feet. "But I'll help you with the chairs and taking stuff inside." He started gathering plates, evidently much to his mother's surprise.

"There, you see, we have it all resolved. Maybe you and Edward can enjoy a nice quiet afternoon alone," Lucille said, collecting silverware.

Once everyone was gone and the things brought inside, Colton went to the kitchen and found Emma with her sleeves rolled up and hands busy at work in the soapy water. He took up a dish towel and began taking clean dishes from her as soon as she finished rinsing them.

"That was a lot of fun. I've never really enjoyed family gatherings," Colton began, "but I never had family like those folks."

"They are all such good people. I must admit, however, they make me miss my mother even more. Those were the kind of gatherings she loved best. Roundup was her favorite time of the year because there would be multiple families all together in one place. Families whom we were all very close to."

"I've never known anything quite like it. Coming here has opened my eyes to how family life ought to be. Everything has changed for me in so many ways." He dried the plate and set it aside before taking another Emma offered.

"I never appreciated family when I was young. They were just people who interfered in my life. My folks always had chores and a list of rules. I couldn't see then how they were trying to teach me responsibility. Their rules stifled my desires, but now I see how they were trying to keep me safe. I look back and see myself for the rebellious and ungrateful child I was, and it breaks my heart."

"But, Emma, you didn't act as you did in order to fulfill your desires to be rebellious and ungrateful. You were merely trying to experience life and try new things. You wanted something different for yourself."

"But what they wanted for me was far better than what I wanted for myself. I was too blind to see it. If I'd have lived as directed by my folks—been obedient and refined as they wanted me to be—I'd have never had a shootout at my wedding."

"You don't know that." Colton added another plate to the stack and turned to face her. "We can't know how things might have been, only how they were . . . how they are now. If you hadn't been the kind of person you were, I might never have met the only woman I'll ever love."

Her cheeks flushed as she turned abruptly to concentrate on the dish in her hands. Colton wanted so much to take her in his arms and hold her, but he held himself back and focused instead on the bowl he was drying. He had to give her time to rethink her feelings toward him. He knew she cared for him. He could tell by the way she looked at him that her previous anger and sense of betrayal were fading. She'd had time to reason things in her thoughts. Their time together Friday night had been a clear indication that she felt love for him.

"I'm sorry if that made you uncomfortable. It's just that I'll be leaving tomorrow and gone for a few weeks. I don't want you to forget about me and how important you are to me. I would hate for some other suitor to seek you out and try to win you over while I'm gone."

"Don't be ridiculous. No one is going to come seeking me out." She started washing the silverware.

"So you might be willing to promise to wait for me?"

She stopped washing the dishes and turned to him. "What exactly are you asking?"

"I'd ask you to marry me if I thought you'd say yes. I'm guessing it's too early for that, though. I know you don't yet trust me, and I understand why." He put the dish towel aside. "I just don't want someone else to get ahead of me in trying to win your heart."

"That won't happen." She barely whispered the words.

Colton took hold of her wet hands. "Do you promise?"

Emma studied his face for a long moment. "I promise."

He grinned, feeling real hope. "Will you kiss me as a pledge?"

Again, she looked at him as if searching for something. Colton was almost convinced she'd say no when she finally nodded her consent.

Tenderly, he took her face in his hands and gazed into her dark brown eyes. He prayed she'd recognize his sincerity and honesty. Prayed that God would let her see his heart and know the truth. Pressing his lips to hers, Colton pulled Emma close, marveling at the way they fit together so perfectly. They were made for each other.

Emma couldn't contain her elation as she gazed at the check given her by the Union Pacific official. It was her share of the Benton family railroad. There was enough money here to keep Rosie and Rob for the rest of their lives.

"This envelope contains the Union Pacific stock certificates." The man handed her the envelope and then gave one to Colton. "Yours are here with your brothers' stocks, and the checks are included. Each are written out as you directed."

"Thank you. That concludes our business together, and now I've a train to catch." Colton took the envelope and placed it into a leather satchel. He got to his feet and offered his hand to Emma. She was still rather dumbfounded by the amount of money that had just been exchanged. She allowed Colton to help her to her feet, nevertheless.

She offered the UP man a smile and put the check in her purse. "It was a pleasure to meet you."

Once they left the office and headed out into the depot, she realized anew that Colton would soon be leaving Cheyenne. His train to Denver was due shortly. He'd already checked his trunk.

"I hope your brothers are pleased with the transaction. I don't see how they couldn't be, but given all that you've told me about them, I suppose they could be upset when they learn that we didn't marry."

Colton shrugged. "They'll have their say and complaints, then they'll take the checks and stocks and go off to do whatever it is they have planned to do. In time, they'll either be great successes or miserable failures. Either way, they will be out of my concerns."

"They won't like it that you plan to move to Cheyenne, will they?"

"I hardly think they'll care. As I told you, I plan to dissolve any of our shared business dealings. Most I'll simply give to them. I want nothing more to do with Dallas and think it will be for the best that we manage our own accounts without outside interference."

Emma nodded. She knew this was part of Colton's attempt

to assure her that he wasn't doing the bidding of his brothers. Any further future for them was going to be based purely on their feelings for each other and nothing more.

Colton glanced at the clock. "I should probably board the train. They'll be leaving soon."

"Yes, I suppose so. I need to go the bank and get this check deposited."

"Don't forget, I set up a completely different account for it. Just as you asked."

She managed a smile and held up the envelope. "And these will go into the safe-deposit box under my name."

"Right. That way you won't have to worry about them should there be a fire or if someone breaks into the house."

He glanced over his shoulder and then again at the clock. "I'll be back as soon as possible."

Emma felt strangely close to tears. She didn't want him to go. She knew he felt the same way. "Please be careful. Rosie would be quite upset if something happened to you." She met his dark eyes. "I would be too."

He smiled. "That encourages me."

"You hardly need encouragement. Now go, before you miss your train all together."

He raised her hands to his lips and kissed her fingertips. Glancing up, Emma saw the passion in his eyes once again and felt her stomach do a flip. Goodness, what was it about this man that so completely captivated her?

Once he'd gone, Emma gathered her senses and made her way from the depot to the bank. She was quite eagerly received by the bank president himself. Her check was even more welcome. The entire process took less than ten minutes, including the time to put her stocks in the safety box. With that completed, she headed for home, wondering how in the world she was going to keep herself occupied for the next few weeks.

She didn't have long to wonder, however. As soon as she got home, Rosie quickly drew her outside and busied her with cookie production. By the time that first evening concluded, Emma was exhausted and had little time to think about Colton. Although it was his impassioned gaze that she remembered as she fell asleep.

Colton gazed out the window as the train made its way into the Dallas station. He'd been traveling for five days, having had an overnight stop in Kansas City. Soon he'd be back in the house he'd called home for most of his adult life. Only it wasn't home any longer. The only people he truly cared about were waiting for him in Cheyenne.

The grueling heat had been unbearable the farther south they traveled, and the humidity and stormy weather had only served to make him even more miserable. He longed for the dryer climate of Cheyenne, along with the milder temperatures.

Hailing a cab, Colton waited for the driver to load his trunk before climbing into the open carriage. He gave the man his address, then settled back against the hot leather. He wondered what he'd find at home. Would his brothers be there to greet him? He'd telegraphed them to indicate when he'd arrive. He knew they were more than anxious for their share of the railroad money. He smiled, almost chuckling to himself. They'd be there.

Things looked the same around town and through the neighborhoods as they made their way to the famed Benton house. There was plenty of noise and action taking place around them. The traffic was quite vexing for the driver, whom Colton heard swear more than once. Dallas was growing by leaps and bounds.

When they finally reached their destination, Colton was pleased to find one of the houseboys hurrying out to take charge of his luggage. He flipped the driver ample coinage for the ride and tip, then hurried up the walkway to get inside and out of the sun.

"Mr. Benton, welcome home," the housekeeper greeted him at the door. "Your brothers are in the library."

Colton nodded. He really wanted to go take a tepid bath, but getting rid of his brothers first was more important. He went straightaway to the library, wasting no time.

"I see you got my telegram," he declared, entering the room with his satchel in hand. "I'll make this brief." He went to his desk and opened the satchel. He took out the checks and handed one to each of his brothers. "Your share of the sale." Then, without waiting for them to comment, he pulled out the envelopes. "Inside are your shares of stock in the Union Pacific."

"Right to business, as always," Walter said, laughing. "But you won't get away without telling us of your success with Tommy's widow."

"My dealings with Tommy's widow are none of your concern." Colton gave him a hard look. "However, Emma and Rosie are both doing well. Our sister is to marry a police officer who has spent the last few months courting her and teaching her to read and ride horses. He's an exceptional young man who loves our sister dearly, and I've given him permission to marry her. They will do so on the first of September."

His brothers looked at him as if he'd just announced his ability to fly.

Ernest regained his thoughts first. "Marry her? He wants to marry a mindless ninny like our sister?"

"You would rethink that comment if you had spent time with Rosie these last few months. In the short time since we've been gone, she has flourished like no one I've ever seen. Emma has taught her many skills, including cooking. Although Mrs. Olson had a fair hand in that as well."

"Who in the world is Mrs. Olson?" Walter questioned.

"Emma's cook. Now, if you don't mind, I'm sweltering and would like a bath."

"You can't leave us without telling us whether or not you married Emma." Ernest looked at Colton with narrowed eyes. "This is most important."

"Why? If I had married her, the money and stocks would be mine, not yours."

"You know why it's important. There is more to do with it than just money and stocks. There are other investments that Tommy inherited."

"Furniture and jewelry, as well," Walter added.

"Not to mention paintings and other art pieces." Ernest was starting to sound angry. "We have a right to know what's going on."

"Nothing is going on. I did not marry Emma, although I plan to. Certainly not for the reasons you would like, but for real and true love. The money is in her account, and her share of the Union Pacific stocks are in her safekeeping. I intend to sign a prenuptial contract that will allow her to keep whatever she has prior to our marriage."

"But that money should have come to the three of us," Walter insisted. "That's why we sent you to Cheyenne."

"You didn't send me, Walter. I went of my own desire to oversee the safety of Emma and Rosie. Your interference and scheming in all of this nearly caused me to lose the woman I've loved since Tommy first brought her into this house."

Ernest chuckled. "That's a marvelous scheme. I suppose you told Emma that and delighted her with hours of conversation about how you pined away for her even as she planned to marry our brother."

"That is quite the perfect game, I must say. You no doubt had her panting after you." Walter grinned in such a way that ended any patience Colton might have shown him.

"The truth is that I care deeply about Emma and am very much in love with her. I won't have you speaking ill of her, nor suggesting anything untoward. You have your money and stocks and should go. I will be in Dallas only long enough to arrange the packing and shipping of Tommy's, or rather Emma's things, as well as my own. Oh, and the sale of this house. You might recall I've already paid you for your share of the place, so there is nothing you will gain by the sale. I plan to arrange for my other business dealings as well, some of which will benefit you. So I advise you to stay on my good side. Once this is completed, I will return to Cheyenne, where I intend to make my home until my death."

He looked at them both, feeling rather satisfied at their shocked expressions. "Now, if you'll excuse me."

"But you cannot just walk away," Walter said. "We wanted you to come in on several projects with us."

"That may well be, but I'm not at all interested."

"But you haven't even heard what they are," his brother protested.

Colton shrugged. "My values in life have changed. I've made my peace with God, as our mother used to encourage us to do. I, in turn, encourage you to follow my example and explore that path for yourself. I have never known such peace and satisfaction as I've experienced in turning to God rather than my own devices."

"You can't be serious." Ernest looked at him with great disdain. "Religious nonsense has no room in the life of a businessman. Let the women in our lives seek solace in such things."

"Church is a social obligation," Walter offered. "Nothing more."

Colton had no interest in arguing the matter. "All I can say is that seeking God has given me great peace of heart and happiness. I hope you'll give it a try for yourselves because, frankly, I've never known two more miserable beings than you."

22

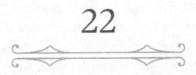

Fourth of July was usually the grandest of celebrations in Cheyenne. Not only because they celebrated America's independence from England, but because this was the day the Union Pacific rolled into the area and started the city's existence. The official date of the town's incorporation was in August, but a great many folks still celebrated on the Fourth of July. This year, however, the big regional Firemen's Tournament was being hosted by Cheyenne, and people from all over the territory as well as the states of Colorado and Nebraska had turned out.

The town citizens had been encouraged to decorate their houses and businesses in grand style using streamers and banners, preferably of a patriotic or celebratory fashion. Emma and Rosie had done up the front of their house with red, white, and blue banners and hung Chinese lanterns from the lower branches of the entryway pines.

There were multiple celebrations set up for both days, with the second day hosting the Union Pacific's cornerstone laying ceremony and a grand parade. Having read the morning paper, Emma had to chuckle at the instructions for all the various people who were to march. It would be a wonder if there was anyone left to watch the parade. The line was to start with the United States soldiers, then the Wyoming Militia, followed by the Cheyenne fire department, and then the visiting fire departments. The list went on and on with civic leaders and state officials included, as well as civic organizations and citizens of Cheyenne.

Emma was glad to read that the parade would take form on the west side of town rather than the east, near her neighborhood. But that was tomorrow. Today was entirely different, and she needed to hurry in order to make it to where the church ladies were setting up the bake sale.

At exactly nine o'clock, Emma, Rosie, and Mrs. Olson stood ready and waiting as the bake sale was officially opened. Crowds were already swarming the streets, and lines had formed with eager firemen and cowboys all focused on buying homemade treats.

Emma helped the other women of the Methodist church to man some ten tables. Children had been commissioned to restock empty places with goods that had been secured in nearby wagons. It had actually been necessary to have a few of their men stand guard to keep less honorable folk from stealing goods right out of the wagons.

Someone counted over three hundred dozen cookies, fifty loaves of bread, and just as many pies and cakes, along with other goodies. And true to every other year, the entire array of foods was bringing some men close to fighting in order to claim their prizes.

"Did you make these cookies, pretty gal?" an older firemen from somewhere in Colorado asked Emma as he handed her his money. His bright blue uniform with gold braid trim suggested he held a position of great importance.

"I helped in making several things here, and I know that you'll be happy with whatever you choose."

"I'd like to choose you!" he said, giving a whoop. "How about you join me for the picnic lunch?"

Emma handed him his change and smiled. "I'm already spoken for, sorry."

The next man in line was a younger cowboy. He pushed the firefighter to the side. "It's my turn, old man!"

Emma wondered if he meant for cookies or sweet talk as the man began telling her how he'd always been partial to brown-eyed women.

Thankfully, by eleven o'clock the goods had all been sold and the tables emptied. Rosie had been put in charge of the children, and she seemed to have had the best time helping to replenish the tables since she wasn't yet very good at making change. She had laughed and talked with everyone, and Emma had occasionally noted her showing off her engagement ring to some eager, would-be suitor.

Once the tables were wiped down and the money handed over to Reverend Bright, the ladies rejoined their families and enjoyed the day of festivities. Emma found her stepmother and father, while Rob claimed Rosie and headed off to where tables of food had been set up for the citywide picnic.

"Everyone was certainly enthusiastic about the goodies," Lucille declared as they made their way to the food. "Some of those fellas acted like they'd been denied sweets all their lives and were making up for lost time."

Emma's father looped his arm through Lucille's. "Seemed to me they were more interested in the pretty girls waiting on them."

"I had several proposals and dozens of invitations to dance and watch fireworks," Emma admitted. Of course, the entire time she couldn't help but think of Colton and wonder how he was doing in Dallas. She worried that his brothers would try to convince him that he'd made a big mistake and demand he come back to Cheyenne to force her to give him her share of the UP money.

But she had the utmost confidence that Colton would tell them to mind their own business. Seeing him leave had served to make her all the more certain of his intentions toward her. She could only believe that God was the one responsible for eliminating her fears where Colton was concerned. God and Rosie. Rosie spoke of her brother in a most positive way, assuring Emma that he was being completely honest now. That he really did love Emma. Rosie's nightly reflections on Colton brought to mind Tommy's shared stories as well. Both had spoken of Colton in high regard and had always added their concerns that he was a lonely man.

"Father used to tell him that a wife and family would only serve to divide his attention, though having an heir to train up was equally important, and a man in his position needed to learn to handle both." This had come from Tommy, but Rosie had said something equally focused.

"Father said families were a bother and told Colton to think a long time before getting involved with a woman. He even used to say that Colton should let him pick the woman—someone not too fussy or fancy, someone who could take orders." The latter had made Emma smile. Colton knew she wasn't very good at that, and yet he still wanted her.

After the picnic lunch, they watched a couple of the firemen races. It was nearly three when Emma suggested her father and stepmother adjourn to her house, where they could rest until evening when the celebration would include more food, a dance, and fireworks.

"Thanks for letting us stay the night with you," her father said, putting his arm around Emma as they made their way up the walk to the house. "We're getting kind of old to make the trip here, spend the day partying, and then drive back to the ranch."

"That's for sure," Lucille said, rubbing her shoulders. "Sometimes I think good times are almost more work than regular days on the ranch."

Emma paused on the front porch. "You make a good point. In my wilder days, I'm sure I expended more energy racing around to have a good time than just staying on the ranch and performing chores." She frowned as memories came to mind. "I wish someone could have convinced me of the truth back then."

"What do you mean?" her father asked.

Emma smiled, but inside her heart was burdened. "I guess I mean that I wish I could have appreciated what I had. I regret the time I lost with you and Mama. I wish I had known how important that time would be . . . how short."

"That's often the way it goes," Lucille replied. "I didn't know my son's life would end so soon, nor my husband's. Just as your father didn't know that your mother would die so unexpectedly. None of us knows the number of our days. That's why we need to cherish each and every one of them. Treat each other well and show love at every opportunity."

"I can certainly see that now." Emma leaned against the brick column. "I have so many regrets."

"I'll let you two have some time alone. Seems you've been wanting to speak to your father for a while now," Lucille said, heading to the front door. "I'll just go rest."

Emma gave her a nod, grateful that her stepmother always seemed to understand her needs. She had told Lucille of her desire to have a long talk with her father when they'd gone out to help with the roundup. There simply hadn't been a good time.

Once Lucille was gone, Emma motioned her father to take a seat. "Do you mind delaying your nap a bit?"

He shook his head and took the seat closest to her. "Not a bit. What's on your mind?"

"Mama. I miss her so much. I have such regrets for how I treated her and the pain I caused her. Caused you both. The other day, Mr. Vogel said he and the other lawmen in town used to joke about what antics I might try next. Sounds like some even bet on my foolishness."

Her father smiled. "I had heard that. Of course, you were just a child."

"Was I still a child at eighteen when I left town to go live with Clara? Because I was still acting as one."

"You were a handful, that's for sure. I'm not saying you shouldn't be sorry for any bad behavior in the past, but you certainly can't live a productive life in regret. What purpose would that serve? You've grown up. You've seen the error of your ways and changed."

"But it took nearly being killed at my own wedding to do so. And, Papa, that was just a few months back."

"Half a year, or nearly so. The important thing is that you realized that you weren't getting anywhere and changed your route. Your ma would be proud of you, Emma. You've put the Lord first, and that's all she ever wanted for you and your brother and sister."

"I know that was important to her. If only I could have given that to her before she passed away. I just hate to think of her being sad or living with regret because of me. Maybe even wishing I'd never been born."

"Your ma never felt that way. I can guarantee you that much."

Emma sank onto the porch at his feet. "I want to live a better life and do what is pleasing to God and to you. I know if I please you and God, then maybe Mama will be happy too."

He put his hand on her shoulder. "Emma, no matter your behavior, you were always loved. Your ma and I were blessed to have you as a daughter. Sure, there were some times when you were a little difficult, but it never stopped us from loving you. Seek to please God. That's all that really matters. But just remember, it won't guarantee an easy life. If anything, the devil will fight you all the harder and try to steal your attention and loyalty."

Emma knew he was right. She reached up and grasped his hand. "I know, and it terrifies me."

"Now, you don't need to go being afraid of old Nick. He has no power over you that you don't give him. When you belong to the Lord, He'll help you to flee the devil. The Bible tells us that God didn't give us a spirit of fear."

"But of power and of love and of a sound mind," Emma murmured. "I remember that Bible verse from Second Timothy, one."

"Exactly so. It was a favorite of your mother's when we first came to live in Cheyenne. She was so afraid."

"I remember some of those times." Emma looked up at her father. He seemed to be looking past her at nothing in particular.

"She tried to hide it. She didn't want you children to know because she didn't want you to be afraid like she was. She feared Indian attacks. She'd experienced such things when she was young, and it worried her that you'd go through that as well. Remember how nervous she was when we heard about Custer being killed by the Sioux?"

"I do remember. But everyone was afraid. We had no idea of what might come our way or where those Indians might show up next. I remember you and Mama told us where to hide if there was trouble, and you made that secret room up in the attic."

"I did. I figured better safe than sorry. Still, the best thing we did was pray."

"I remember. I wasn't walking with the Lord, and I wished I could feel close to Him. But I figured that He'd given up on me. I was fifteen and should have known better than to act the way I did."

"I recall you weren't so critical of prayer time during those days," her father said, giving a bit of a laugh. "Sometimes God has to let things go the way they do in order to get our attention."

"Well, He's got mine now. Colton's too. I'm so glad he changed his mind toward God."

"He's a good man, Emma. Smart too. Just like you. I figure you two would work well together."

Emma pulled back a bit. "What do you mean, Papa?"

"I think you know. The man is in love with you, and I think your feelings for him run in the same direction."

She heaved a sigh. "They do. I never expected it."

"Folks seldom expect love." He chuckled. "I sure never figured to fall in love with a shy, pigtailed preacher's daughter, but I'm mighty glad I did. When I lost her, the emptiness of our house liked to swallow me whole. Lucille was a healing balm to me. I know she'd tell you I did the same for her after she lost Frank. God just has a way of puttin' folks together at the right time."

Emma leaned her head on her father's knee. "He does."

"I've never been to a dance," Rosie said as she and Rob took a moment to themselves. "I'm glad you taught me how to two-step. I'm not very good at it, but it was fun to try."

"I was never all that interested in dancing. Seemed like most of the girls I knew were excited for it, though, and so I let my ma show me how."

"Well, we don't ever have to dance again if you don't want to."

"Tomorrow night is the firemen's ball, and it's fancy dress.

I heard that you have a mighty pretty dress all ready for the affair. I can't let that go to waste."

Rosie shook her head and walked a few steps to distance herself even more from the others. "I'm afraid of that dance. I'm not very good at waltzing. You know that."

Rob came up behind her and pulled her back against him, wrapping her in his embrace. "I don't care if we dance or don't. I've never been in love like this. You are all I've ever wanted in a wife, and I've planned to marry me a gal since I was a little fella. I'm not exactly sure why, but I always knew I wanted to marry and have a family."

"I didn't figure I could have that, and it was so lonely. It wasn't until Emma came that I had a chance to do much of anything. I thank God for Emma."

"I do too," Rob whispered again in her ear before giving her a quick kiss on the cheek.

Rosie had never known such happiness or excitement for the future. There had been so many bleak moments in her life when she had asked God why she was even alive. Why had He bothered to bring her back to life if she was only going to be a burden to everyone around her?

She turned to face Rob. "I didn't think anyone would love me. My own family only tolerated me. They sure didn't want to spend much time with me. We've only known each other a short time, Rob. Are you sure you want to spend the rest of your life with me?"

He surprised her by roaring with laughter. Rosie was glad they were standing away from everyone else. With the music playing again, no one seemed to have heard. If they had, people might wonder what in the world she'd said to make him laugh so much. It would be embarrassing to admit what she had asked him. Of course, Emma said a person didn't have to tell everything just because someone demanded an answer. How was it she told Rosie to answer when people pried? Oh yes, she remembered. *"That is a private matter."*

She realized just then that Rob hadn't answered her question. Tilting her head, she fixed him with a look. "Well?"

He grew serious. "I am very sure, Rosie. I know I'm just twenty years old, and some folks might think that's too young for a man to know his mind, but like I said, I've been planning to marry since I was five. I used to talk to my ma about it. You can ask her if you don't believe me."

"Why wouldn't I believe you? You've always been good to tell me the truth."

"And I always will, Rosie." He touched her cheek. "I won't ever lie to you, even when the truth is hard. I promise."

She smiled and nodded. "I promise you the same thing."

"Don't ever doubt my love for you."

"I don't doubt it. I mean, not really, but I know I'm not like everyone else. I might embarrass you."

He pulled her close and kissed the top of her head. "I doubt that, but I might embarrass you. You can never tell."

"I would never be embarrassed by you." She paused for a moment. "Well, maybe if you were teasing me in front of a bunch of people. Sometimes that scares me."

"Then I never will. Rosie, I don't care what anyone else thinks about you, although if they say anything bad, they might get a fist in their face. You're perfect for me, and I like to think I'm perfect for you. There's a lot we have yet to learn, but we've got time."

Rosie knew he was right. She'd already learned so much, and who knew what else she might be able to do? No matter what, she had promised God she would always seek His help when she felt particularly unable to meet the demands of the people around her.

The dance music ended, and partners were being exchanged for the next dance. Rosie glanced back up at Rob.

He was smiling again. He really did love her, and he was always so patient with her when teaching her things.

We're going to have a good life together. I just know we will. There might be hardships at times, but we're going to work through it, and God will show us what to do.

"What's going through that pretty head of yours now?" Rob asked. "You look like you're plotting something."

Rosie laughed. "I'm not plotting at all, just thinking about how happy I am and how happy we're going to be once we're married."

"I don't have to wait until then. I'm already the happiest man in Cheyenne."

Colton was already tired of traveling, and yet he was still at least two days' train ride from home. It seemed that the journey was taking forever. The darkness of western Kansas made the trip seem never-ending. He imagined that Emma and her family were celebrating in grand style at the Firemen's Tournament. He'd heard at the Bible study that Cheyenne would spare no expense, and that it required two days of celebration just to fit in all the events. How he wished he could be there instead of on this train. Not to share in the festivities, but because he longed for Emma's company. The idea of the town filling with hundreds of eager firemen did not exactly comfort him. Between the influx of firefighters and cowboys, the already high number of single men would no doubt leave the single ladies with more attention than they could manage. Still, there was nothing to be done about it. Had it taken less time to arrange for the sale of the house, he might have already been home and able to stake his claim.

But did he really have a claim to Emma? She had promised to wait, but did she take it as seriously as he did?

Colton tipped his hat down over his eyes, hoping to sleep. There had been no available berths in the sleeper car, so he would have to attempt to sleep sitting up. When they reached Denver in the morning, he had a meeting to attend with several men who hoped to interest him in investing in a new method of food processing and packaging. It appeared to have merit. If food could be preserved for longer periods of time, it was to everyone's benefit. It would delay him another day, but he'd promised Emma he'd give her good investment ideas, and this one looked promising.

The rhythmic rocking soon lulled Colton to sleep and filled his dreams with images of Emma. He always seemed to find himself taken back to her wedding. He had been helpless to keep her or Tommy safe. Watching his little brother take a bullet to the head had been the most horrific thing he'd ever experienced. That was, until he saw that Emma had been hit as well. Knowing he might well lose them both was more than he could bear.

He rallied himself briefly to clear those images from his mind. Falling back asleep, Colton tried to refocus his thoughts on better times—times when he and Emma had happily shared each other's company. How he hated the separation. Hated knowing that she was still struggling to really believe he loved her. His dreams once again turned darker, and he saw Emma waving good-bye as she boarded a train. He ran after her, but she disappeared into the mist that seemed to swallow up everything. He woke with a start, surprised to find it was daylight outside.

He pulled out his pocket watch and checked the time. They'd be in Denver in a very short time. He'd check into a hotel and clean up a bit, maybe even have some breakfast before his meeting. He wondered how long the meeting would take and when the next train to Cheyenne might be.

"Next stop, Denver!" the conductor called as he made his way through the car.

Denver wasn't home, but it was that much closer.

23

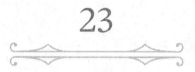

"Did you read the newspaper this morning?" Mrs. Olson asked Emma as she passed through the kitchen to go out the back door.

"I was lucky to finally finish reading yesterday's paper. I wouldn't have even taken time for that, but I wanted to double-check the schedule for the cornerstone ceremony. We should probably be ready to leave here at eight if we're to get a decent place to watch the parade. My folks already left to go to a Stock Growers Association meeting. We're going to meet near Armstrongs' Emporium. I was just on my way to tell Rosie."

"She's out with her chickens. Goodness, but I never did see a girl dote over a flock like she does."

Emma pulled on her sunbonnet. "My mother always loved her chickens. Gave some of them names even."

"But not all of them?"

"No, she said they had to earn their name." Emma chuckled at the memory. She made her way through the mudroom and outside. "We had one she called Henny Ninny because she was such a silly thing. Guess we'll see what Rosie comes up with."

Rosie had already collected the eggs, which were waiting in a basket just outside the fenced area, and now she was singing as she cleaned up the coop.

"You've been busy," Emma said, noting she was nearly done. "I came to help you so we can leave here by eight. Lucille and Papa are already gone. He had business with the Stock Growers Association, and some of the wives were also going to be there, so Lucille went with him."

"I figured you'd want to go early, so I thought to get my chores done first. I didn't even eat breakfast. I wasn't hungry, and besides, there will be plenty to eat at the celebrations."

"No doubt." Emma picked up the basket of eggs.

"Rob and I decided not to go to the ball tonight." She bent to stroke one of the hens, then made her way out of the pen. "We don't like to dance."

Emma breathed a sigh of relief. "That's wonderful. I think I'll forgo it as well. I'm still exhausted from yesterday, and I have no desire to spend the evening dancing with strangers or telling them that I'm not there to dance. Seems foolish to get all dressed up and stand in the corner all night. I'd much rather spend it at home."

"Well, if you don't mind then, I'm going to invite Rob over. His folks must attend the ball because of his dad being the chief of police. His sister is so excited about the ball because Michael Decker asked her to go with him. They're sweet on each other."

Emma nodded. "I heard. What about Daniel?"

"He's not old enough to go, so he's going to spend the evening with the Decker boys." She secured the gate to the pen. "As soon as I wash up, I'll be ready to go."

"Will Rob be coming with us?"

"No, he has to work all day. He started before dawn. There's been some bad people taking advantage of the town with all these extra people. He says it's been really busy."

"I can well imagine. Well, hurry and get cleaned up, and I'll get Mrs. Olson."

The parade and laying of the cornerstone were over by noon, and then the partying really commenced with all sorts of races and time trials for the firemen. One of the most attended was the hose race. Each team of eleven firefighters started with their apparatus and hose and were to race some four hundred yards to couple to the hydrant and actually draw water. There were all sorts of rules as to the size of cart they could use, the length of hose, and other details. The timed test was cheered on by groups of people supporting their favorite team. The men from Laramie seemed to do especially well. It was all great fun, but Emma could also see how important it was for the men to be able to manage the job. This would be critical during a fire, and mistakes would only slow them down.

After that were the hook and ladder races, dry and wet hose races, and a variety of other games that showed off the firemen's abilities. Emma couldn't help but wonder how any of the men would have the energy for dancing later that night.

Emma wearied of the crowds and party atmosphere. She was glad that everyone was having so much fun, but without Colton there to celebrate with her, it seemed to lack any real interest for her. She continued to think about him throughout the day and wondered how he was . . . where he was.

"Are you having a good time?" Rob asked as he caught up to them on the street.

"It's so noisy," Rosie replied, "and no fun without you."

He laughed and told her he was looking forward to seeing her later. "Do you want me to take you out to eat for supper? I heard the Normandy is offering wonderful selections. A bunch of the fellas were talking about going there."

"No, Mrs. Olson said she's laying out a feast for us all

our own. Just come on over when you get off work." Rosie glanced back at Emma. "That's all right, isn't it?"

"Of course." Emma gave the couple a smile. "We can have supper and play games or just enjoy the quiet."

"We could read a book together," Rosie said, pushing her sunbonnet back a bit. "I always love a good story."

"I'm sure we'll figure out what to do with the time," Emma's dad said. "I think going to bed early might be how I celebrate."

Emma laughed. "Like Rosie said, just come on over when you get off work, Rob. We'll hold supper until you arrive."

There was some sort of ruckus on the street ahead. Rob gave them a shrug. "Got to go do my job."

"I'm just as happy to head back to the house," Lucille said, looking to Emma's father. "What about you?"

"That would please me to no end."

Emma nodded and looked to Rosie. "Let's go home. Mrs. Olson might need some help with dinner."

"Sounds good to me. It's so hot today, anyway." Rosie took a handkerchief and dabbed it to her neck.

At home, Lucille and Papa immediately went inside to seek out something cold to drink, while Emma and Rosie went to see if Mrs. Olson needed help out in the summer kitchen.

"Everything is going just fine," she reported. "I have a large roast of beef in the oven. I started it before we left this morning and just added potatoes and carrots and lot of onions. I know your father and Rob both like onions."

Emma laughed. "They do. I'm partial to them with a roast myself."

Rosie shook her head. "I like them raw, but not all cooked. They get all soggy and feel funny in my mouth."

Mrs. Olson stirred a pot on top of the stove. "I'm with Rosie. Never could abide a slimy vegetable."

After making sure everything was under control, Rosie

went to check on the chickens' water, and Emma went inside to the surprising coolness of the house. She pulled off her bonnet and went to the icebox for the pitcher of lemonade and saw that Mrs. Olson had smartly made two.

The drink was nice and cold, and Emma thanked God for such luxuries. She remembered times as a child when there were no such things to be had. She'd longed for shaved ice with lemon juice and sugar when they'd come to town.

"You look mighty deep in thought," her father said as he came into the kitchen.

Emma reached for the pitcher. "Are you back for more?" She nodded at the empty glass in his hand.

"You know it. I was parched."

She poured him more lemonade, then put the half-empty pitcher back in the icebox. "I was just remembering how we had nothing like this on the ranch when I was little. We'd have ice sometimes until the end of May, but after that we went without cold drinks."

"It's true. I know it will be a mess of worldly imposition and cost, but I think I'll be glad when we get electricity on the ranch. Doubt I'll live to see it, though."

Emma shrugged. "You can never tell. Folks used to say that about Cheyenne as a whole. Twenty years ago, they said we were too far from the rest of the settled world to have any modern conveniences."

"True enough. Now here we are with electricity and water running through pipes to each house."

"It's a great city that I have a feeling will only get greater. I heard them say in the cornerstone speech that the Union Pacific intends to add a thousand jobs, which could bring more than three times that many people to the area. We're definitely going to be able to reach the sixty thousand people that they say they need for the territory in order to achieve statehood."

"And they chose all their delegates on Monday for the constitutional convention in September," her father added. "I'd say we'll get the federal government to recognize us as a state soon enough."

"I suppose the governing officials are thinking they have Montana, Washington, and North and South Dakota coming in this year, and they don't need to add any other states. But I figured since we were just next door to other states, they'd include us." Emma shrugged. "I guess they'll get around to us when it's time."

"All things come in God's timing and no one else's," her father said, smiling. "That includes finding the right mate."

"I just want to make sure it's God's choice. I didn't choose so well for myself the first time around."

"Colton's completely different from his brother, Em. I never felt right about you marrying Tommy Benton, but everything is different with Colton."

"Maybe the fact that you approve of him should be proof enough for me. I know you're a very wise man, Papa."

"Well, whether I am or not, I think you'd best be making up your mind about that fella. He's soon going to be back here, and I think it's very possible he'll come with a proposal and maybe even a ring."

Emma didn't want to pretend she didn't think the same thing. "I think you're right." She chuckled. "Maybe I will be married before Wyoming becomes a state."

"I'm glad you decided to come back to the ranch with us," Lucille said as Rosie and Emma rode alongside the wagon Friday morning.

"Rosie wanted a good long ride to prove she could handle herself, and I couldn't think of a better way for her than to take one out here to the ranch. And with you and Papa along, I knew we'd be safer than coming out alone. I know it bothers Colton, and probably Rob as well, when we make trips out here without a man along."

"We can all ride back in on Sunday for church."

"Gary said he'd manage the chickens and yard. I think he's sweet on Mrs. Olson," Emma said, glancing at Rosie. "Don't you think so?"

"I do. I think he likes her cooking a lot."

They laughed at this, but Emma couldn't help but wonder if there might be more than just Rosie's wedding in the near future. Papa thought her own would be held, but Emma seriously wondered about the wisdom of marrying twice in the same year. A part of her figured it might be wise to wait a full year. Another part declared it silly to wait when one knew what their heart truly desired.

It had been a bit overwhelming to come to the conclusion that she wanted Colton for her husband. The process of going from widowhood, to seeing how foolish her life had been, to learning what truly mattered and then realizing the potential of true love . . . well, it was an awful lot to contemplate.

They took the narrow wagon road that led to the house. As it came into view, Emma couldn't help but remember all the years she had dreaded coming home. Now it was a welcome sight. How she wished she could have appreciated it back then.

When they came to a stop, a couple of cowboys came out to manage the horses and wagon. Emma handed over her hired mount and dusted off her split skirt. Rosie was quite excited. She threw her leg over, kicked out of the other stirrup, and slid down the side of her horse.

"That was wonderful. I love riding horses." She pulled off her wide-brimmed hat. "And I love this new hat."

Emma laughed. "They do keep the sun from burning your face." She removed her own hat and let the breeze cool her face.

"Did Rob teach you about caring for the horses after a long ride?" Papa asked.

"He did. Do you want me to go take care of Rufus?" Rosie asked, nodding toward her rented mount.

Emma's father shook his head. "Nah, today we'll let the boys do the work. I know you gals have plans for talking about the wedding. I've got plenty of work to keep me busy, so you ladies have fun." He helped Lucille from the wagon and then tipped his hat. "I'll see you for lunch."

Emma smiled. "He was always good about getting out from under foot when Mama had womanly things to discuss."

"I think most men are good at that," Lucille said, dusting off her clothes. "Weddings are one of those things they'd just as soon leave to us to figure out. They do good just to show up on time for the actual event."

They walked toward the house, but then Lucille stopped and looked at them quite seriously. "Something occurs to me. Rosie's soon to be married, and perhaps you will as well, Emma."

"Everyone seems eager to marry me off." Emma knew, however, there was no sense in denying it.

"Why not?" Rosie asked. "Colton's in love with you. I know he wants to marry you soon."

Lucille continued on. "Neither one of you have a mother to talk to you about getting married, and . . . well, the expectations of a wife."

"What expectations?" Rosie asked.

Lucille reached out and patted her arm. "Exactly. You know, I feel bad that I didn't think of this until now. I'd like to fill in for your mothers, if you'll allow me to. I suppose your sister might have talked to you before your wedding, Emma, but I might have something new to add."

"Clara tried to talk to me about wedded bliss and wifely duties, but I wouldn't have any of it," Emma admitted. "I wasn't listening to anyone, as you might recall. So I, for one, would love to receive your advice."

Rosie looked at Lucille and smiled. "I would love for you to be my mother. Can I call you Mama since I never really had my own mother?"

Emma could see her request touched Lucille. Tears formed in the older woman's eyes.

"I'd be honored if you called me Mama. However, I'm certain Marybeth Vogel will want you to call her Mama as well. Why don't you call me Mama Johnson, and that way you can still call her Mama."

"I'd like that a lot, Mama Johnson." Rosie gave her a hug.

"Can I call you Ma?" Emma asked, feeling a connection with Lucille that hadn't been there before. "I always called my mother mama or mother, so Ma would be something completely different and just for you."

Lucille looked at her with such a tender expression that Emma was the one to tear up. "I know how much you loved your mother. I loved her so dearly, and she'll always be an important part of our lives. I think she would like it if you called me Ma. I know I would." She reached out and drew both girls into her arms. "Not long ago I lost a son, but just look. God has given me daughters to fill that void."

Colton stood in front of Emma's house, wondering where in the world they might be. He had knocked and knocked, but nobody answered. He hadn't told them when to expect him back, so he couldn't fault them for not planning on welcoming him home. He had confided in Emma that his trip would probably take him at least a month, and arriving back four days shy of that time, he had intended to surprise them. But the surprise was his. No one was home. Where could they have gone?

He left his suitcase and satchel on the porch and walked around to the back. He knocked at Gary's apartment, but again no one answered. Apparently, he'd gone out as well. Colton frowned and made his way around the back of the house.

"Who goes there?" a deep male voice questioned. Rob Vogel came around the corner, shoulders squared, looking ready to spring.

"It's me, Colton Benton. Are you on guard duty?"

"I saw someone sneaking around to the back of the house and figured it couldn't be for any good reason." Rob laughed and stuck out his hand. "Good to have you back, Colton."

"Good to be back—I think. Where is everybody?"

"The girls went out to the ranch to spend a couple of nights. Rosie wanted help planning the wedding."

"I wish they wouldn't ride out there alone. Or wait, did Gary go with them?"

"No, I believe he has gone to town to buy a new shirt. He asked Mrs. Olson to dinner and then worried he wouldn't look good enough."

Colton chuckled. "I wondered if he would get around to asking her out."

"He finally did. I think if he hadn't, she might have done the deed herself."

"She's none too shy about speaking her mind, so you're probably right." Colton felt a sense of disappointment as the truth of the situation settled over him. "Do you know when the girls plan to get back?"

"They'll ride into town in the morning with Mr. and Mrs.

Johnson. It's Sunday, you know. Everyone will be headed to church."

Colton realized there was nothing he could do but wait for morning. It would be foolish to ride all the way out to the Johnsons' when he wouldn't arrive before dark. He had thought of nothing but Emma the entire trip home, and now he would have to wait once again to see her.

"Well, I suppose I'll just head back to the boardinghouse and settle in for the evening."

"I have a better idea. Since we're going to be family and probably spend a great deal of our time together, why don't you and I go to dinner and get to know each other better?"

"What do you mean that we'll probably spend a great deal of our time together? You newlyweds won't want me around."

"It won't be a matter of what I want. Rosie is very close to Emma, and I know she'll be a part of our daily life. And I figure since you're not only Rosie's brother but will no doubt soon be Emma's husband, you'll be around as well."

"I won't deny that I mean to marry her. I'm planning to propose right away, in fact. I brought one of my mother's rings to offer incentive to say yes."

"She'll say yes. I'm absolutely certain. Now come on, what about going to supper with me? Afterward, if you want, there are some horse races planned, oh, and a prize fight if you like that sort of thing."

"I don't care for races and despise fights."

"See there, we already have that in common. I've had to intercede in way too many fights to enjoy watching men beat each other to a pulp. And the only time I like racing a horse is when I'm on his back. Supper, then?"

Colton smiled. "Sounds good. Let's go."

24

Emma, I'm sorry we can't ride back with you." Lucille had just gotten word that Charlotte was sick, and she wanted to go tend to her. "Please give the pastor our regards."

"We will, and thanks for the loan of Jacob to accompany us back to Cheyenne. I know that will make you both rest easier."

"Rob will be happy too," Rosie said, securing her hat. "He hates it when we come out here alone."

"Well, even with there being more and more people moving into the territory, we're still having the occasional problem. I think it makes all of us feel better to know you'll have a little extra help in case of trouble."

Emma kissed her stepmother's cheek. "Well, try not to worry about us, Ma. And please tell Charlotte that I hope she feels better soon."

"I will, and I hope to see you both real soon."

"Papa, you married yourself a good woman." Emma kissed his cheek, then allowed him to help her into the saddle.

Rosie had already bid them both good-bye and was holding Rufus under control. She patted his neck to calm him. "He's more than ready to go," she said, laughing. "I wish we could let him run, but I'm not good at gallops just yet."

"No galloping in this heat," Emma's father said, shaking a finger. "Be kind to your mount."

"Yes, sir!" Rosie turned the horse toward the drive as Emma came abreast of them on her horse. "Rob has told me that more than once. He said you never know when they might save your life."

"I agree. You all be careful."

"We will, Papa." Emma adjusted her hat, then gave a wave as she moved her horse out.

Rufus matched Emma's mount, and the girls took the lead with Jacob following behind. Emma remembered meeting the young cowboy the year before. He seemed rather shy, and when she tried to engage him in conversation, he replied with simple yes and no answers. Now he was far more capable of carrying on a conversation without stumbling all over his words.

It was a beautiful morning, although it was already getting hot. There wasn't a cloud in the sky, and all around them the ground showed signs of drought. Ma had told her they were doing something called dry farming and having pretty good luck with it. They were anticipating putting up a good-sized crop of hay in the next couple of weeks. Since the terrible winter of '86–87, the ranchers who continued raising livestock had learned that they were also going to have to maintain winter feed, just in case. They were also learning various techniques to grow it themselves due to the high cost of bringing it in. Emma was very impressed with what her father and stepmother had already accomplished. They, along with Lucille's daughter Charlotte and her husband, had formed a tight working association, and together they were making all sorts of improvements to increase the herds and benefit the ranch.

They'd been riding about half an hour when Rosie spoke up. "I just can't get over how the land stretches out forever. I love it all." Rosie pointed. "Look, there are a couple of riders coming on the road."

They were just specks on the horizon. "You've got good eyes, Rosie." Emma put her hand to the edge of her hat to shade the sun a bit more. She hadn't even caught sight of the motion. "I'll have to be more vigilant."

Jacob pulled up and around them. "Hang back, I'll see who it is. Could be trouble, looks like they're picking up speed."

Emma stiffened a bit in the saddle. She had her rifle sheathed and within easy grasp. She thought of pulling it and placing the weapon across her lap, but at the same time she didn't want to appear aggressive. But what if she needed to appear aggressive? What if the two riders were up to no good?

Rosie's excitement put her mind at ease, however, before she had to decide. "It's Rob and Colton!" She urged the horse forward, passing Jacob to trot toward the two men.

"Jacob, it looks like you won't have to ride all the way to town, after all." Emma came up alongside him and smiled at the young man. "That's Rosie's brother on the right and her fiancé on the left."

They slowed their horses to a stop. Jacob looked at her for a moment. "Are you sure, ma'am? I can still go with you."

Emma laughed. "Yes, I'm quite sure. Rob Vogel is one of Cheyenne's police officers and quite good at his job. We'll be just fine. Please let my father and stepmother know that we're in good hands."

"I will." He tipped his hat and headed back to the ranch.

Emma couldn't deny her own excitement at the vision of Colton riding toward her. She urged the horse forward, ignoring her father's opinions on galloping. Rosie was just reaching the two men, and Emma could hear her excited greetings as she drew closer.

"Colton, I'm so glad you're back! Rob, what a surprise!"

She looked over her shoulder as Emma approached. Emma kept her gaze fixed on Colton. He was grinning, and so was she.

Rosie continued in her energetic way. "We were headed into town to go to church. Emma's folks were going to come with us, but Mama Johnson—she said I could call her that now—she heard that her daughter is sick and wanted to go help her. They decided to send Jacob with us so you wouldn't worry."

"That was good of them," Rob replied before bringing his mount to a stop not far from Rosie. "Did you enjoy your long ride?"

"I did. It was so much fun. I feel like I could do this for days and days."

Rob laughed. "I've done it for days and days driving cattle, and it's not as much fun as you might think." He turned his horse to come along side his fiancée. "But I think the company of this ride back to town will make the trip tolerable. If you don't mind, Emma, Colton, we're going to ride on up ahead." Rob didn't wait for an answer but moved out with Rosie following suit.

Colton made a circle around Emma and came up on her right side. The horses were from the same livery and seemed comfortable with each other. "I think Rob wants to sweet-talk my sister all the way to church."

Emily curiosity got the best of her. "And will you sweet-talk me all the way to church?"

"Would you like me to?"

She laughed and started the horse walking. Seeing Colton again assured her that she really had forgiven him and let the past go. Now all she wanted was to move forward toward their future.

"I was saddened to return and not find you home," he told her as the horses matched paces.

"I wish you would have telegraphed to let us know you were coming. I would have not only stayed home, but we would have planned a big supper with all your favorites."

He looked at her oddly. "And how would you know what all my favorites are?"

"I've paid attention. You're particular to pork chops, creamed peas, and pecan pie. Throw in some hot coffee and dinner rolls with lots of butter and you are happy as a man can be."

Colton roared with laughter, causing Rob and Rosie to glance back from their place ahead. They quickly lost interest, however, and resumed their focus on each other.

Emma slowed her mount a bit to let the space between couples grow a little longer. Colton slowed his horse as well. For a few minutes, neither said anything. Emma couldn't figure out how to start a conversation about the two of them. She wanted to tell him how much she'd missed him—that absence did indeed make her heart grow fonder. But what if absence had made him rethink his affection for her? What if she had missed the chance to accept Colton's love? The very thought made her frown.

"Is something wrong?" Colton asked.

She turned to look at him, shaking her head. "No. Why do you ask?"

"You looked upset . . . worried. I thought maybe something happened while I was gone, and you didn't want to tell me about it."

"No. That is to say . . . well, yes, something has happened. And I do want to tell you about it. I guess I was just a little worried as to how to go about it." She shook her head. It wasn't like her not to speak her mind, but having the opportunity to explain her heart, Emma felt suddenly shy.

"I always think it's best to just say what's on your mind. Lay your cards on the table, so to speak."

She glanced up and met his gaze. "I've always thought that as well."

He kept looking at her, and Emma found it impossible to look away. Still, she said nothing. She heard Rosie laugh and glanced to where the couple had stretched the distance to about one hundred yards. She felt confident that she could say what needed to be said and not be overheard if she chose.

"I . . . I've been thinking a lot about my life and . . . well, I . . ." She stopped and pulled back on the horse's reins. Colton stopped as well and waited for Emma to continue. She swallowed the lump in her throat. "I want to marry you."

He looked at her blankly for a moment. Emma felt her heart lurch. Had he changed his mind? Had she just created a most embarrassing situation?

She shook her head. "I suppose our time apart changed your mind. Your brothers probably talked to you and decided that since I knew about their plan that you shouldn't go through with it. They probably fear my actions against them because of knowing the truth. Or maybe they found another way to get what they wanted." She looked away, afraid of what she might see in Colton's eyes. "I know that when I was in Texas, I wasn't the most reliable person. I was wild and seldom serious. I didn't want to dwell on the responsibilities of life. I can't blame them for not thinking I'd make you a good wife, based on the person that I was. And maybe your brothers think it embarrassing that I should want to marry you so soon after Tommy's death, but as I told you, Tommy was more of a playmate than a husband. Neither of us were very serious about anything, as you know full well." She paused, but still wouldn't look at him. "I do wish you'd say something."

"I would if you'd be quiet long enough."

He sounded amused, and Emma looked up to find him smiling. "I was rambling a bit, wasn't I?"

"Just a bit." He chuckled. "You didn't need to say anything past the statement that you wanted to marry me. I feel like I've been waiting a lifetime to hear it. You've made me quite happy, Emma. I very much want to marry you."

She gave a long sigh. "I was worried that I'd ruined my chances with you." The horses were growing restless in the heat, and Emma gave the gelding a quick stroke on the neck. "We should keep moving."

Colton nodded and once again kept stride with her as she moved out. Emma wished they'd had a better place to discuss the future. She thought about waiting until they got home but knew that would never do. She was far too excited to hear what he had to say. She wanted to make plans for their future and waiting seemed like agony.

"I'm glad you haven't changed your mind about me," Emma began. "I'm still quite surprised that all of this has happened. I thought for the longest time that you didn't even like me, but knowing that you had such strong feelings for me, it all makes sense now. Every time you moved away from me or refused to engage me in casual talk—that time in the garden when we ran across each other, and you all but bolted for the house."

Colton laughed. "I remember that day well. I came around the corner and ran right into you. I took hold of you to steady you and keep you from falling backward, and I didn't want to let go. It scared me pretty bad."

It was her turn to laugh. "I thought the look on your face was one of disgust. Like you had touched something most undesirable."

"Not at all." He looked at her, and the passion was once again in his eyes. "I never wanted more to hold a woman . . . to kiss you."

"I've never had the feelings that I have for you," Emma admitted. "It's all so strange. When I combine that with all the new feelings I have for God, it's almost more than I can bear. Everything has changed in my heart and mind."

"I know what you mean regarding God. I never thought I'd think the way I do, but I can't help but remember my mother's faith, and now I finally understand. She had lived all her life with the conveniences money could buy. She had beautiful things and didn't have to do much for herself, but her faith was more important than all of that. A relationship with God mattered to her more than fine jewels. I put my faith in money, as my father had done, yet it always seemed so insignificant compared to her faith in God. Now I realize the truth of it. My trust was falsely planted."

Emma nodded. "As was mine."

"So now we are both on better ground," he said, reaching out his hand to her.

Emma clasped his fingers. "I love God dearly, and because of loving Him, I believe it has allowed me to love you more than I ever thought possible."

"I love you, Emma. I've loved you for so very long, but now that love is all the sweeter because of making my heart right with God." He squeezed her fingers. "Marry me?"

She nodded most enthusiastically. "Yes. I will happily marry you."

That day, after attending church and announcing their engagement, Emma and Colton settled onto the porch settee and enjoyed the coolness of the evening. Colton had been waiting for a special moment to give Emma his mother's ring, and now seemed perfect.

He slid from the settee and knelt before her with ring in hand. Emma's eyes were wide in wonder as he held up the large emerald ring.

"This belonged to my mother. It was one of five special rings she had made. One to represent each of her children. I think Tommy's was in with the jewelry he gave you. Anyway, she wore those rings with great pride and used to tell me that when she wore them, she prayed special prayers for the mate they would one day marry. She even believed there might be someone for Rose. If Rosie hasn't already shown you her ring, you should ask her about it. She loves that our mother thought of her that way. But this ring she wore for me and prayed for you—for us. I want to offer it to you now as a pledge of my love and faithfulness. Will you accept it?"

"Oh, Colton, I would love to." She held out her hand.

He slipped the ring onto her left hand. "Wear it here until I replace it with gold on our wedding day."

"Look." She held up her hand. "It fits as if it were made for me."

"It was," he replied. "Designed with love, just for you." He stood and pulled her to her feet and into his arms.

He kissed her tenderly, then stood back. "Just promise me that we don't have to wait too long for our wedding."

"I don't see why we should."

"Maybe we could even have a double wedding with Rosie and Rob?"

Emma gave a light laugh. "Double weddings run in my family. My father and Lucille married the same place and time as Lucille's daughter, Charlotte, wed Micah Hamilton."

"Do you think we could talk Rosie and Rob into it?"

"Why ask me? Let's go inside and see what they have to say about it."

Colton didn't even wait for Emma but bolted to the screen door. "Rosie!"

25

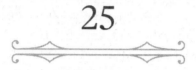

The Benton-Vogel weddings were held after church on the first of September. Rosie and Emma both wore new gowns of pale blue silk and looked very nearly like twins with their dark brown hair carefully pinned up in identical styles.

Colton had been anxious to get to this day and speak his vows. The moment he saw Emma walking down the aisle, he breathed a sigh of relief. This was really happening. He was really going to marry the woman of his dreams. Still, he couldn't help but remember his younger brother's wedding. The tragic outcome had certainly allowed for this day to be possible, but he missed Tommy. Missed his laughter and excitement. They had completely underestimated the young man, just as Emma had suggested. While in Dallas, Colton had managed to speak to the man who had advised Tommy on several investments. Listening to the man talk about his brother, Colton realized that they hadn't known who Tommy really was, nor what he was capable of doing. Just as they hadn't believed Rosie was able to be anything more than a child.

Now Rosie stood at the altar, a young woman talented in

so many ways. When he thought of how they'd hidden her away as if ashamed of her, it grieved Colton. What might she have accomplished if someone had believed in her as a child? Of course, their father would have curtailed her education even if she hadn't endured the circumstances of her birth. He felt women were only good for bearing children to give a man his much-needed heirs.

The ceremony itself took very little time. Colton slipped a beautifully etched gold band onto Emma's finger while Rob did likewise with Rosie. The pastor pronounced the couples married and encouraged the grooms to kiss their brides. Colton didn't need further urging. He pulled Emma into his arms and gave her a kiss that he hoped promised her everything his words had failed to say.

When he pulled back, he felt Emma stiffen. She turned to glance down the aisle and then back at him. Her expression was one of concern.

"There's no one coming to hurt us," Colton whispered. "The past is gone."

She glanced sidewise again and then nodded. He heard her sigh. Colton took hold of her hand and gave it a squeeze.

"I'm so happy you shared this day with us," Rosie said, coming over to give them both a hug. "Now we're double sisters, Emma."

"That we are, Rosie." Emma hugged her, and then Colton did likewise.

Rob stepped up and gave Emma a hug. "Congratulations."

"And likewise to you, Rob," Emma replied.

Rob turned to Colton and stuck out his hand. "Now we're truly family."

"Then give me a hug." Colton grabbed the younger man and embraced him. "Take good care of my sister."

"I promise you, I will. She's the love of my life." Rob stepped back and took hold of Rosie. "Nothing ever felt quite right before she came to Cheyenne. Now I feel like all the missing pieces are in place."

Colton took hold of Emma again. "As do I. It took forever to find her, but now that I have, I don't intend on ever letting her go."

Many of the congregants came forward to congratulate the couples before Edward Vogel reminded them that there was to be a lawn luncheon and reception at their place. It was nearly one thirty before everyone sat to enjoy a meal together.

Not everyone from church came to the Vogels', but there were still quite a few people who wanted to join in the festivities. Colton found the men of his Bible study and their wives were among those who gathered, as well as the folks from his boardinghouse. A lot of the people who came for the luncheon, however, were friends of Emma's and her family. From here and there he heard stories about Emma's antics when she was younger, but none of the stories were told in anger or hurt. Even Emma was able to laugh with most of the reminiscent partygoers.

By three o'clock, the party was still going strong, but Colton managed to get Emma away from the crowd. They made their way across the street to Emma's house. Colton carried her across the threshold.

"Traditions have never been all that important to me," Colton said, setting her down, "and I know they really aren't that important to you, but I will only ever marry this one time, so I figured why not uphold some of the customs."

Emma laughed. "I think traditions are becoming more important to me. Some things are just special." She put her arms around him and placed her head against his chest.

"I know the party is still going on, but I wanted to show you something important," Colton began. "Come, sit with me for a moment."

Emma straightened and met his gaze. "Something more important than holding me?"

He chuckled. "Believe me, I intend for there to be plenty of that in our days together, but I wanted to share this with you." He led her to the sofa and sat down beside her. "I didn't want there to be any misunderstandings or confusion about our financial situation." He pulled some folded papers from his pocket. "I actually meant to come earlier today and talk to you about them before church, but you and Rosie told me you'd be much too busy to have me here, and supposedly it's bad luck to see the bride before the ceremony."

Emma shook her head. "I never said that. I don't believe in luck anymore—bad or good. God directs my steps and future."

"I agree." He handed Emma the papers. "The first one is my agreement that everything you brought into the marriage will remain yours to do with as you please. The second is a revision of my will leaving everything I own to you upon my death. Keep them in a safe place for the future."

"I'm truly touched that you would concern yourself with such matters on our wedding day." Emma glanced at the papers momentarily, then folded them up. "I have something of my own that I wanted to show you before we give it to Rob and Rosie because I want it to be from both of us."

Emma went to the little desk and rolled up the top. She opened a drawer inside and pulled out an envelope.

"I had this prepared and have something to admit to you. I didn't tell you my plans because . . . well, I didn't want you or your brothers to give Rosie difficulty over it. Now I know that you wouldn't have done such a thing, but when I first decided it, you and I were rather at odds."

"What is it?" He couldn't imagine what she was talking about. Why would he give Rosie difficulty over anything?

She held the envelope up. "I want us to present this to

Rob and Rosie when no one else is around. I changed the name on that bank account you set up for the Union Pacific money. It's Rosie's money now. The stocks will also be hers, as well as all the family jewelry that I was left by Tommy."

"Emma, that's a lot of money and valuables. You don't need to do that. Tommy wanted you to have it."

"But we don't need it, and Rosie should have been made an heir. Now she'll have her own inheritance, and she certainly deserves your mother's jewelry more than I do. This can be our wedding present to them."

Colton was deeply touched that Emma would give up a fortune to his little sister. He was also ashamed that she should have to. "You are the most generous person I've ever known."

She smiled. "I still have plenty. Tommy's other investments are doing quite well. In fact, if you feel up to the task, I would just as soon have you take them over for us. I know nothing about investments and finance. I don't want to keep my accounts separate, Colton. I am your wife and proud to be so. Furthermore, I trust you completely."

He took her into his arms and held her close. "I love you more than life itself, Emma."

She raised her face to his. "And I love you, Colton Benton."

"I don't understand," Rosie said, looking to Emma. "What does this mean?"

The party was finally over, and the foursome was getting ready to head off to the train station to catch the evening passenger service east for their wedding trip abroad. Colton had managed to arrange a private car for them to travel in style.

"It means you are a very wealthy woman, Rosie," Colton replied. "Emma wanted to make sure you got your fair share of the Benton inheritance. It was important to her and Tommy, and to me."

Emma looked to Rob. "I know that you aren't an overly prideful man, Rob. I think you can see for yourself that this is my way of righting a wrong. Nothing more. Nothing less. Rosie deserves a share of her family's fortune, and I am quite well provided for." She looked at Colton and smiled.

"I'm just as shocked as Rosie," Rob said, glancing at the papers Emma had given them. "I never figured to be married to an heiress. It's going to take some getting used to."

"Well, there is one more aspect of this that Emma and I discussed." Colton looked at Emma.

"That's right. We know you two haven't had much luck finding a house and wonder if you'd like to have my house. Especially since Colton and I have our new house being built over on Ferguson."

Rob put his arm around Rosie. "What do you think?"

"I love this house. I think we should buy it with some of this money Emma gave me."

He nodded and looked to Emma and Colton. "It would be ideal with the house just across the street from my folks. That way when I work evenings or nights, Rosie will have someone close by if she needs them."

"Our place should be completed by the time we all get back from our trip abroad, so we could even arrange for your things to be moved in while we're gone." Emma noted the time. "For now, we'd best get the rest of our things and get to the train station. Our adventure is about to begin."

"I'm so happy," Rosie said, hugging her husband.

Emma laughed and did likewise with Colton. "I'm looking forward to our grand adventure and all the fun we're going to have. This time with a balance of responsibility with the good times. And hopefully, none of our pleasures will cause pain to anyone else."

"I promise you we'll see the world and dance and do whatever pleases you. I like that you are so full of life, and I want to have a good time with you."

"And I want to enjoy life with you, Colton. Like Rosie, I'm so happy. Maybe for the first time in my life."

"But certainly not the last time, if I have anything to say about it," Colton whispered in her ear.

Emma grinned and gave him a quick kiss on the lips. "I'm sure you will."

If you enjoyed *Designed with Love*,
keep reading for a sneak peek of

A MOMENT to LOVE

AVAILABLE FALL OF 2025

Prologue

The war had come to an end. After four years of conflict and bitterness between the North and the South, General Robert E. Lee had surrendered the day before to Ulysses S. Grant at a place called Appomattox Courthouse. For all his ten years, Spencer Duval could only remember the country at war, and he really had no idea of what surrender might mean for the country.

His father, Harrison Duval had been gone much of the time during the conflict, working for the Pinkerton Agency, hunting down deserters, profiteers, and other criminal type who sought to benefit from the country's condition. Spencer and his mother, meanwhile kept the home fires burning in Philadelphia while they prayed for Pa's safety as he performed his job. They prayed too for the war to stay far away from city of "Brotherly Love." Nothing was more terrifying to Spencer's mother than the thought of a war being fought in their hometown. It was frightening enough to both when the Battles of Gettysburg and Hanover had taken place just two years earlier. Now that the end of the war had been announced, Spencer could only feel a sense of victory and celebration, as most of the crowd did. His father, however, said there was still a lot to do. That gave Spencer's mother very little to celebrate. She worried that his job with the Pinkertons was even more dangerous than fighting in the war.

"It's good that this war has finally come to an end," Spencer's father said as the people around them continued to celebrate. He'd only been home a few days, and even then, it was only because the man he was hunting had been seen in town. Spencer had been intrigued by his father's stories of Eugene Astor, a bounty jumper. These were men who pretended to sign up to fight in the war only to take the bonuses offered and flee. Astor and his brothers had made a career over the last four years of robbing the government this way. Theirs was a treasonable act, and Astor's two younger brothers had already been killed, refusing to surrender when caught by the Pinkertons. Only Astor remained, and he had proven nearly impossible to locate, much less to capture.

Pa tightened his hold on Spencer's shoulder. Spencer looked up to see his father's jaw clench. It was a sure sign that he'd spotted something.

"Do you see him, Pa?"

Spencer had been instructed to not gawk around looking for the man. Not that he knew what Eugene Astor looked like. Pa had figured a man in the crowd with a boy at his side wouldn't be seen as a threat—definitely not thought of as a Pinkerton. He had explained to Spencer what they were doing and why.

The idea of being a part of his father's covert operation had excited Spencer to no end. He longed to grow up and follow in his father's footsteps. He wanted so much to be a Pinkerton and root out criminals. When his father was able to be home, Spencer had listened to his stories for hours while Pa had also worked to show Spencer tricks of the trade. Now Spencer got to see him working up close. It was the proudest day of his life.

"No, I thought I did, but it wasn't him."

A man took the podium atop the outdoor stage and began. "Friends, we have come here today to give thanks to God for putting an end to this horrific and abominable war. Let us pray."

Spencer noted most everyone bowed their head in reverence, but Pa took the opportunity to sweep the crowd. He didn't miss a thing, and Spencer tried to be just as astute. Pa always told him to look for the thing that was out of the ordinary—the person or object that didn't belong.

Every man in attendance had removed his hat, including Pa, with exception to one. That man now eased across the farthest gathering of people. He wasn't at all remarkable in appearance, but the fact that he wasn't praying with the others struck Spencer as odd. It struck his father as infinitely more. He took off, weaving his way through the audience. Spencer had his instructions for just such an occasion. He was to move closer to the stage and stay there until his father returned for him. But something in Spencer refused to be obedient. He followed his father instead.

The man who'd been moving through the back of the crowd disappeared down the alley. Pa gave pursuit, and Spencer did as well. Somewhere among the people was Aloysius Gable, another Pinkerton who was Pa's best friend. Spencer glanced around, wondering if Al had already maneuvered around to corner Eugene Astor.

The prayer was finished, and the speaker introduced someone to great applause. Spencer didn't care, however. He was struggling to keep up with his father. It dawned on him more than once that he needed to stop and return to the stage. His father had made it clear that he wasn't to follow him. It was far too dangerous. Astor hadn't been known to kill, but now that he knew his brothers were dead, there was no telling what he might be compelled to do. He just might be of a mind to seek revenge. Pa and Al even discussed the possibility that Astor would seek to shoot down some of the men speaking that day. One of the men had been among Harrison Duval's team searching for Astor's brothers. When they had been fired upon by Calvin Astor, it was this man who had claimed the death shot. He was also a war hero and slated to speak to the crowd since he was home recovering from a wound that had taken his left arm.

Pa disappeared momentarily, and Spencer strained to see where he'd gone. He was headed for the alley, and so Spencer kept moving toward it, hoping that once he cleared the mass of people, he'd once again see his father.

He broke through a group of older women who chided him for his rudeness. He tipped his cap and pressed on. There would be time to apologize later. Right now, he had to find Pa. He stepped into the alley, seeing nothing. The speech giving and applause erupting behind him made it difficult to listen for telltale signs of activity, but Spencer finally heard what sounded like bootsteps running. He sprang forward hoping he might reach his father and Al just as they caught their man.

The sound of gunfire slowed his pace only momentarily. Spencer knew his father was armed. Al, too, carried a gun. But it was a single shot he heard. No exchange. Whoever had fired had either hit his mark or was prevented from firing again.

Something came barreling around the corner. Spencer pressed himself against the brick wall and watched as a couple of stray cats yowled and a large wooly dog came bounding down the alley. The stench of trash assaulted Spencer's nose as the cats ripped through some unmentionable slop and dashed across the toes of Spencer's boots. The dog followed, not giving Spencer a second glance.

There was shouting around the next corner, and Spencer refocused on why he'd come in the first place. He crept down the alley, doing his best to be silent and invisible. The alley T'd at the end, and Spencer knew he'd have to go right or left. The voices were coming from the right, and so he figured that was where he'd find his father. He hugged the wall with his cheek flat against the brick. In complete silence, he stretched his neck just far enough to peek around the corner.

"You're done for, Astor. Give up like a man and accept your consequences." Spencer's father stood facing the man he'd been searching for throughout the war. Spencer saw the man matched the description his father had shared prior to their outing. He was medium build with brown hair combed straight back, and a scar edged the left side of his lower jaw. He was dressed as many of the politicians and businessmen who'd amassed around the stage. Three-piece brown suit with a frockcoat that hit mid-thigh. White shirt, black tie, and scuffed black boots. He also held a revolver, not so unlike the one Spencer's father held.

"We are at a stand-off, Pinkerton, but I will end that momentarily. If I'm not mistaken, you are one of the men who helped corner my brothers. Poor Calvin and Amos." He gave a tsking sound. "Cut down in their prime, and for what?"

"For lying to the government. For signing up to fight, taking the bonuses offered, and then deserting. Last count I had, you and your brothers pulled that scheme nearly two hundred times in as many towns."

Astor smiled. "And that was worthy of death? We did what we had to in order to keep our mother fed and housed. If we'd left to fight in that senseless war, she'd have been alone. What did we do that harmed anyone? What did they do that was worthy of death?"

Spencer watched his father. His gaze never left Astor. He stood completely still, gun leveled at the man's heart. Astor did likewise. Neither seemed to so much as blink.

"You broke the law and deceived the government. You weren't the only bounty jumpers, but you were the busiest."

"You can hardly fault a man for being good at what he does," Astor said with a slight shrug. "But that still isn't call to kill two young men who'd never harmed a single soul in their lives."

"They were the first to draw their guns and fire. They refused to surrender and meant to kill us."

"Out of desperation to remain alive."

"We wouldn't have shot them if they'd surrendered." Spencer noted the tone of his father's voice. He wanted an end to this matter . . . a peaceful solution. His father hated taking a life and would much rather take Astor in alive. At least he hadn't dropped to one knee. His father routinely knelt when certain he would have to fire his weapon. It was just something he had always done. The fact that he hadn't moved gave Spencer hope that maybe Astor would give up.

"No, you would have hanged them for treason."

"This is at an end, Astor. You're under arrest. Drop the gun."

For just a moment, Spencer thought the man was going to comply. Then something like icy fingers went up Spencer's spine. And everything seemed to happen at once. Pa went down on his knees as Astor's eyes narrowed.

"No." The single word sounded along with the shot that rang out.

Spencer watched his father's head lurch. The revolver fell from his hands. Without thinking, Spencer screamed and ran to him. "Pa!" He grabbed hold of his father's shoulders and pulled him back. The life had gone out of his eyes. He was dead.

"No, Pa. Don't die. Pa!" Spencer cradled his father's bloody head and rocked back and forth, mindless of Astor.

To his surprise, the man came and knelt beside them. "The score has been settled, son. This is a day to end all wars."

Spencer stared at him from tear-blurred eyes. He memorized everything about Eugene Astor in that moment. His score might have been settled, but not Spencer's. One day he would find Eugene Astor and make him pay for what he'd done.

A shout and several voices sounded from somewhere behind Spencer. Astor got to his feet and fled down the alley. Spencer could still hear the man's voice. Still see his blue eyes search Spencer's face as if looking for an answer to a question he'd not posed.

The score hasn't been settled, Mr. Astor. This war isn't over.

Tracie Peterson is the award-winning author of over one hundred novels, both historical and contemporary. She has won the ACFW Lifetime Achievement Award and the Romantic Times Career Achievement Award. She is often referred to as the "Queen of Historical Christian Fiction," and her avid research resonates in her stories, as seen in her bestselling HEIRS OF MONTANA and ALASKAN QUEST series. Tracie considers her writing a ministry for God to share the Gospel and biblical application. She and her family make their home in Montana. Visit her website at TraciePeterson.com or on Facebook at Facebook.com/AuthorTraciePeterson.

Sign Up for Tracie's Newsletter

Keep up to date with Tracie's latest news on book releases and events by signing up for her email list at the link below.

TraciePeterson.com

FOLLOW TRACIE ON SOCIAL MEDIA

Tracie Peterson   @AuthorTraciePeterson